Advance Praise

"A compelling and intriguing blend of 80s nostalgia and contemporary horror, featuring a plucky wisecracking teenage protagonist and an enraged demon from her past whose entire purpose is to possess her body and devour her soul. With plenty of snappy and witty dialogue and a cast of unforgettable, believable characters—including a beautiful enigmatic witch steeped in the ancient traditions of her mysterious Cuban ancestors—Reefe hits another grand slam out of the park with The Ghosts of Glenn Dale."

> — Kerry Alan Denney, multiple award-winning
> author of *Soulsnatcher* and *Jagannath*

The Ghosts of Glenn Dale

The Ghosts of
Glenn Dale

Mark Reefe

Apprentice
House Press
Loyola University Maryland

First Edition

Hardcover ISBN: 978-1-62720-534-4
Paperback ISBN: 978-1-62720-535-1
Ebook ISBN: 978-1-62720-536-8

Design by Abby Benner
Editorial Development by Carlos Balazs
Promotion Development by Molly Gels

Published by Apprentice House Press

Apprentice
House Press
Loyola University Maryland

Loyola University Maryland
4501 N. Charles Street, Baltimore, MD 21210
410.617.5265
www.ApprenticeHouse.com
info@ApprenticeHouse.com

Also by Mark Reefe

Spindle Lane
The Road to Jericho
The Valley of Hinnom
El Sendero

"Be yourself; everyone else is already taken."
- Oscar Wilde

CHAPTER 1

October 9, 1988

It had been a month since the witch moved to Spindle Lane. Her flawless mocha skin, seductive smile, and exotic accent fooled everyone – everyone except me. I knew better because I saw that smile twist into a smirk when she thought no one was looking. I also noticed the lights in her house burning into the wee hours of the night when all non-witches were fast asleep. But most damning of all, while peeking through her window, I watched the witch burn sage and chant some fiendish spell in Spanish. Unfortunately, I had opted to take French in high school. "Why French?" was a question I often asked myself lately. I mean, what were the chances of me bumping into some hot French guy in Bowie, Maryland? *Absolument zéro.* Anyway, whatever Ms. Maya Suárez Martinez was brewing up was no doubt wicked, and I planned to get to the bottom of it.

It didn't help the witch's case that she moved into the

house previously owned by the Butcher of Bowie. The place had been empty for ten years, ever since they discovered the mess of bones and satanic stuff in Edward Hutchinson's – aka the Butcher of Bowie's – basement. They never found Mr. Hutchinson though. The old man had up and vanished a couple of days before the police were tipped off about his murderous habits by an anonymous caller. I remember little about him save for his wrinkled smiling face. I guess looks can be deceiving.

Crouching low, I glanced up and down the street. It was unlikely there would be traffic on Spindle this late on a weeknight, but better safe than sorry. The smoky smell of a nearby fireplace tickled my nose as I crept behind the hedge of laurels that lined our front porch. What I was about to do wasn't the type of thing most sixteen-year-old girls did, but I wasn't like most girls my age. If I ever forgot this, my best friends Theresa Petruzzo and Jackie Engert were quick to remind me of my well-earned status as our resident troublemaker. I had known Theresa since grade school and even though she now lettered on both the girls' softball team and on track, she preferred hanging out with Jackie and me instead of with the jock clique. As for Jackie, she was the complete opposite of Theresa. A cheerleader and fashion fanatic, she would have been welcome with the A-listers at Bowie Senior High any day of the week, but for some reason she also rebelled against the natural order of things. It might have been because underneath the makeup and pom-poms, she had a twisted sense of humor and preferred the company of like-minded people over the bourgeois drama that passed for life as one of the in-crowd. Not quite jocks, not exactly freaks – and definitely not geeks – we were our own thing, and we traveled between the cliques as we pleased.

Across the street and two houses down was the target. A few clouds lingered in the sky, but the crescent moon was bright, giving off enough silvery light for the shadows lining both sides of the lane to stretch long. I stuck to them until it was time to make my move. After a glance up and down Spindle, I bolted, making it to a pool of moon shadow next to the witch's house. There I crouched and sucked in the cool night air. Goosebumps popped up on my arms as they did every time I stepped foot on her property.

A puff of breath escaped my mouth as I whispered, "Almost there." Standing, I sidled my way along the wooden fence that enclosed her backyard. The witch erected it the first week she moved in. It was her first shady act. She had no kids and no pets but almost immediately had the fence installed. Who does that unless they have something to hide?

The twisted crabapple tree that grew beside the witch's fence provided the perfect roost from which to spy on her every move. After climbing up about four feet, I peered over the obstruction and through a large sliding glass door that opened into her dining room.

"What the hell?"

Two-by-fours and wiring stood where drywall had

been ripped away, and the house's cement slab foundation was exposed, the linoleum having been scraped up and tossed in a corner. Piles of crumbled plaster, shredded wallpaper, and splintered wood were scattered throughout. The place was beyond trashed.

Burning candles sat in a small circle on the floor, and a thin veil of smoke enveloped everything. The witch was kneeling before them and scribbling something on the floor, but I was too far away to make out her devilish doodling. I needed to get closer.

With the speed and grace of a sloth, I shimmied onto a large branch that jutted out over the fence. The rational side of my brain knew what I was doing was dumb, but that ninety-nine-pound weakling stood little chance against the T-Rex that was my adventurous side. Closing my eyes, I dropped to the ground.

I landed with a soft thud. No turning back now. Adrenaline shot through my veins as I dashed to a cluster of azaleas that stood twenty feet shy of the glass door. As luck would have it, the backyard sloped upward giving me a good vantage point. Staying low, I sucked in a couple of deep breaths and tried to keep my cool.

The witch's drawing was made from chalk. Arrows shot out in the four cardinal directions, and strange swirls were sketched between them. A large circle bisected the arrows, encapsulating all of the swirls in the process. The witch was now walking around her handiwork, chanting while holding a wad of smoldering weeds in her left hand and a pointed stick in her right. After circling it three times, she knelt and placed the stick in the center of the drawing. It lay there motionless for several seconds before twitching, first left and then right.

"No freaking way," I whispered.

Like the needle of a compass, the stick spun wildly, alternating directions as if struggling between two invisible magnets. A tingling sensation crept up my spine as I stared, mesmerized by the spectacle. An alarm clock rang from somewhere in the recesses of my brain, urging me to bail, but it was no use. The T-Rex was calling the shots.

The stick stopped suddenly, its pointed end aimed past the sliding glass door, through the azaleas, and directly at yours truly. I looked up and locked eyes with the witch. Sweet Jesus.

Breaking from the bushes, I darted to the fence and scaled up it and into the tree like a jungle cat. In my less-than-graceful rush to get down the other side, I slipped and landed hard on my butt. After struggling to my feet, I executed a gimpy—Hunchback of Notre Dame—style sprint back toward home. Once up the trellis and through my open bedroom window, I climbed in bed and pulled the sheets up around my head. Trying to calm my breathing, I watched the deserted street below.

Could the witch have seen me hiding in the bushes? Even with the moonlight, it was pretty dark out, and her lights were on inside. The reflection would have made it nearly impossible to see out.

Minutes passed as I kept vigil over Spindle Lane,

turning my gaze just long enough to catch the glowing green digits on my clock. It was 12:15. My butt would be dragging in homeroom and for most of history and chemistry, but on the bright side of things, it was officially Friday.

Footsteps interrupted my train of thought.

Below, the glow of a streetlamp caught the shadowy figure creeping up the street. In an upturned palm, the witch held the pointed stick, and with each step she took, its tip pivoted ever more toward my house. Dread welled in my gaseous gut.

A few steps more and the stick was pointing directly at my house. The witch turned and looked up to my window. Our eyes met once more.

A tiny fart escaped me.

CHAPTER 2

The grin on Theresa's face was hard to miss as I climbed into the back seat of her Malibu.

"Late night?" she asked.

As if I didn't know the dark patches under my eyes made me look like a junkie or zombie—or even better—a junkie zombie. Stare-downs with neighborhood witches tended to affect one's beauty sleep. Fortunately, old hocus-pocus must have gotten bored because she bailed after a minute or so. Why she followed me home in the first place was a question for another day.

"Bite me, Petruzzo."

Riding shotgun, Jackie decided to join in the fun. "Oh my, such language from such a *pristine* girl."

Even though I was a huge fan of John Hughes' *The Breakfast Club*, I was not in the mood. Stifling a yawn, I responded half-heartedly. "I'm not *that* pristine."

Jackie waved a makeup compact over her head. "If you give me a few minutes, I could make those raccoon eyes vanish. Y'know, you have nice cheekbones and a decent enough complexion. All you need is a little touch-up. Some eyeliner wouldn't hurt either. Ever thought about crimping your hair?"

Theresa rolled her eyes and said, "Don't try and turn Kate into one of your little Barbie doll friends, Jackie. She looks fine without all that junk on her face."

"Whatever," Jackie said, scowling at Theresa. "One of these days you'll both come begging to me for a makeover, and when that day comes, I may not be so obliging."

Theresa put the car in drive and gave it too much gas. Narrowly avoiding my neighbor's trash can as we hurtled down Spindle, she said, "Aaanyway. On to more important stuff. I hope you're not thinking of wimping out on us tonight, Kate. Mike's been hyping it up all week. He said it will be awesome."

Theresa's boyfriend, Mike Casey, was a bit of a thrill seeker and was always trying to reel us into one of his hair-brained adventures. Since the beginning of the school year we had already toilet papered the principal's house, spent a night ghost hunting at Crybaby Bridge, and changed the Bowie High School marquee from "NEW STUDENTS WELCOME" to "SEND WET NUTS." The last one seemed much funnier at the time. His current scheme involved a late-night visit to the infamous Satan Church, which I had totally forgot about.

"Ugh, is that tonight?" I asked.

"Jake is gonna be there," Jackie teased.

Jake Shaw. The way his wavy brown hair curled just above his icy blue eyes was to die for. "He is?"

My friends busted out laughing.

"Could you be any more obvious, Kate?" Theresa asked.

"What? I didn't say anything weird."

"It's not what you said, doofus. It's how you said it." Jackie repeated my words, being sure to stretch out the ending. "He *iiisss?*"

"I didn't say it like that."

"Yeah you did." Theresa added.

"Whatever. I guess I'm up for it. But listen up, I have some freaky news to share about the witch."

"Oh, you mean the Caribbean Queen?" Jackie asked.

The Caribbean Queen was the honorary title bestowed on Ms. Martinez when she first moved to my street. I guess it was fitting considering her glam looks and the way the men in the neighborhood fawned all over her. "Yep. So last night I caught her in the middle of some freaky Voodoo ritual in the middle of her dining room."

"How'd you see that?" Theresa asked.

"Well, I was hiding behind the bushes in her backyard."

Jackie stifled a giggle and attempted a lame impersonation of my mother. "Kathleen Marie Dwyer, you should be ashamed of yourself. A good girl doesn't peep into other peoples' houses."

"I actually agree with Jackie on this one," Theresa

said. "You've been obsessed with that woman ever since she moved here, and now you're hiding in her bushes. What if you got caught?"

I had no time for their judgment. There was juicy stuff to spill, and I sure as heck wasn't gonna let common sense or good advice get in the way of it. "Hold that thought. So anyway, I was watching her, and she had some candles lit, and she was burning something while chanting. I think it was sage."

"Are you sure it was sage?" Theresa asked.

"Yeah, maybe it was some other type of plant," Jackie added. "You said she's from Jamaica, right?"

"No, she's from Cuba according to my dad. Now zip it, and let me finish. Anyway, she put this stick on the ground and it started spinning all by itself. It did that for about ten seconds before stopping and pointing directly at me."

"The stick was pointing at you?" Theresa asked.

"Yep. Then I look up and see the witch staring at me, almost like she can see me hiding in the bushes."

Jackie smiled. "Maybe she was just looking outside in the direction the stick was pointing."

"At first I thought that too, so I hauled butt out of there."

"And?" Jackie asked.

"And the witch followed me back to my house using the stick like it was some sort of magic compass. It was creepy as all hell."

Jackie flipped the mirror on the car's sun visor open

and tilted her head left and then right, assessing her cosmetology skills. "And then what?"

"She split."

Satisfied with what she saw, Jackie closed the mirror and blurted, "Ooh, ooh, I just came up with a new nickname for your neighbor! I say we call her Voodoo Witch."

Theresa's nose scrunched. "That sounds a little redundant. What about Voodoo Queen?"

"That's even better," Jackie said.

Although I love my friends dearly, there are times I would have no qualms about smothering them in their sleep. "Call her what you want, but if I end up on the back of a milk carton, you two know where to look first."

"Maybe she's possessed by the Butcher of Bowie's ghost." Theresa joked.

"Why would she be possessed by the Butcher of Bowie?" Jackie asked.

Sometimes I forgot that Jackie had moved to town over the summer and was not yet intimately familiar with the local folklore. "She's living in his old house," I said.

"Oh my God! You're shitting me. *That's* the Butcher of Bowie's house? I knew he lived around here, but I didn't know the house was actually on your street. That's wicked."

"Yep. My brother even mowed his lawn."

"Which brother? Steve or Chris?"

Whenever I mentioned my brothers, Jackie was sure

to follow it up with a hundred questions. She could have her pick of half the guys at Bowie High. Why she was so interested in the two of them was a mystery to me. I suppose they were good-looking, but they were so old. Chris was twenty-five and Steve was twenty-seven, and they worked together traveling across the country selling stuff. I say stuff because exactly what they were selling changed each time I talked to them. One week it would be vacuum cleaners and the next encyclopedias. The sad truth was we weren't nearly as close as we used to be. Growing up, I remember my brothers always looking out for me and including me in any neighborhood fun. That changed shortly after Chris graduated high school and informed Mom and Dad that he would be taking some time to travel the country before going to college. As if that news was not tough enough for our parents to take, when Steve left Loyola in the middle of his junior year to join his younger brother, I was pretty sure my folks were going to stroke out. It took years for things to calm down between them, and the fact that neither of my brothers returned to finish college only made matters worse.

"I think it was Chris that mowed his lawn," I said.

"Kate and I weren't friends at the time," Theresa chimed in. "But I remember my parents talking about it. Some people even joked that the Butcher of Bowie was actually the Goatman."

Most everyone who lived in Bowie, or in Prince George's County for that matter, knew about the

Goatman. He was our local boogeyman, and he had been haunting the lonely backroads and woods of the county for as far back as I could remember. Despite having grown up listening to the stories of his murderous exploits, the mention of his name always sent chills raking up my spine.

"Earth to Kate. Come in, Kate."

I turned to Jackie. "Huh?"

"You all right?" she asked. "Looked like you were orbiting Pluto."

I had spaced out again. It was happening more often, ever since the strange dreams started. They were so vivid, so true to life that they seemed more like memories. I could smell, taste, and feel things in them. But most disturbing was the flood of emotions which accompanied them. In the last one I was chasing a boy with a giant hammer in my hands. Gripping the nicked wooden handle of the weapon, I pursued my prey as a terrible rage bubbled up inside me. I was screaming, and I was sure to kill the boy if I could catch him. It was seriously messed up.

I snapped out of it. "Pfft. Just a little tired. I'll be chill after I catch some sleep in social studies."

Ignoring the blaring horn from the car she had just cut off, Theresa looked at me and said, "So what do you think the Voodoo Queen is up to?"

I stifled another yawn and muttered, "Not sure, but now she knows I'm onto her, and that's bogus."

"Maybe you can do some kind of test on her to see

if she's just possessed or really a witch," Jackie said. "You could get her to drink some holy water or eat some garlic."

"Don't encourage Kate," Theresa chided. "What she needs is some sleep and a boyfriend to keep her from peeping in her neighbor's windows like some pervy old man."

Jackie snickered. "Yeah, maybe Jake can keep you busy tonight so you don't go wandering off."

I decided to let Jackie and Theresa entertain each other at my expense until we reached the school parking lot. It was way too early in the morning to have to deal with this level of stupid, and I needed to conserve my energy—at least until social studies.

CHAPTER 3

As if the primed Cutlass Supreme blasting Run-DMC while pulling into my driveway wasn't loud enough, Mike felt the need to announce their arrival with three blasts from the car's horn. Because of his lame stunt, my parents didn't let me leave until I promised to inform Mike that any future beeps would mean a call to his parents and me being grounded.

I was ready to lay into him when I noticed Jake sitting behind the wheel of Mike's car.

He put his hands up and offered an embarrassed smile as I approached. "Sorry. It wasn't me honking. It was the jackass riding shotgun."

Mike leaned over Jake and stuck his crew cut head out the window. "Hey, Kate! Where's the Voodoo Queen? I want to see if I can score me some ganja."

It was going to be a long night. Scowling at Mike, I said, "Slick move with the horn, McFly. Do it again, and I won't be seeing any of you until senior year."

The smile on his chiseled face turned upside down. "I'm sorry. Mike bad." He ducked back in the car and reemerged out of the other side. "Allow me to make it up to you with a night of thrills and chills, but be forewarned, not all those who venture to the Satan Church return."

A whiff of fruit punch hit me as I slipped behind Mike and squished into the backseat next to Theresa, who was squished next to Jackie.

Theresa waited for Mike to sit before lightly smacking the back of his head. "Sorry about that, Kate. I keep telling my dummy boyfriend your mom gets pissed when he honks, but he doesn't listen."

Rubbing his head, Mike turned around and winked at Theresa. "It's a good thing I'm so good-looking; otherwise, you would have dumped my ass by now."

"The night's young, dork. I still might."

"Here," Mike said shoving a thermos in front of me. "A peace offering for the pretty lady. It's my finest jungle juice yet, guaranteed to put a smile on your face and hair on your chest."

From the punch-stained grin he was sporting, it was obvious Mike had already downed a fair amount of juice. "Maybe later. I don't think I want to get busted boozing it up in my parent's driveway."

"I'll have some," Jackie blurted.

Mike handed the thermos full of trouble to her. "That's the spirit. Show these party-poopers how to have a good time."

Theresa and I watched Jackie take a big gulp.

Her blue eyes popped wide as Jackie fell into a coughing fit. Between gasps for air she wheezed, "Holy crap! How much vodka did you put in that thing?"

Mike giggled. "Aw, c'mon. It's a good mix, fifty percent Hawaiian Punch and fifty percent Absolut."

"And that's why I'm driving tonight, ladies," Jake said as he pulled out of the driveway.

For the next twenty minutes, we sang along to Jake's mixtape of U2, Social Distortion, and Joan Jett while cruising down Route 301 in search of the exit that would eventually lead us to the infamous Satan Church. Everyone but Jake had sampled some of Mike's punch by then, and we were halfway through *I Hate Myself for Loving You* when Jake interrupted.

"This is it!" he shouted over the music as we approached a four-way intersection. "From what I've been told, if we turn left here and keep going straight, we'll find it."

"Well, how far do we have to go?" Theresa asked.

Jake hunched his shoulders as he pulled onto a two-lane country road. "Not sure. My friend Andy said we'd be on it for a while, but he didn't give any specifics." He turned the stereo down to a whisper. "I suppose we'll know it when we see it."

A hush descended as everyone stared out of the windows watching the number of homes dotting the landscape slowly dwindle, gobbled up by the surrounding forest until all that was left was the occasional lonesome farmhouse. It remained like that for almost ten minutes before Jake spoke up. "You know, I must have passed by this road a million times, but I swear I've never been down here, at least not this far."

Mike took a swig from his thermos before adding, "That's because there *is* nothing down here."

Jake stopped the car. "Check it out."

I glimpsed over Mike's shoulder and noticed we were at a crossroads. In front of us the road ran straight until disappearing into an ocean of black. To our left and right was the same. A single sign stood on the far side of the intersection.

DEAD END ROAD.

"That's not creepy as all hell," Jake muttered.

Mike turned to the backseat and said, "This is gettin' good. One way in. One way out."

I looked at my friends. Jackie was smiling, but Theresa's face was wrinkled with worry.

Theresa spoke. "I'm not sure about this. What if we get lost or the car breaks down? We'd be stuck in the middle of nowhere."

"Chill, babe," Mike said putting a hand on Theresa's leg. "Nothing's gonna happen to you ladies with me and my boy Jake protecting you. This will be awesome. Trust me."

Jake twisted the rearview mirror so he could see in the backseat. "Andy said we'd see a dead end sign, so we're on the right trail. It's up to you guys though. We can keep going, or we can turn around. No whoop either way."

Where Mike was pushy and annoying, Jake appeared laid back and reassuring. I didn't realize I was staring at him in the mirror until he winked at me. Thank God it was too dark for him to see me blush.

Jackie leaned in close to Theresa. "C'mon, Smeresa. Think of the cool stories we can tell everyone at school. We found the legendary Satan Church and lived to talk about it."

Theresa plucked her boyfriend's hand off her leg. "Okay, okay. Just get your funky fruit punch breath out of my face. If Kate's good with it, I guess I am."

Despite Mike's lame promises, I found the idea of continuing into the unknown in search of a church of devil worshippers oddly exciting. "Let's do it. Worst case scenario, we offer Mike up for sacrifice if we get caught."

The Cutlass's high beams sprang to life as we crossed the intersection and entered into the unknown. Jake drove cautiously along the narrow, winding road as the last glimmers of light vanished like snuffed out candles, replaced by the encroaching woods. Minutes passed and the car fell eerily silent as we weaved our way through utter blackness, relieved only by the car's headlights.

I was gazing out into the gloom when Theresa flicked a flashlight on for a split second. Catching my reflection in the car window, I stopped breathing. As the light went out, I put a hand to my mouth to confirm what I already suspected. The face in the window had been smirking, but I had not. Before I could process what I'd witnessed, Theresa spoke up.

"Where the hell is this place? The sign said it was a dead end road like an hour ago, and we're still driving."

"There it is," Jake said.

The church was small and simple, with no decoration save a steeple and tiny cross just above its gabled entrance. If not for the fact that it was in the middle of nowhere, illuminated by a lone streetlamp at the end of a long country road that had seemed to go on forever, it would have been inconspicuous, completely forgettable. But considering both the setting and the mood, the plain little building looked as ominous as the Death Star.

Jake slowed as he pulled the car around the looped driveway in front of the church and parked. "End of the line."

"Oh snap!" Mike yelled. "That is definitely it."

Pointing to a small trail in the woods to the right of the church, Theresa said, "Is that the path you were talking about, the one they go down to bury the remains from the human sacrifices?"

I was about to ask Theresa why the hell she was encouraging her crazy boyfriend when she silenced me with a wink and smile. Sometimes I forgot how much she enjoyed stoking Mike's imagination and getting him all riled up.

"Yep, that's it all right. Talk about the perfect place to get rid of bodies. No one would ever find them down there."

Though I enjoyed a death-defying adventure as much as the next thrill seeker, I felt the need to point out some of the more glaring problems with Mike's Satan Church theory. "Hey, Sherlock, last time I checked, satanic churches don't have crosses on them."

A smug smile grew on Mike's face as he shook his head. "Oh, Kate, Kate, Kate. So pretty, yet so naïve. If you're in a satanic cult, you're not exactly gonna advertise it. The cross is probably meant to throw law enforcement off the trail. I bet that thing pops right off when their hellish rituals commence."

"Or," Jake interjected, "someone just hits a button inside the church, and the cross turns upside down."

I knew Jake was also having fun at Mike's expense, but something was undeniably cute about the way he was doing it. Maybe it was because his electric blue eyes stayed fixed on me the whole time he was talking.

Mike grabbed Jake's shoulder and squeezed. "That's it! I bet that's what happens." Mike pointed to Jake. "See, this guy gets it."

"Why do I feel like I'm in an episode of *Scooby-Doo?*" Theresa asked.

Jackie took a swig from Mike's thermos, let out a fruity belch, and said, "If we are, then I'm Daphne. You two bitches can fight over who's Velma."

"Theresa can be Velma," I said. "I've always wanted to be Scooby. He has a great sense of humor, is loyal to the bone, and can eat as much as he wants without gaining a pound."

Jake turned off the engine and killed the lights. "So we're here. Now what?"

The passenger side door swung open as Mike shouted, "We investigate!"

"What do you think, Scoob?" Jake asked. "Should we take a peek around just to shut him up? Maybe there's a pantry in the church we can raid."

I wasn't overly fond of prowling around an old country church in the dead of night, but the thought of getting a little alone time with Jake swayed my decision. Doing my best Scooby impression, I answered, "Rokay."

"Cool." Jake turned to Theresa and Jackie. "How about you two?"

Theresa scowled at Jackie, who was swigging from the thermos. "Go on ahead. The booze hound and I will catch up with you."

"Yeah, you two go on and scat," Jackie said between giggles. "Scoot on out of here, and find someplace dark so you can smooch." She puckered her lips and started making kissy sounds.

I made a mental note to kill her later.

Ignoring Jackie's taunts, Jake exited the Cutlass and motioned for me to follow. By then Mike had already disappeared around the side of the building.

Bitter cold awaited as I exited the car. Hugging myself, I shivered. "Wow, it's chilly."

A plume of breath billowed from Jake's mouth as he said, "Would you like my jacket?"

He was both cute *and* sweet. "No thanks. It's just so

much colder here than when we left that it surprised me. I'm good now though."

"It tends to be chillier out in the country," Jake said. "I bet—"

"Guys! Check this out!" Mike's shrill voice blasted from behind the church.

Jake rolled his eyes as he grabbed my hand. "Let's see what that knucklehead has stumbled on."

His grip was firm but gentle. Fortunately, it all happened so fast there was no time to worry about whether my palm was sweaty. I was pretty sure it wasn't, but I knew thinking about it was a surefire way to get it as damp as a sponge. I shook my head and muttered, "Get a hold of yourself, dummy."

"Did you say something?" Jake asked.

"Nope," I answered a couple of octaves too high and way too fast.

Jake and I led the way with Theresa and Jackie not far behind. We found Mike at the back of the church standing in front of a door. To the left of it was a small window smudged with grime.

Pointing frantically at the window, Mike said, "Check it out. There's a bunch of black robes in that room. I bet they wear them when sacrificing virgins."

Theresa slipped past us and made her way to the window. "How about you let a grown-up take a look." Cupping her hands to the sides of her head, she peered in. "There's a desk and some chairs. I do see clothes hanging from the wall, but it's too dark to make out what color they are."

"They're black. I'm telling you," Mike protested.

Stepping back, Theresa frowned and said, "It's probably the sacristy and those are probably the priest's vestments."

Mike put his hand on the doorknob. "There's one way to find out."

Jake chuckled. "It's gonna be locked, butthead."

"But it's not, amigo. I already tried it."

"No way," Jake said.

A Cheshire Cat smile grew on Mike's face. "Yes way. So, who's up for a little exploring?"

Jackie hiccupped before shouting, "I'll go!" Pushing her way past Jake and me, she blared, "Out of the way, ladies. It's time to kick some Satan ass!"

This would usually be the point in the night where I would try and talk some sense into Mike before he got punched in the face, kicked in the nards, or worse, but Jake was still holding my hand, and I was a tad distracted.

We watched Mike turn the knob.

The church began to glow. It took a few seconds for me to realize the light was coming from an approaching car. We watched in shocked silence as it was followed by another car and then another.

"Oh shit!" Mike yelled.

"Keep it down," Jake whispered. "They haven't seen us yet, only the Cutlass."

He let go of my hand and pointed to the plot of land

behind the church. "We'll hide back there in the dark. Let's move."

Following Jake's lead, we took off into the open field and complete darkness.

Seconds later I heard a thud to my right followed by Mike's cursing. Next came a yelp from Jackie.

A hand grabbed my arm and pulled me to a stop. "Careful. There's something out there."

It was Jake's voice. As my eyes adjusted, I noticed dozens of objects surrounding us, sprouting two to three feet from the ground. I approached the one in front of me and touched its cold hard surface. Running my fingers across it, I felt engraved letters. "It's a gravestone. We're in the middle of a frigging graveyard."

The sound of car doors slamming echoed through the night air. "You might as well come out! We know you're there!"

The guy sounded like he wasn't much older than us. If I had to guess, I'd say he was a member of the church we were about to trespass into. Jake and I ducked behind one of the larger headstones and watched.

I counted six of them. Their silhouettes, partially shrouded by exhaust fumes, stretched against the glow cast from the headlights of their cars, making them look like giant stick figures.

"We can wait all night!" one of them shouted.

From our right came Jackie's voice. "Oh shit. Oh shit. Oh shit."

"Mike," Jake whispered, "you and T okay?"

"We're chill," he answered from our left side. "Bruised the shit out of my leg on one of those stupid rocks. They're everywhere."

"Gravestones, Mike," Jake answered. They're gravestones. We're in a graveyard."

"Ohhh."

"I think we're safe for now," Theresa said. "I'm pretty sure they can't see us back here."

We watched as the shadows circled the church and then searched Mike's car. They continued taunting us, but never ventured beyond the periphery of the church. Apparently, they weren't as sure of themselves as they pretended to be.

Mike was now cursing under his breath, and Jackie had begun crying.

After letting out a long sigh, Jake stood and said, "I've had enough of this. I'm going up there and say it was just me, that I got lost and was looking for someone to give me directions, or something like that."

Despite our desperate situation, I found myself not just calm and clearheaded but energized from the evening's events. Standing beside Jake, I said, "I like your style, but the story needs work. Better we say you were looking for a quiet place to park and stopped here. When we saw the headlights, we got spooked and hid."

Jake cleared his throat. "I have to admit, your story is better than mine, but what makes you think they'll buy it?"

What Jake couldn't see in the dark was me

unbuttoning the top of my blouse and mussing up my hair. "Call it a gut feeling. I can be very convincing when I want to."

"Hold on," Mike whispered. "Look, guys. They're leaving."

We watched in relief as the shadows got in their cars and rolled one by one back down the country road.

"Son of a bitch," Jake said.

I heard Theresa close by Mike. "Why would they just up and leave?"

"Schweet!" Mike crowed. "They must have gotten bored, probably left to go tip some cows or do some other redneck shit."

The tremolo in Jackie's voice was thick. "Maybe it's a trick. Maybe they're just waiting for us around the bend."

We stood in the graveyard in silence for upward of thirty seconds before I blurted, "So is this the part where someone is supposed to say let's get the hell out of here?"

"Kate's right," Jake said. "Let's split!"

The five of us broke into an all-out sprint toward the car. Jackie, Theresa, and I dove into the backseat seconds before Jake hit the gas.

"Ow!" Mike cried as he flopped in beside Jake and shut the door. "You ran over my toe!"

Ignoring his friend's whining, Jake kept his foot on the accelerator as he banked a hard right. In the backseat we slid left, right, then left again as Jake hugged the curves of the road like he was Bo Duke. About a mile from the church, he eased up.

"I think you broke my damn toe," Mike complained.

Jackie moaned. "I think I'm gonna barf."

"Chill, guys," Jake said. "Just a couple more turns and then it's a straightaway all the way back to the highway."

"Mike, this is the stupidest thing you've even gotten us into!" Theresa shouted.

"Night's not over yet," Mike replied while gently massaging his foot. "The way I see it, we're all in one piece, and we now have one hell of a story to tell. Frankly, I think you all should be thanking me for this amazing—"

Mike's voice died in his throat as a string of headlights flashed on. A quarter mile down the road a row of cars was parked across both lanes, blocking our escape.

"Well…shit," was all I could think to say.

CHAPTER 4

Five cars were parked across the road and shoulders. The assholes were shining their high beams at us.

Instead of slowing as most sane people would do, Jake hit the gas.

"Oh shit!" Mike yelled as the car approached sixty.

"I'm definitely going to be sick!" Jackie shouted.

While Jackie struggled not to barf and Theresa dug her nails into my thigh, I stared at Jake in the rearview mirror in quiet fascination. His eyes scanned the road ahead as if searching for something. Steady hands gripped the wheel as a smirk grew on his face. Oh damn, he was about to do something crazy.

"Hold on everybody!" Jake shouted as we swerved off the road and into a soggy field of harvested corn. With the exception of our driver, everyone was now screaming. The car bounced and sloshed its way through the soft earth as we skirted past the makeshift roadblock. Once around it, Jake turned the mud-covered Cutlass back to the road. As rubber met asphalt, we rocketed forward.

Mike shouted, "Whooeee! Now that's what I'm talkin' bout!" He rolled down the passenger window and stuck his head out of it. "Bite me, you cousin-kissing jackasses!"

I watched Jake glance in the rearview mirror. He was as quiet as a mouse but his smirk had spread into an ear-to-ear grin. "Where'd you learn to drive like that?" I asked.

"Here and there. I used to drag race back in Poughkeepsie. It's one of the reasons we moved. Any of them following us?"

I wanted to ask him more about Poughkeepsie, but now wasn't the time. No matter how much it was killing me to learn about his mysterious past, it would have to wait. I hated waiting. Peering through the mud-splattered rear window, I said, "Doesn't look like it. I think you surprised them."

"That makes two of us," Theresa said.

"Are you *sure* they're not following us?" Jackie asked.

"We're only half a minute from the highway," Mike said. "Even if they were, there's nothing they can do once we hit the main road. We could just head to the nearest police station or public place." Snapping his fingers, Mike turned and looked at Theresa. "Belzer's. We'll go to David Belzer's."

Theresa's response was a groan.

"That's a great idea!" Jackie shouted. "His parents

are out of town, and he's having a keg party. We'll be safe there."

"And drunker," I said with a tinge of sarcasm in my voice. "Don't forget that."

Jackie scowled and stuck her tongue out at me.

"What say you, Mario Andretti?" Mike asked Jake. "Up for a little well-earned celebration? It's not every day you get to save your friends from a group of Satan worshippers."

Jake snorted. "Those clowns are no more Satan worshippers than my parents are. They're probably just a bunch of guys who are ticked off at all the high school kids poking around their church."

"Could be. Or it could be that we just narrowly avoided becoming the next ritual sacrifices at one of their black masses. I guess we'll never know, but my story sounds much more interesting, so I'm sticking with it. Now back to the question, chum. Up for a cervesa or four?"

"Mmm. I don't know." Jake looked at me in the mirror. "What do you think?"

I opened my mouth to speak but hesitated. Afraid I might squeak and come off a little too eager, I just nodded and smiled.

We could hear the music over a block away. Apparently, Wang Chung was telling everyone to have fun tonight. After finding a place to park along the car-packed street, we made our way into party central. The scene was intense. The football team had taken over control of the kitchen and the keg and was busy serving up beer bongs to anyone brave or stupid enough to try one. In the dining room a lively game of quarters was taking place between some foreign exchange students and members of the audiovisual club. The family room was now home to a bunch of freaks and band geeks who were arguing over what to play next on Belzer's hi-fi system.

As soon as we got through the door, Jackie made a beeline to a group of cheerleaders who lingered near the kitchen entrance, close enough to get beers from their jock boyfriends but far enough away where they could talk about them without being overheard. Mike and Theresa were the next to scram, heading out onto the back deck for a little privacy after filling their solo cups with suds. With our friends out of the picture, a sudden awkwardness swallowed me. From the way Jake was fidgeting, I knew he felt it too.

"So, can I get you a beer?" he asked.

Whether it was the thrill of our off-road adventure that had built up my thirst, I didn't know, but a beer sounded like the best idea I had heard all night. "Yes, please!" I shouted over the music.

Closing my eyes, I leaned against the wall and listened to INXS play over the stereo while waiting for Jake's return. As Michael Hutchence claimed that he needed me tonight, a hushed word echoed in my mind. *Raga*. It sounded strangely familiar to me.

"Here you go."

I jumped at the sound of Jake's voice. "Wow, that was quick."

"Really? Thought it had taken a while myself. The line for the keg was pretty long." Jake frowned as he handed me a beer. "You okay? Looked like you were in some kind of trance for a minute there."

After taking a sip, I nodded. "I'm good. Just zoned out for a sec. It's been one crazy night."

Jake chuckled. "Right? I don't know where Mike gets his ideas from, but one of these days they're going to get him in trouble."

I never considered myself much of a beer drinker, but I had to admit the stuff they were serving up tonight was good, damn good. "Is this some fancy type of beer? Maybe an import or something?"

Shaking his head, Jake said, "Tastes like Bud to me."

"Hmm. Maybe I'm just thirsty." I took another sip, reevaluating my beverage preferences with each sampling. It was so frothy. It was so filling. It was so…gone.

"Wow. You sure were thirsty," Jake said grinning. "Would you like another?"

As good as it was, I was already jonesing for more. "Buurress, please," I said through a burp. My hand shot up to my mouth in horror. "Oh, God. That's so embarrassing."

Jake stifled a laugh and said, "No problem. Here, have mine while I get us a couple more. Hopefully this will help quench that thirst of yours."

Jake slipped away, leaving me to my shame.

Something was definitely up. Maybe the adrenaline rush I'd felt at the Satan Church was somehow fueling my appetite. Looking down, I noticed I was already halfway through the beer Jake had given me. That had to be it. I was still riding high from our adventure. The sight of a bowl of pretzels on a nearby table caused my tummy to rumble. With my free hand I grabbed a fistful of the salted snacks and began popping them in my mouth. By the time Jake got back, the brew and pretzels were gone.

"Here," he said, handing me another beer. "Looks like I made it back just in time."

Before I could respond, David Belzer's head popped over my shoulder. "Hey, homies! Did you check out my bodacious sound system? It's got a hundred watts of power, fifteen-inch woofers, and a Pioneer disc player. Cost over two grand for everything, but it was so worth it."

David's parents were attorneys who worked long hours and traveled frequently. To make up for their absence from his life, they showered David with expensive gifts. The stereo was simply the latest in a long line of toys and was far from the most extravagant. That award had to go to the Corvette he got on his sixteenth birthday. It was the prevailing opinion within our group that the lack of attention and affection he received at home fueled David's need to be admired. It's not that he was a bad guy. He was just stuck up. *Real* stuck up.

"It's cool, David," Jake said with the tiniest smile on his face.

"Damn right!" David shouted. "Now what's this I hear about you breaking through a roadblock of devil worshippers? Mike gave me the play-by-play, and it sounded awesome. Of course if we were driving my ride they never would have come close to touching us. Zero to sixty in just over five seconds, dude."

Maybe it was the fact that he was interrupting my time with Jake or maybe it was due to the multiple beers I had downed, but whatever the reason, I felt a compelling urge to mess with David Belzer. "Zero to sixty, huh? Well, from the looks of it when we came in, it won't be going anywhere anytime soon."

The smug smile dropped from David's face. "Huh?"

"You got some flat tires, *dude*. Pretty sure it's all four of them."

"Someone let the air out of my tires?"

"More like slashed them. I think I saw a switchblade sticking out of one of the front tires. Can you think of anyone who would want to do that?"

David's pasty face was slowly turning red. "Slashed? Are you sure? It must have been Greg Cummings. That loser has been jealous of my ride since I first drove it to school. It's not my fault he's got a suck job Fiero."

Doing my best to fight back a smile as David stormed off to investigate, I turned to Jake. "Where were we?"

Jake smirked and said, "Funny, I didn't notice any flat tires on David's car. Come to think of it, I don't remember even passing it on the way in."

"Sorry, my patience for snobs must be at an all-time

low tonight."

"What happens when he finds out his car is fine?" Jake asked.

"Meh, I'll just say I mixed up his douche mobile with someone else's, and then you'll add that I've had a lot to drink tonight, and that will be that."

"Got it all planned out, do ya?"

The beer was starting to kick in, but I still had a mean thirst. Placing a hand on Jake's chest, I said, "Not all planned out, but I do have some ideas…"

"Really?"

"Ah yep," I said pointing past Jake and toward the kitchen where one of the Bowie Bulldog's linemen had just finished off a funnel of foaming Budweiser. "I think I'll start with one of those."

CHAPTER 5

The face staring at me was mine. It had the same hazel eyes, an identical button nose, and sported a pouty replica of my mouth, but something lurked behind it that was not me. Reaching up, I touched the mirror's cool surface. As I pulled my hand back, I watched my reflection's lips curl into a ghoulish grin.

Jerking awake, I quickly remembered why sunlight sucked. I drew the blinds closed to block its headache-inducing rays and opted to stay in bed for the rest of the morning. When I finally summoned the energy to venture beyond the confines of my room to try and stomach some Saltines and ginger ale, I was greeted with a note taped to the outside of my door. It read:

> *Decided to let you sleep it off this morning. Your mom was livid and ready to let you have it, but I convinced her to cut you some slack. Don't make me regret it. This is your one strike, kiddo. Any more and you'll be*

grounded until graduation.
                              ~ Love, Dad.

P.S. Mom's working at the library, and I'm running errands.

Nothing like getting busted by your parents to start the day off right. Doing a superb impression of a zombie, I ambled my way down to the kitchen and grabbed a can of ginger ale from the fridge. Glancing out of the window over the sink, I was pleasantly surprised to find the day was now overcast. From the look of the darkening sky, a storm was brewing.

Based on the blurred bits I could remember, it had been a crazy night. Feeling good and flying high after our narrow escape from the devil worshippers – or pissed off rednecks depending on your perspective – I had decided to try a beer bong for the first time. I remember downing two of them before things went dark.

Summoning up the courage, I dialed Theresa's number. On the third ring she picked up.

"Hello?"

"How bad was I?"

Laughter bubbled over the line before Theresa responded in a sarcastic tone. "Who is this?"

I was *not* in the mood. "You know who this is, smartass, so out with it. What's the damage?"

"Well, we all partied pretty hard last night, but I have to admit, you were in rare form."

"That bad, huh."

"Depends on your definition of bad," Theresa said. "After setting a record for consecutive beer bongs, you raided Belzer's kitchen and began stuffing your face. I'm pretty sure you killed an entire box of Twinkies. Next, you hijacked the sound system, popped in a Def Leppard disc, and started singing. You moved to a different person for each song, forcing them to sing along with you."

I felt a lump form in my throat. "No way."

"Yes way. But it gets *sooo* much better. When you got to Jake, the song was *Pour Some Sugar on Me*. Your performance was fantabulous. Jake did pretty good too."

The lump plopped into my stomach. I was going to be sick.

Theresa continued. "After the song, you planted a kiss on him, mentioned something about making a run to Hardees, and dragged him out of the party. That was the last I saw of you. Jake showed back up about an hour later to bring the rest of us home. He said he had already dropped you off."

"Oh God."

"If it makes you feel any better, he refused to tell us what happened. We pried and pried, but all he would say was it was none of our business. He was smiling though."

"Oh God."

"Don't sweat it, toots. Sure, you were a bit much last night, but to tell you the truth, it was kind of fun watching you blow off some steam and go buck wild. And in case you haven't figured it out, Jake is totally into you."

My churning stomach started to settle. "You think so?"

"If he wasn't, he would have been running for the hills by now."

Closing my eyes, I let out a deep sigh.

"So you don't remember anything after you two left the party?" Theresa asked.

"It's all a blur. I think I remember the singing though."

More giggles travelled over the line.

"Shut up, T. It's not funny. I can't remember a damn thing from after the party."

"Well…I guess you have to call Jake then."

Just the idea caused my stomach to start gurgling again. "He probably thinks I'm a complete freak."

"If it makes you feel any better, we all do."

"What!"

"Just messing with ya. Seriously though, next time take it easy on the beer bongs. It's hard enough keeping an eye on Jackie; I don't have the energy to babysit both of you."

After promising Theresa I would fill her in on the details, I hung up and stared at the phone for the next five minutes while trying to summon the courage to call Jake. What the hell was going on with me? No one could ever accuse me of being a prude, but I was no party girl either. I was the wallflower watching everyone else get wasted and making fun of them for it. I was also a bit of a doofus around hot guys, but apparently not last night. The phone almost slipped out of my sweaty hand when

I picked it back up to call Jake.

He answered immediately. "Hello?"

"Hey, it's me, Kate."

"Hey, I thought about calling but figured it might be better to let you sleep in."

"Thanks. That was nice of you."

"No problem."

An awkward silence followed as I fumbled for the right thing to say. I opened my mouth not sure what words were going to spill out, but Jake beat me to the punch.

"So how are you feeling?" he asked.

"A little like one of the cast of *Gremlins*. You know, afraid that if I'm exposed to direct sunlight, I might melt. Also, for some reason everyone sounds like Gilbert Godfrey to me."

Jake's laughter came over the phone. It was a good sign.

"Here's the thing," I said. "I don't normally drink that much, and I'm having a little trouble piecing everything together from last night. So…"

"I kind of figured on that. What's the last thing you remember?"

"I think maybe doing a little singing."

More laughter. *"Pour Some Sugar on Me?"*

Beads of cold sweat sprouted on my hands and face. "Yep. I remember that thanks to Theresa. But after that things get a bit…fuzzy."

"So you don't recall ripping my shirt off and all the hickeys?"

Oh God. Whatever words I was planning to utter were drowned in a tidal wave of sheer panic. I was officially a slut, a sweaty slut.

"Hey, still there? I was just kidding. Sorry, I couldn't resist."

Breathing a sigh of relief, I said, "You're a butthead."

"I know. It was just too good to pass up. Nothing happened. I mean, we did kiss a little in the car, but when I went to change the radio station, you passed out. After getting you home, I was able to rouse you enough to get you to the front door. Once you were inside, I split."

Praise Jesus, I wasn't a slut. "That's it?"

The response was muffled laughter.

"What's so funny?"

Jake stifled the laughs. "It's nothing really."

"Apparently, it's something. C'mon, out with it."

"Well…you have the cutest snore. That's all."

So I snore. Yes, it's a little embarrassing, but it could have been much, much worse. "Jake, I have to tell you, what you saw last night was not the real me. I'm not usually that crazy. I'm not sure what got into me."

"It's okay. Last night was nuts, and you let loose a little. It's completely understandable and you have nothing to be embarrassed about. I've done much worse."

It was nice the way he was trying to make me feel better. "Oh yeah?"

"*Oh* yeah."

"You'll have to tell me all about it sometime."

"How about next Friday?" he asked. "They're

showing *Halloween 4* at the Cineplex in the Marketplace."

"Sure." Once more my response was too high-pitched and too fast. I cleared my throat and made sure the next words were slower and lower. "Sounds like fun."

"Awesome. As for today, drink lots of water and take some Motrin. Also, don't eat anything heavy."

Jake's sweetness was such a turn on. And for some reason he still liked me after I made a complete ass out of myself. "Thanks, doc. Will do."

As soon as I hung up, the phone rang. Thinking it was Jake, I answered asking, "Did the doctor forget something?"

"Kate Dwyer?"

It was a woman's voice. "Who's this?"

"You have a bad habit of snooping into other people's business."

The words were spoken with a smoky island accent. It was the Voodoo Queen.

"You know who this is, don't you?" she asked.

"Yes."

"Come to my house in exactly ten minutes, no sooner, no later. Do you understand?"

In addition to being bossy, she was intentionally cryptic. But seeing as I was already on thin ice with my folks and if one of the neighbors complained about me, I would probably be grounded for the next year, I had no choice but to comply. "Yes."

"Good."

The line went dead.

CHAPTER 6

A serious case of the heebie-jeebies overwhelmed me as I stepped foot on the Voodoo Queen's porch, made that much worse by an accompanying rumble of thunder from a gathering storm. Shivering, I grabbed the cast iron door knocker. After the third bang, she answered.

The woman's sculpted face was expressionless, but her dark brown eyes gripped me tight. "Kate Dwyer. It's so nice of you to come to the front door...for once."

"Yeah, sorry about the other night. I—"

The Voodoo Queen placed a finger to her mouth. "Quiet, child. Let me have a look at you."

She put a finger under my chin and gently tilted my head back, examining me in silence. After several seconds she nodded and said, "As I thought. Please, enter."

At a loss for words and still wee bit hungover, I followed her through the front hall and into a thick haze that hung in the air. The smell of burnt grass was strong. "Are you cooking something? Hope it's not breakfast."

The Voodoo Queen's laughter was soft and almost musical. "It's sage, child. I use it to help cleanse this house."

"Of what?" I asked.

She turned and looked at me like I had a hole in the middle of my forehead. "Of evil. This house is sick with it."

We entered a dimly lit dining room stacked high with unopened boxes. The Voodoo Queen motioned to one of four wicker chairs that surrounded a glass-topped table. "It's time for us to talk, Kate. Please have a seat while I get us some coffee. You look like you could use some refreshment."

As my host disappeared into the kitchen, I sat in one of the chairs and assessed the surroundings. To the best of my memory, I had never been in the house before, but I was having wicked déjà vu. The view into the backyard through the sliding glass door was so familiar to me, and somehow I knew the room off the dining room to my left had been a study, even though the door to it was now shut. I could see its book-lined walls and a paisley patterned throw rug in my head.

She reappeared a minute later with two small cups. Sitting opposite me, she placed the coffee on the table. "This is café cubano. It's stronger and richer than what passes for coffee around here."

"Thanks, Ms. Martinez."

"You can call me Maya."

I took a sip and closed my eyes as creamy sweetness

gave way to a wallop of roasted heaven. "Wow. This is a lot better than Folgers."

"I'm glad you like it. Why were you in my backyard the other night?"

Her directness caught me off guard. Swallowing hard, I said, "Sorry about that. It's just that this house has been empty for the past ten years and there are lots of stories about how it's cursed and even haunted. Then you show up, a single woman moving into this big house, and then the first thing you do is fence off the backyard. It was all too tempting. I had to snoop. In case you haven't figured it out yet, this street is really boring, a total snooze fest. So when you came along, there was finally someone interesting to check out."

Maya took a sip of her coffee and said, "In other words, to spy on."

Raising my cup to my mouth, I muttered, "I guess you could call it that."

"And what was it you thought you saw two nights past?"

There it was, the big question. She wanted to know if I knew that she was a witch. "I didn't see much." That was a lie. "It was kind of smoky in the house." That was the truth.

Maya's eyes narrowed. "Why do you and your friends call me the Voodoo Queen?"

I barely managed to choke down the coffee in my mouth before stammering, "I—I—"

"Don't lie to me, child. I heard all of you yesterday."

We were busted. "Well, I might have seen some stuff. You drew a few arrows on the floor and were spinning a stick. What were you doing anyway?"

"Voodoo Queen," Maya spat out, ignoring my question. "That's the most ridiculous thing I've ever heard. As if I would be involved with such nonsense."

"So you don't cast spells or anything like that?"

"Of course I do! I am a yaya, a priestess of Palo Mayombe."

"Wait, seriously?"

"I never joke about Palo Mayombe. It was taught to me by my mother who was taught by her mother and so on for generations."

"So let me get this right," I said, grinning. "You're Maya the yaya?"

Maya's face was as stone. "And?"

As quickly as it arose, my grin vanished. "Uh, nothing, nothing. That is so cool. I *knew* you were a witch. What were you doing the other night? Some kind of séance? I heard the Butcher of Bowie killed at least a dozen people, and they found the victims' bones somewhere in this house."

"Tell me, Kate, what do you remember about the man called the Butcher of Bowie?"

"Not a whole lot. From what I've been told, he mostly kept to himself. I vaguely recall him stepping in once to stop a neighborhood bully from beating me up. He seemed like your run-of-the-mill friendly old man."

Maya put her coffee down. "I would like to try

something with you. It's a simple incantation, but it requires your cooperation. What do you say?"

"You're not going to go all *Serpent and the Rainbow* on me and turn me into a zombie?"

The yaya frowned. "Not unless it is absolutely necessary."

"Really?"

The frown remained etched on her face "No. Despite what you may have learned from television and the movies, making zombies isn't something we do. What I want to perform is a cleansing spell. Think of it as a shower for your soul."

"If it will help get rid of my headache, sure."

Maya went into her kitchen and was back half a minute later. She was holding a bowl with an egg in it in one hand and a blue candle and pack of matches in the other. "This spell is intended to purge any unclean energy from you."

She placed the candle on the kitchen table and lit it before saying, "Give me your hand."

I stuck my right arm out.

Maya gently flipped my hand palm up and placed the egg in it. "Hold this close to your body and shut your eyes. Imagine all of the negative energy flowing out of you and into the egg, and do not open your eyes until I tell you to."

If someone told me this morning that in a couple of hours I would be sitting in the Butcher of Bowie's house holding an egg while a witch cast a spell on me, I would have said they were tripping. Closing my eyes, I listened as Maya chanted in Spanish. Why the hell did I have to take French? Stupid, useless French. While pondering my academic choices, a sudden stomach spasm almost caused me to drop the egg.

"Open your eyes, Kate."

"That felt weird."

Maya held out her hand. "Give me the egg."

The priestess muttered something else in Spanish as she cracked the egg and emptied its contents into the bowl. Though the yolk was pitch black and hard, like it had been boiled and covered in oil, the white of the egg remained clear and runny.

"Yuck. I think your eggs may have gone bad," I said.

Maya stared stoically at the egg for several seconds before looking up and flashing me a smile. "The spell is done."

I opened my mouth, but she continued before I had a chance to press her.

"You would be wise to stop wandering onto other people's property uninvited. Where I am from that could get you shot."

"Where's that? Cuba?"

Maya blew out the candle and removed it and the bowl from the table. As she went into the kitchen, she said, "Miami. But my parents are both from Cuba. They came to America before I was born. My mother was a yaya in her village and her mother was before her. I come from a long line of powerful priestesses."

"That's cool. So what other kinds of spells can you cast? Can you put a curse on your enemies or get someone to fall in love with you?"

When she returned this time, she was holding a polished red stone with intersecting arrows and strange glyphs carved into it. "This is a good luck charm," she said handing the quarter-sized rock to me. "Take this, Kate, and keep it with you at all times. It will protect you from those who would do you harm."

A warm, prickly feeling radiated from my hand as I held the stone. Irritated by the sensation, I pocketed it. "So what do I do? Throw it at them?" I asked.

Maya did not look amused as her gaze fell to my pants pocket. "Do not lose it."

"I – I won't. I was just kidding about the whole throwing thing."

The yaya's eyes met mine. I felt their power as they took hold of me. "How have you been feeling lately? Have any unusual thoughts or urges entered your mind?"

I couldn't lie to her, not with those eyes staring at me. They would know the second any false words slipped out of my mouth. I was sure of it. "Well, I did get pretty wasted last night and make a bit of an ass out of myself. I made out a little with this really hot guy. His name is Jake. Anyway, I liked him before I got sloshed, so it's not too weird that we hooked up. But now I'm a tiny bit worried he might think that I'm a slut – which I'm definitely not. Don't get me wrong though. I'm no prude either. Basically, I'm fun and laid back, but not easy. Does that make sense?"

A smirk grew on Maya's face. "That's not exactly what I meant. How about members of your family? Notice anything peculiar about the way they have been behaving?"

"You mean my folks? Not really. They're your typical nosey, overbearing parents. Nothing strange there."

"And your brothers?"

"How did you know that I have brothers?"

The smile on Maya's face melted away. "I must have heard it from one of the neighbors. They said you have two older brothers."

"That's true, but I haven't seen Chris or Steve in almost six months. Mom and Dad are hoping they can make it for Christmas, but I'm not betting on it. They work a lot. Seems they're always on the road, traveling from one town to another selling this or that. Let's just say we're not exactly tight anymore."

"I see."

Maya fell silent as if reflecting on what I said, which was weird to me because it really wasn't that interesting. After a few seconds, she continued. "You seem like a nice girl, but I have much to do, and I can't allow you or any of your friends to be a distraction. I'm looking for something important, and disturbances are unwelcome. Do you understand?"

Things were just starting to get interesting, and I was getting the brush off. "Maybe I can help with whatever it is you're looking for. After all, I know the area and the people."

"That is out of the question!"

The shout caused me to jump in my seat. "I think someone needs to ease up on the Cuban coffee. I can take a hint."

A small smile returned to Maya's face. "There are things you don't know, Kate, and it is not my place to educate you. You would be wise to keep the stone with you at all times and leave me to my work. But should you find yourself in any sort of trouble, come see me at once."

CHAPTER 7

Thunder rumbled in the bruised sky above as I walked home, and an autumn wind scattered dead leaves up and down Spindle. As if the pending storm wasn't ominous enough, a little girl was standing alone in the middle of the street directly in front of my house. She couldn't have been more than five or six, and her overalls and Dutch boy haircut looked like throwbacks to a much groovier time. She stared at me with glassy eyes, and a strangely nostalgic feeling overwhelmed me. Slowly I came to realize I was looking at my past self.

Freezing in my tracks, I debated going back to Maya's but quickly reconsidered. If I was a gambler, I would have bet the farm that I was the only person who could see this younger version of me. Someone or some-*thing* was messing with my head, and I needed to know who or what it was.

"Hello," I said, approaching her.

The girl smiled and waved a pudgy hand, beckoning

for me to follow as she turned and headed toward our backyard.

I shadowed her in quiet fascination, not at all surprised when she walked through the backyard fence. Opening the gate, I saw her patiently waiting for me on the other side. "Where are we going?" I asked.

Putting a finger to her mouth, the girl silenced me as if she was about to share some great secret. She went to the far side of our tool shed, rounding it to the five-foot-wide patch of lawn that separated it from the fence.

My instincts were telling me she was not a ghost or spirit but rather a vision from deep within my subconscious that was trying to communicate with me. Since they hadn't steered me wrong to date, I decided to continue. When I turned the corner, she was waiting for me.

With the queerest grin on her face, she pointed to the ground beneath my feet.

"Is something buried there?"

The girl nodded.

"And I'm guessing you want me to dig it up. It's nothing gross, I hope."

The smile vanished as she stabbed at the air around my feet with her tiny finger.

"Okay, I get it. Can you at least give me a clue? I'm not a fan of getting dirty for a bunch of bones. It's not bones, is it?"

The girl shook her head.

"If it's not bones, is it treasure of some sort?"

Her smile returned, stretching until it curled up

Grinch-style toward her ears.

"Really?"

The girl nodded.

A chilling wind played havoc with my hair. Spitting long brown strands from my mouth, I asked, "This isn't some kind of twisted trick you're playing on me?"

Slow and deliberate, her head turned left then right.

I disappeared for less than a minute to grab a shovel out of the shed, but when I returned the little girl was gone. Truth be told, it didn't surprise me. I suspected that having delivered her message, she might up and poof away. Another rumble of thunder rolled across the sky as a drop of rain hit my hand. I didn't have long before I got soaked.

After digging furiously for several minutes, I heard a pop followed by a crunch. Pulling the shovel out, I noticed a bunch of orange flakes mixed in with the dirt. Leaning down, I picked up one of the slivers and held it to my nose. It smelled like old cardboard and...nacho cheese. Putting my hands in the hole, I sifted through old tortilla chips and pulled out a faded plastic bag. The word Doritos was barely visible on faded alternating orange and yellow blocks. "What the hell?"

I sifted deeper into the damp dirt with my hands and started pulling out bag after bag of crushed potato chips, Fritos, and Cheetos. Mixed in with the salty snacks were packs of stale Devil Dogs, Twinkies, and Suzy Qs. From the retro look of their wrapping, the junk food must have been in the ground for years. Some of the packages were intact, many were torn, but most were completely mushed. The junk food graveyard made no sense. There was no canned food or anything nonperishable dumped in the hole. It was as if the person burying the stuff had no idea that the food wouldn't last, especially the way it was just tossed into the hole with no protection. Looking down into the center of the mess, I noticed a rotting bundle of cloth. I reached for it but paused as a dark thought crept into my head. What if food wasn't the only thing buried here? The shape of the bundle was about the size of a baby.

Not sure what to expect, I grabbed a nearby stick and poked the object as more raindrops fell. It gave a little in some places but not in others. Placing a hand on the muddy cocoon, I felt for familiar shapes under the fabric. My heart paused as I found what felt like an arm and then a leg. Could someone have actually buried a child in our backyard? The rain was coming down harder now. Using the stick again, I managed to roll the package over and start peeling the layers of cloth from it. Soon a clump of muddy hair revealed itself.

Dropping the stick, I put my hand to my mouth in horror. "Holy shit."

I stared at the outline of a tiny head in shock and disbelief. It was a child. Looking down, my eyes focused on an exposed hand of pink flesh. But wait…that wouldn't make sense. If the body was buried when the rest of the food was, the skin and organs would have decomposed a long time ago. After a dry swallow, I grabbed the stick and poked the hand with it. It was hard. I tapped the arm a couple of times. *Thunk, thunk.* Flipping more of the cloth away, I noticed another arm and a pair of pudgy legs, all perfectly intact. "What the hell?"

Reasonably sure what I was looking at had never been alive, I picked up the mottled mess. The doll had seen better days, having been reduced to a filthy piece of nylon barely holding together plastic arms, legs, and a head. I wiped the soil from its face and gazed into painted blue eyes. It was Baby Jackie, the doll I had since I was five. But it couldn't be. Baby Jackie was up in my room, tucked safely away in my closet. The doll's face lit up as lightning flashed and a tremendous boom broke overhead.

CHAPTER 8

Saturday nights I was usually out with my friends stirring up some kind of trouble, but Friday's fun and my morning encounters with Maya, the six-year-old version of me, and zombie Baby Jackie had left me wiped out. As such, I decided that filling in the hoard of rotten food in my backyard would be my last bit of adventuring for the day. After a very long, very hot shower, a night vegging out in front of the tube and stuffing my face with all things sugar was the plan. A bowl of Rocky Road ice cream smothered in chocolate sauce usually satisfied my sweet tooth, but I found myself strangely unsatisfied and ended up back at the freezer grabbing what remained of it. After emptying half a can of Hershey's syrup and a mountain of Reddi-Wip into the half-gallon container, I went to town while watching *The Lost Boys* on videotape. I was about halfway through the movie when my eyelids started to grow heavy.

I was little again, barely tall enough to see over the

foot of the bed. There was a boy sleeping in it that was no more than fourteen or fifteen years old. He woke and looked at me with cold eyes. "What are you doing here?" he asked. The voice was Chris's, but he was so young.

"Watching you sleep." The words came out of my mouth, but they didn't sound right. They were rough, almost gravelly.

"Remember our agreement, Raga," young Chris said. "No more snooping or else I have to talk to you-know-who. I don't think you want that, do you?"

The image went hazy. When it cleared I was in our kitchen, but it looked different. Storage cabinets stood where the dishwasher should be, and the floor was covered in brick-patterned linoleum instead of the green accented tiles Dad put down years ago. I was rummaging through the pantry grabbing handfuls of Hostess fruit pies, Twinkies, a jar of pickles, and a tin of deviled ham. Plopping the food on the kitchen table, I tore into it. The fruit pies were the first to go, quickly followed by the pickles and mounds of deviled ham, both of which I gobbled up using my bare hands. I was *crazy* hungry, grunting while wolfing down everything in sight. Even though it had to be a dream, I tasted the gooey cherry filling of the pies mixed with the saltiness of the pickles. Pausing mid-chew, I looked up to the younger version of Chris. He was smiling as he downed the contents of a tiny plastic cup full of purple liquid. "What's that?" I asked as pie crumbs spewed from my mouth.

For a moment Chris looked like he was going to barf,

but after taking a deep breath, he said, "It's a little treat I'm giving myself seeing as I don't have much longer."

Once more the scene blurred, but this time it transitioned to something familiar. I was chasing the boy again, except I now recognized him as Chris. Filled with rage, I threw the wooden hammer at his legs, causing him to trip and fall. Moving in over him, I picked up the hammer and hoisted it over my head. With a bloodcurdling scream, I brought it down.

I jerked awake. A salty-sweet tang lingered in my mouth, like I had chowed down on a dinner of ham and pineapple upside down cake. Running my tongue over my teeth and along my gums, I searched for remnants of food to no avail. Plastic wrappers and empty tins rolled off the bed and onto the floor as I pushed myself up in bed. My stomach gurgled loudly, like it was angry at me.

"Blech. What the heck?"

Peering over the bed, I spied the pile of wrappers that once contained snack cakes and fruit pies but now held only crumbs and smears of frosting. I didn't remember heading back downstairs for a late-night snack. Hell, even if I had, the combination of food was bizarre – I didn't even like fruit pies. My stomach rumbled again.

Crawling out of my nest of gluttony, I stumbled to the bathroom and downed a couple of antacids before brushing my teeth with a double dose of Crest. I rinsed thoroughly and gazed in the mirror. "Raga," I whispered. Chris called me by that name in my dream, but it wasn't really me he was talking to. It was the same word that had echoed in my head at Belzer's party.

"Kate, are you up?" Mom shouted from downstairs.

I opened the bathroom door. "Yes."

"Chris is on the phone. He wants to talk to you."

This was unexpected. It wasn't my birthday, and we were still a ways off from any holidays, so why was my brother calling? Once back in my bedroom, I picked up the phone and said, "Got it, Mom." Chris and I both waited for the click before talking. To my knowledge our mother had never eavesdropped on our conversations, but neither of us wanted to take any chances and have something slip out that was better kept between siblings.

I opened the conversation. "Hey, dorkus. Long time no talk."

"I know. That's my bad. Business has been...hectic, and there hasn't been much time for Steve or me to reach out. That's no excuse, but if it makes you feel any better, Mom already read me the riot act."

"Maybe a little better. So to what do we owe the pleasure? You guys finally score big in the vacuum sales business? Plan to retire and buy some hacienda in South America?"

"All right, all right. Very funny. Seriously though, how are you doing?"

"Me? I'm fine." The words came out flat. It had been a strange couple of days and my mind was elsewhere, trying to make sense of the weird dreams I'd been having, as well as my bizarre new eating habits.

"What's up, Kate? You don't sound like your usual

annoying self."

Chris had always been good at reading me. Even over the phone, he knew something was up. I shook my head to help clear it. "I'm good. It's just been a little crazy around here with school and everything. That's all."

"Yeah, Mom *may* have mentioned that you had a little fun Friday night."

Of course she did. "Look, it was just the one time and was really no big deal. It's also not something I'm interested in being lectured about from my part-time brother."

"Ouch, that was kind of mean."

Mean, yes. Appropriate, perhaps. After sighing, I said, "Sorry, I just don't have the energy now for a lengthy phone conversation about my life."

"I get it. How about we catch up next week? Steve and I will be in town then."

An out of the blue call from my brothers was unusual, but a visit from the two of them for no apparent reason was something else entirely. The Dwyer brothers were constantly on the road, traveling from town-to-town selling this or that. If I didn't know any better, I'd guess they were drug runners, but that wasn't their style – at least I didn't think it was.

"What's wrong?" I asked. "Are you guys broke or something?"

"No, it's nothing like that."

"Is Steve okay?" The worry in my voice took me a

little by surprise.

Chris chuckled. "Big bro is fine. Maybe just a little burnt out from our time on the road. It hasn't helped that sales have been slow."

"So what is it this time? Girl Scout Cookies? Amway?"

"I wish. Maybe we'd have a little more luck with those. No, we're selling Tupperware."

"Tupperware?"

"Yeah, you know. Keep your food fresh and all that junk."

Sometimes it sounded like he just plucked an idea from out of the air. "Is that your sales pitch? Keeps your food fresh and all that junk."

"Steve handles most of the sales. I take care of the orders and paperwork."

Drug runners. They're definitely drug runners. Okay, maybe not drug runners, but they sure as hell weren't selling Tupperware. I decided to switch subjects instead of talking about their fake Tupperware sales. "So, this might seem like a strange question, but did we get in any fights when we were younger?"

"Fights? Nah, not really. You threw temper tantrums every now and then, but that's what kid sisters do."

"That's not what I'm talking about. Did we ever get in any fight fights? Like ones involving me chasing you with a wooden hammer?"

I grimaced, waiting for the hysterical laughter that was sure to follow.

The line went silent.

"Chris? Hello? Dorkus Maximus?"

Awkward laughter echoed over the phone. "What, you mean, like in a *Tom and Jerry* cartoon?"

"I'm serious. I've been having a recurring dream where I'm holding a hammer and chasing you and one of your friends. I throw it and trip you up. Then, right before I'm about to cave your head in, everything goes black."

"That doesn't ring a bell. I think I would remember my kid sister chasing me and Kevin around with a hammer."

"I didn't say it was Kevin."

Chris's response took a couple of more seconds than it should have. "You didn't?"

"Nope."

"Are you sure?"

"Yep."

"Well, who else would it be?" Chris said. "It's not like I had a bunch of friends growing up. Don't try and make something out of nothing."

As far back as I could remember, Chris had no shortage of friends. "So none of that sounds familiar to you?"

"Like I said, I'm pretty sure I'd remember something like that. Have you had any other weird dreams?"

"None where I was trying to kill you." I thought about last night's pig out and the accompanying dream. Some people talked in their sleep, others actually walked. Me, I binged on sweets in my sleep. I was a sleepbinger. "There was this one dream. In it I'm chowing down on anything I can get my hands on, but the more I eat, the hungrier I get. Freaky, huh?"

"Yeah, freaky."

My brother sounded distracted. "Chris?"

"Huh?"

"You okay?"

"Sure, I'm fine as wine. Hey, why don't you say hi to Steve. Hold on."

He was gone without so much as a goodbye or smell ya later. I could hear whispering in the background before Steve picked up.

"Hey, Kate. How's it going? Hear you've been having some strange dreams and eating a lot. If Mom finds out you're getting high in the house, she'll go ballistic."

"Very funny," I said, deciding it was time to change subjects to something less embarrassing. "But enough about me. How are you doing? Selling a lot of Tupperware?"

"Actually, it's been a bit slow. That's one of the reasons we're coming home. It's time to take a break from the road. I was finally able to convince Genghis Khan of that."

"Chris been working you too hard? Let me know, and I'll give him an earful."

Steve laughed. "I bet you would. But enough about all that boring junk. What's up with you? Heard you've turned into quite the party girl. Any boys mixed up in your recent hijinks?"

"Hijinks? Geeze, so I stay out a little late one night

and now everybody thinks I've turned into some kind of deviant."

"Hey, some of my favorite people are deviants, so watch it. But back to the question. What's his name?"

For as far back as I could remember, Steve was easier to talk to than Chris. He was more laid back, not as judgmental, and less big brotherish in general. "Jake."

"Don't think I've heard that name before."

"Nope. He's one of Mike's friends. He transferred to Bowie for his senior year."

"A transfer student? Very mysterious. What happened at his last school? Did he get kicked out for fighting or maybe smoking in the bathroom?"

"Don't know, but I'd like to find out."

"You just sounded like Lorraine from *Back to the Future*. Hope Jake doesn't turn out to be your time-traveling kid."

"That's gross, Steve."

"I'm just sayin'."

In the background I heard Chris mumbling. Seconds later Steve was back on the phone. "Gotta go. Genghis just reminded me we have a customer we have to meet. Love you and see you soon."

The line went dead before I could say goodbye. My brothers may have had Mom and Dad snowed, but those two clowns were going to come clean with me during their visit, even if I had to beat it out of them.

As I contemplated the most efficient methods for extracting the truth out of the two of them, my eyes turned to the bedroom window. On it a message had been scrawled in an oily, black fluid. It read:

```
The witch lies
Governor's bridge
Sunset
Come alone
```

The day had started out strange and was getting stranger by the minute.

CHAPTER 9

As much as I loved Theresa and Jackie, I decided to do as instructed and go it alone. The way I figured it, there was little point dragging them into something that was almost guaranteed to be a wild goose chase. Odds were it was Mike or maybe one of his friends that wrote the message to mess with me. That said, I did opt to bring a can of pepper spray in case the author turned out to be a pervert…or Mike for that matter.

The autumn sun was already sinking below the tree line when I pulled my parent's Plymouth Reliant off to the side of the road just prior to Governor's Bridge, better known as Crybaby Bridge by everyone at Bowie High. It was one of the first haunted places Mike took Theresa and me to before Jake and Jackie joined our motley crew, and legend had it that a woman had thrown her baby over the bridge and into the river a long time ago. Some people said she was a single mother who couldn't afford to feed her baby, others thought she was a witch offering the child as a sacrifice, but whatever her reasons, all three of us swore we heard the wail of the child above the gurgling of the river on that terrifying night. For that reason, I considered Mike the prime suspect behind the mysterious message written on my window.

The jean jacket I was wearing provided little warmth from the cool wind gliding off the muddy Patuxent to greet me. Shivering, I crossed the front of the bridge and started down a worn path along the riverbank. After walking for several minutes, I heard the distant metallic thumping of a car crossing the old truss bridge. Realizing I was some ways from the road and in a perfect spot to be kidnapped, robbed, stabbed and dumped in the river, etcetera, etcetera, I slipped a hand in my jacket and gripped the pepper spray.

With each passing minute, the likelihood of Mike's guilt slipped more and more from my mind. Though he liked a good joke more than most, Mike didn't have a lot of patience when it came to pranking someone, and we were well past the "gotcha" point for one of his gags. Something else was going on.

Up ahead to my left was a small grove just beyond a cluster of brush and brambles. Something was strangely familiar about it, but I knew I had never been this way before. Pushing past the branches and stepping over evil-looking thistles, I came to the clearing just in time to see streaks of dying sunlight slip between the trees, painting the ground in alternating lines of orange and black. In the middle of the striped field was a circle of bare earth. My mind started to buzz as if a honeybee had flown into one of my ears and gotten trapped there. The closer I got to the circle, the louder the buzzing became until it sounded like an entire hive was in my head. Something was buried in the center of it, and it was calling to me. Leaning forward, I reached out to touch the patch of dirt.

"Yow! Son-of-a-biscuit!"

A jolt of electricity leapt from the ground, zapping me just as sure as if I'd grabbed hold of an electric fence.

Massaging numb fingers, I stared at the ground looking for exposed wires or anything else that could explain the shock. "This is so freaky."

As the sun dipped lower and darkness grew, I discovered a reddish glow emanating from my left jacket pocket. Reaching in, I retrieved the stone Maya had given me. It was warm to the touch and radiated a brilliant orange light. The buzzing in my head diminished to a mere whisper as I held it in the palm of my hand. "What the frig?"

The rustling of leaves drew my attention to a thicket a half dozen yards to my right. Shoving the stone back in my pocket, I asked, "Who's there?"

Though the forest went silent, I could feel the weight of eyes on me. Pulling the can of pepper spray out, I shouted, "If that's you, Mike, you're a few seconds away from getting a face full of mace! This isn't funny!"

In my gut I knew Mike wasn't out there, but I didn't want to admit it. To do so would be to acknowledge that some roof-climbing nut job had lured me to the middle of nowhere for God knew what.

Sticks snapped behind me. Whatever was lurking in the dark was fast. "This is super lame, you butthead! If you don't show yourself, I'm out of here!"

A bone-chilling cry echoed in the forest. It was a deep, hollow sound, one that I was sure couldn't come from a human throat. I was being toyed with, taunted.

I swallowed hard to keep my heart from jumping out of my throat as I considered my options. The car was too far away to make a run for it. My instincts told me I would be ambushed long before I got there.

"Kate." The word crept over my shoulder like a spider. Spinning around, I caught a pair of luminous green eyes staring at me before they blinked out, vanishing into the dense undergrowth.

Those were *not* human. They seemed almost cat-like. Dammit, why the hell did I decide to come out here alone? It was stupid, a rookie mistake. I had all but served myself up to the creeper in the woods like some ditsy teenager in a cheesy horror movie. Shoving the pepper spray in front of me, I shouted, "So are you gonna come on out where I can see you or stay hidden like the chickenshit you are?"

Clawed hands parted the greenery, allowing a shadow to emerge. Tall and thin, it stretched upward well above my five-foot-three frame. Vaguely human-oid, it was covered in jet black fur that glistened in the twilight. Something grew from the shadow's head, drooping down along its shoulders. Were those ears?

The shadow's green eyes took hold of me. It extended a long black arm and spoke in a hushed voice. "Time to go."

I couldn't look away from those terrible eyes. The world around me turned gray, and my head grew foggy. I was walking toward it. Try as I might to stop, the message wasn't getting through to my legs. My tongue went limp as I mumbled, "No go."

"Yes," the creature hissed.

A few steps more and I was within arm's reach of it. Sharp teeth gleamed as the creature smiled. A clawed hand opened and beckoned me to take hold.

Blue smoke exploded in the creature's face as a voice from behind me boomed, "Back to the shadows with you!"

Howling in pain, the beast clawed at its face as it slipped back into the forest.

"Come, Kate," the voice said. "It will be back soon."

My head slowly cleared. Turning, I saw a hooded figure approach.

Grabbing my hand, the figure pulled me back to the bare patch of earth. "Do precisely as I tell you, and ask no questions if you want to survive. Understand?"

I knew the accent. "Maya?"

The witch leaned in close. Her eyes burned with intensity. "*Do you understand?*"

"Yeah, sure. I—I mean, yes."

Maya pointed to the circle. "Step in the center, and

do not leave it until I tell you it's safe."

Like a swimmer testing the water, I tried sticking my big toe into the circle. "Damn!" I shouted as a wicked shock nipped it. "The circle won't let me in. It's got some kind of energy field around it."

"The evil must have taken root," Maya muttered.

"Excuse me? Exactly what evil are we talking about?"

Ignoring my question, Maya said, "Take the stone and hold it tight. It has the power to subdue the darkness within you."

How Maya knew I had the stone was a question for another time. For now, following her instructions seemed like the smart thing to do. I grabbed the red rock and immediately felt its warmth. With my fingers wrapped tightly around it, I closed my eyes and once more attempted to step into the circle. To my surprise and relief, my foot touched ground with no resistance.

"Now, child! Get into the damn circle!" Maya shouted.

A terrible shriek pierced the stillness of the night.

The witch turned her attention to the surrounding forest. Reaching beneath her robes, she pulled out a cool-looking machete with strange symbols etched into it. "By Zarabanda and Nsasi, you shall not have this girl! Leave now, and I will spare you!"

Leaping from the shadows, the beast bounded toward Maya. In the blink of an eye, it was upon her, swiping at her flesh with a clawed hand.

But Maya was too fast. Pivoting with the grace of a

ballerina, she ducked and sliced the creature's ribcage.

With a pained cry, it spun away and vanished into the forest.

"What the hell is that thing?"

"Quiet," Maya ordered.

The witch's head swiveled left then right as she searched the shadows for the creature. "This is strange."

"You don't say?"

Maya cast me a sideways glance. "The beast hunting you is not evil by nature. It's a pooka. They can be mischievous and cause small amounts of damage, but true violence is not their way. Something must be controlling it."

"You mean like another witch?" I asked.

"That is possible."

This time I saw the pooka first. It darted out from behind Maya and was heading straight at her with its arms extended. "Turn around!" I shouted.

The pooka slashed Maya's arm, causing her to drop the machete.

"Fae be damned!" she shouted falling to one knee. "This creature is of the forest. It has the upper hand here."

Grabbing her weapon. she struggled to her feet. "I must even the playing field, quickly."

"Maya," I said pointing to three long gashes on her left bicep, "you're bleeding."

"So I am," she responded indignantly.

Maya was tough as nails, but she was at a

disadvantage and wounded to boot. And here I was absolutely worthless, stuck in a magic circle with nothing to do but play the part of a damsel in distress. Wait… maybe there was a way to help after all.

"Maya, this circle offers some kind of protection from evil, right?"

The witch nodded while catching her breath.

A screech echoed in the surrounding woods. The pooka was preparing for another attack.

"So, what if you use me as bait?" I asked. "You know, lure that thing out and get it to come full on at me? If it gets anywhere near the jolt I did, that might be enough to send it howling for the hills."

A smirk grew on Maya's sweaty face. "Very clever, Kate. But we won't be using you as bait."

"Won't I be safe though? It's just—"

"Shh," Maya said, stepping into the circle next to me. "If this creature gets the best of me, you must run as fast as you can to your car and don't look back."

Raising her machete like a baseball bat, Maya shouted something in Spanish to the pooka. Whether it was the tone she used or that the pooka happened to be bilingual and didn't appreciate her choice of words, I'll never know, but either way, Maya's challenge had the desired effect. The creature responded with an earsplitting shriek and broke cover, making straight for us.

Fighting the urge to curl up into a fetal position, I watched the beast pounce, stretching its clawed fingers toward us as it opened a gaping mouth. That's when I lost faith in our plan, convinced that Maya was the appetizer and I the main course. To her credit Maya never flinched.

Like a bolt of lightning, a brilliant light flashed temporarily blinding us. A high-pitched squeal immediately followed, accompanied by the stench of singed fur.

"Oh God," I said placing a hand over my nose. "That smells *so* bad. Like a bunch of barbecued cats."

"Blessed be Zarabanda. It worked," Maya whispered.

"What worked? Where is it?" I said as my eyes adjusted.

"There," Maya pointed to a smoking mound of fur.

We watched as the pooka staggered back to its feet. Its eyes fell upon us, but I saw no evil behind them. The creature looked bewildered, as if waking from a long dream.

"Begone!" Maya shouted while shaking her blood-stained machete.

Mewling, the crispy and confused beast slunk back into the shadows, leaving the rank smell of burnt fur in its wake.

Maya turned to me. A couple of droplets of blood speckled her check. "Are you okay?"

"I think so. I feel a little tingly all over, but other than that, I'm fine." Motioning to my cheek I said, "You have a little blood…"

Maya smiled. "An unfortunate occurrence. I do not enjoy spilling the blood of bewitched creatures."

"Is that thing gone?" I asked, nodding toward the

forest.

"For now. Whatever spell it was under has been disrupted, at least temporarily. We will not be seeing it again tonight."

"Tonight?" I said. "How about never? I would be very happy never seeing a pooka again, thank you very much."

The smile left Maya's face. "I cannot offer such assurances. It seems you have a talent for attracting dangerous things. Tell me, why are you wandering alone in such an odd place?"

Though I never considered myself a devious person, the guilt of not trusting Maya caused me to speak in half-truths. "Someone left me a note. It said to meet them here at sunset."

"Why?" Maya asked, her eyes gazing into mine.

Looking to my feet, I feigned ignorance. "I don't know. That was all the letter said."

"I see," she replied.

The witch's tone suggested she wasn't buying it. I tried to think of some bit of information to add to my story to make it more believable, but before I could, Maya crouched down and began digging.

"What are you doing?" I asked.

Ignoring me as she scooped up dirt, Maya mumbled, "This must be the place."

"The place for what?"

"Ah!" Maya shouted, holding something small between her thumb and finger.

"What is it?"

She stared at the object as if it was the most fascinating thing she had ever seen. "A nail," she answered.

I leaned in close. Tiny bits of clay stuck to the rusted piece of metal. It was weirdly shaped too, square-headed like a tiny railroad spike. "Why would someone bury that here?" I asked.

The witch rolled the nail across her fingertips. "It's a long story, one to be shared another time. What's important now is how this can help us."

Maya was being cryptic, but my ever-growing knowledge of witches taught me to stay out of their way when they behaved as such. I watched her retrieve a black candle and box of matches from the satchel slung over her shoulder. She lit the candle and began whispering in Spanish while drawing a glyph of intersecting arrows on the ground.

"Quick, Kate, hand me my machete. The beast's blood must be fresh for this to work."

I did as she asked, watching in anxious silence as she worked her witchy ways.

Smoke curled into the air as Maya scraped the old nail across the bloodied blade of the machete and then held it just above the candle flame. Closing her eyes, Maya leaned over and inhaled, allowing intertwining tendrils of smoke to waft into her nose. How she could stand the pungent metallic odor was beyond me. Once more she chanted in Spanish.

After several seconds, her eyes popped open. "The

pooka was not trying to kill you."

Pinching my nose to keep the smell out of it, I said, "Could've fooled me."

Maya blew out the candle and shoved the nail back into the earth. "You were to be abducted. For what purpose I cannot say, but someone wants you alive."

"Well, I guess that's better than dead."

The yaya stared at me but said nothing.

"Right?" I repeated in a nasally voice.

"Perhaps."

Releasing my nose, I said, "I forgot to ask how you found me."

"I have been watching you since the first night I caught you spying on me," she said, wiping the blade of her machete across the grass. "You are attracting the attention of forces that are better left undisturbed. Until we figure out why, it would be wise for you to refrain from going out alone to remote locations based on notes left by strangers."

Somewhere beneath the dripping sarcasm, Maya was holding out on me. I was also ninety-nine percent sure I wasn't followed earlier. Aside from the fact that I didn't see anybody behind me on Spindle, Governor's Bridge Road was a lonely little stretch of pavement that would have been super difficult to follow someone on without getting busted. "Okay, granted. That wasn't the smartest move I've ever made, but c'mon. How the heck was I supposed to know tall, dark, and creepy was trying to kidnap me?"

"Promise me you'll be more careful from now on and not go out unaccompanied."

Why Maya had taken so much interest in me was anyone's guess, but she did just save my bacon, so I guess I owed her. Also, I still felt a tad guilty about not trusting her. "Okay."

"And remember to keep the charm with you at all times. It masks your presence from those who would seek to do you harm."

"It was also the key to entering your magic circle here. Why was that? Why couldn't I get in without the stone?"

"Much has been said tonight, Kate, and there will be a time and a place to talk more." Maya pointed her machete toward the woods. "But there are many eyes and ears in the shadows, and our words are better kept between us."

CHAPTER 10

Pizza, greasy tater tots, applesauce, and a blob of no-bake chocolate peanut butter gooiness. School lunches were awesome. I started with the sweet stuff and worked my way backward to the pizza. At this rate I was going be on Jenny Craig before Thanksgiving.

"Anyone catch the news last night?" Mike asked the group.

When none of us bothered to answer, he took it as his cue to continue. "They found another body on Fletchertown Road. That makes three people killed in Bowie since June. *Three.*"

"I thought one of them was killed in Crofton," Jackie said.

"Crofton smofton," Mike replied before slurping some of his lime Jell-O up with a straw. "It might as well be Bowie. They're right next to each other."

"So what's your point?" Jake asked.

Mike's eyes narrowed as he shook his head in mock

disgust. "Seriously? Hello, McFly! Anybody in there? We have a serial killer on our hands. I bet they'll find another body in the next two weeks. See, the killer's gonna start getting bold because he hasn't been caught. Just like that Night Stalker guy in California."

Jake nudged my arm. "You believe this knucklehead?"

I was too busy trying to enjoy my lunch to pay attention to the conspiracy theory, satanic cult, crop circle crap Mike was spouting. "I like to tune Mike out while eating. It helps with the digestion." I moved in close to Jake and stretched my arm out, snatching the no-bake cookie from his tray. "You weren't gonna eat that, were you?"

"Uh, I guess not."

I gave him a peck on his cheek as payment. "Thanks, hon, you're beautiful."

The school lunches at Bowie High never used to appeal to me, but in retrospect, perhaps I had misjudged them. The mix of the cheesy pizza and super salty tots with ketchup was sublime. Simply put, I couldn't get enough of it.

Theresa crossed her arms and flashed Jake and me a smile. "You two seem to be getting awful cozy. Guess my matchmaking skills worked."

"Our matchmaking skills," Mike said, putting his arm around Theresa. "But on to more pressing matters. I have our next adventure locked and loaded."

A clamor of sighs and groans bubbled from the group.

"Let's not forget our last adventure," I said. "If it wasn't for Jake, we probably would have had our butts kicked by bunch of pissed-off rednecks. Not cool."

"Kate's right," Theresa added. "One near death encounter per month is enough for me. Let's just chill for a bit."

Mike raised his hands, acknowledging defeat. "Fine. Fiiine. I get it. Geez, you'd think I was talking about robbing a bank. You haven't even heard the idea yet."

"So," Jackie said with an impish grin, "what is it?"

Mike leaned over the table and whispered as if the cafeteria walls had ears. "Two words. Glenn Dale."

"You mean the hospital they closed a couple of years ago?" Jake said, blocking my hand from snaking another one of his tater tots.

Theresa shook her head. "He's been talking about this one since we came back from the Satan Church."

I watched the smile fade from Jackie's face. "You okay?"

It took her a few seconds to acknowledge me. "Huh?"

"I said, are you okay? You look like someone just walked over your grave."

She feigned a weak smile. "I'm fine. Just remembered I forgot to do my history homework. Oh well."

Oblivious to everyone but himself, Mike continued. "They say it was a hospital for the criminally insane and that when they closed it not all of the patients were accounted for. Rumor has it there are still a few of them left there, hiding and preying upon anyone foolish enough to enter."

Jake pointed at Mike. "I heard from Matt Harper that the place is actually owned by the government and that they do weird experiments there. Topside it looks like an abandoned hospital but underneath there is this huge complex of secret labs."

It was normal to hear conspiracy theory garbage spewing from Mike's mouth, but to hear it popping out of Jake's was a bit surprising. I gave him a cockeyed glance. "Really? Now you're buying into this stuff?"

"Hey, I'm just repeating what other people have said. It's not like—"

"You're both wrong," Jackie said.

Jackie was usually one of the first people to jump on board Mike's crazy train. She loved the idea of flirting with danger and sneaking off to forbidden places. To hear her poo-pooing one of his schemes was strange to say the least.

"It was a sanitarium for people with tuberculosis, at least that's why it was built," she said. "After improved medications came out to treat the disease, the place started to empty out, so they opened up the doors for people with other kinds of debilitating sickness. They closed it when they found asbestos everywhere."

"Well look who knows so much all of a sudden," Mike said. "What, did you have to do some kind of report on the hospital for school?"

Jackie answered with a meek, "No."

Between mouthfuls of cookie, I decided it was time

to put Mike in his place. "Mike, some people actually know more than you because they're just plain smarter. I imagine that would be the case for pretty much everyone in the cafeteria."

"Or everyone in the school for that matter," Theresa said.

Mike smirked at me. "Yeah, well at least I don't chew with my mouth open, Kate. And since when do you like the cafeteria food? I always hear you saying how gross it is."

The exact same question had been bothering me since I first caught whiff of the baking pizzas and started drooling, but for some reason I couldn't help myself. "Today's food isn't so bad. You just need to add a lot of ketchup to the pizza."

My newfound affinity for cafeteria food and recent sleep snacking episode had me at a total loss – as did my bizarre dreams and last night's near kidnapping. Maybe I was coming down with something. Maybe I had a tapeworm. The more I reflected on it, the more my thoughts drifted back to Maya. The freaky dreams I was having didn't start until after she had moved into the neighborhood and neither had my bizarre dietary choices. Also, the way she shut me down when I started asking her questions about the stone was odd. My hand slipped into my pocket and touched it, the "gift" given to me by the witch. It was warm. She made me promise to keep it wherever I went...

It hit me like a slap to the face. The damn stone. That

was how Maya found me at Crybaby Bridge. She must have used it like some kind of magical tracking device. It was the only explanation. "That *bitch*," I muttered.

"Who's a bitch?" Theresa asked, breaking me out of the spell I was under.

Standing, I looked at my friend. "Sit tight. I'll be right back."

Storming out of the senior lounge, I marched across the hall and into the cafeteria where the underclassmen riff-raff ate. Pulling the stone from my pocket, I went to the nearest window and chucked it out. "Suck on that, Maya."

The warmth left my hand with the stone. I stared at my fingers, wondering how I could have been so clueless. That manipulative psycho, serving me delicious coffee and pretending to be my friend all while conjuring up spells to give me constant nightmares and turn me into a size sixteen. That was just downright mean. But was that really the end of it, or did the witch have something worse in store for me? And what about the pooka? If Maya really was out to get me then maybe the creature was actually trying to rescue me. My head started to ache. Whatever the case, the Voodoo Queen and I were going to settle things once and for all after school.

CHAPTER 11

Pink walls and stuffed animals surrounded me. I was a child once more, squatting on the floor of my bedroom and playing with a doll. The next thing I knew, its head was in my mouth. Biting down, I gave a hard tug with my pudgy little hand, and yanked the doll – minus its head – out. After tossing the headless remains onto a pile of decapitated dolls, I spat the slobbery head across the room. With no more dolls left to ruin, I grabbed a red crayon from my desk and opened the closet door. Plopping down on my stomach, I continued work on a mural drawn on the back wall. Furiously spinning my hand in circles, a pool of red formed beneath several prone stick figures as another figure stood above them with a smile on its face and a bloodied knife in its hand. A rush of air entered my bedroom as the door flew open. Chris was now there, frowning and yelling at me, but he didn't call me by my name. He called me Raga again. As he knelt to snatch the crayon from my hand, the scene faded.

Next, I was in another room in another house being scolded yet again, this time by an old man with silver hair and leathery skin. Even though he looked ancient, I was terrified of him. Leaning in close, he whispered unintelligible words in a low, menacing voice. I watched in horror as the vessels in his eyes ruptured, turning them from hazel to blood red. His mouth sprang open displaying two rows of razor-sharp teeth, and a terrible bleating crawled out of his throat. Crimson eyes spread apart as his face stretched long like a wolf's snout, and tiny snakes sprouted from the sides of his head, coiling round and round to form wicked looking horns.

"Gah!" I shouted.

The chorus of laughter served as a heinous reminder that I was still in school. I blinked as my eyes adjusted to the fluorescent lighting and the laughter receded to giggles.

"Sorry to disturb your nap, Ms. Dwyer. I can only assume that you are already familiar with the subject at hand and have fallen asleep out of sheer boredom. As such, perhaps you can provide some assistance with the conundrum on the blackboard. We need to figure out how many moles are in thirty-eight grams of sodium chloride. Why don't you come up here to the blackboard so the whole class has the benefit of seeing your work?"

James Evans was his name, and boring the hell out of students was his game. He sported typical chemistry teacher attire, consisting of a short-sleeved button-down shirt, overstuffed pocket protector, gray Sansabelt slacks, and a pair of horn-rimmed glasses to round off his ensemble. Sometimes the color of his shirt changed, but the marker stain on his bottom lip was ever-present, always appearing after his inevitable use of the overhead projector.

What made Mr. Evans a terrible teacher wasn't his poor fashion sense or that he was boring – I had plenty of boring teachers – but rather that he took delight in embarrassing his students. In Mr. Evans's class there were definitely such things as dumb questions, and wrong answers were routinely met with responses like, "Don't worry, McDonald's is always hiring," and "Your parents wouldn't happen to be related, would they?"

Yawning, I looked blankly at Mr. Evans's ink-stained mouth. He had called me out to serve as his latest example, but I was neither embarrassed nor intimidated. To the contrary, I felt strangely confident, maybe even a little bit pissed.

"Sorry, Jimbo, had a big lunch, and I think it made me a little sleepy. It had nothing to do with your teaching skills, promise."

His pasty face turned pink. "I'm glad to hear that," he said, holding up a piece of chalk. "Now, if you would be so kind as to show us your solution."

My lip curled into a sneer as I pushed my chair back and stood. Walking to the front of the class like I owned the joint, I started humming the theme to *Jeopardy*. Once next to Mr. Evans, I placed my hand out in front of him and cleared my throat.

The teacher's rosy cheeks graduated to beet red, and for a moment I thought he might have ruptured a blood vessel or two. But he did as instructed and put the tiny white stick into my hand.

I winked at him and went to work. My hand had a mind of its own as it danced across the blackboard in sweeping strokes, left and then right. I was in the zone, possessing a crystal-clear picture in my head of the solution to this particular problem. When my masterpiece was finished, I turned to the class and smiled. "Any questions?"

The stunned silence that followed my rather graphic depiction of our chemistry teacher as a giant penis was music to my ears. In case there were any doubts as to who the spectacled pecker was, I had written his name directly above my work of art with an arrow pointing down. The open-mouthed stares and ear-to-ear grins of my classmates served as a just reward for finally sticking it to one of the biggest bullies in our school. Poor Mr. Evans was beyond words. His hand trembled as he pointed to the classroom door.

I nodded. "Got it. Principal Baker's office. I'll tell him you said hi."

CHAPTER 12

Most kids would have gotten a suspension for the stunt I pulled, but because of my superior academic record and lack of prior offenses, along with Mr. Evans's less than flattering reputation, a week's worth of detention was my sentence. On the home front my parents placed me under ten days of house arrest. I played the role of penitent daughter and apologized profusely, citing Mr. Evans's abusive teaching methods as motivation for my controversial artwork, but deep down I was glad I did it. It served that prick right, pun intended. What really bothered me was I still had no idea where I got the cojones to stand up to him. Somehow all of my inhibitions and anxiety melted away and were replaced by a powerful urge to shut his marker-stained mouth up.

As with most goings-on at Bowie Senior High, my act of defiance quickly took on a life of its own, gradually evolving with each retelling. By the time it circled back to me, as told by Jackie between uncontrollable fits of giggling, I had taken Mr. Evans's infamous marker and decorated his forehead instead of the chalkboard with my artwork. Admittedly, if that thought had occurred to me at the time, Mr. Evans might still be trying to wash a tiny penis off his face.

The only one of our crew annoyed by my behavior was Mike, as it caused our Glenn Dale adventure to be postponed by a week. Of course that didn't stop him from talking about it every chance he got. We couldn't make it through a single lunch without him blabbing about insane patients still haunting the hospital grounds or satanic cults holding human sacrifices deep within the bowels of Glenn Dale.

I wasn't going to let something as lame as the possibility of being grounded until I was college-bound deter me from paying a late-night visit to Maya to wring the truth out of her. She owed me answers as to why she put a curse on me, why she was tracking my every move, and who or what the heck Raga was.

I waited until my folks crashed to sneak out using my never fail terrace route. With no stone for her to track my moves with, I planned to catch Maya off guard so she didn't have time to whip up some bad juju and hex me. I would be direct and force her into coming clean.

Her front door flew open before my knuckles could touch it. Maya's long black hair was tied back in a ponytail and her perfect bronze skin was smudged with dirt. Even filthy she was glam.

"What is it?" she asked, wiping a bead of sweat from

her forehead. "I thought we agreed that you weren't to come over unannounced. Why are you here at this late hour?"

I opened my mouth to let her have it and, instead, began stammering. "I—I—"

Maya shut her eyes and muttered something in Spanish before opening them and waving me in. "Well, don't just stand there."

Defeated, I shut my mouth and entered.

The inside of her house had been stripped down to its bones. In place of walls, wooden studs stood, and the floor in the front hall was nothing more than cement. Cabinets had been ripped off framing and exposed pipes and wires were everywhere. Piles of rubbish sat in corners, and a fine layer of dust had settled on everything, including Maya.

I said the only thing that came to mind. "Wow."

Maya grabbed a towel from the kitchen and wiped down the wicker chair I sat in during my last visit. After cleaning off another chair, she motioned for me to sit.

Ignoring the seat offered – in case she had put some kind of spell on it – I claimed the one closer to her.

A tiny smile blossomed on Maya's face as she sat in the available seat. "What exactly can I help you with?"

I breathed deeply and began. "Look, I'm sorry that I trespassed on your property, okay? I promise it won't happen again. Now could we stop playing games, and will you please remove whatever curse, spell, or hex you put on me so that I can go back to my normal, boring life? I've learned my lesson. Promise."

She frowned. "You think I put a curse on you?"

Apparently, Maya still wanted to mess around, but I was through with her little mind games. "Don't play innocent! I know you're mad at me for sneaking into your backyard, and it's clear you thought you could teach me a lesson by putting some kind of hocus pocus on me. Well it worked, okay? I am sufficiently freaked out. Enough already with the bizarre dreams and cravings and giant killer pookas or whatever you call them. If I keep chowing down like I've been doing lately, pretty soon I'll be wearing nothing but muumuus. In case you haven't guessed, that is *not* a cool look when you're in high school."

"You're having strange dreams and experiencing great hunger?" Maya asked.

So she wanted to play dumb. That was fine. Even if I had to put her in a headlock and noogie a confession out of her, I was going to get Maya to undo whatever the hell she had done to me. "As if you didn't know that. Listen, I'm not leaving here until you fess up and unwhammy me. *Comprendez?*"

A tired sigh slipped from the yaya's lips. "So tell me, Kate, why do you think I have summoned such spirits to plague you?"

I was ready to crack open a can of whoop ass when I paused, noticing things I failed to when first entering the house. The T-shirt Maya wore was sweat stained, and her eyes were smoky, not from makeup but from dust and grime. Here I was all pumped up for a major fight, but seeing Maya exhausted doused the fire in me. When I spoke, I dialed the volume way down. "It all seemed to begin around the time you moved in. It started with the dreams. I'm a little kid in them, and I'm usually doing something terrible like ripping off doll heads or trying to cave my brother's head in with a giant hammer, kind of like the one in *Donkey Kong*. Also, he keeps calling me a weird name in the dreams, Raga I think."

Maya tried to keep it cool, but I noticed the tiny flare in her eyes at the mention of Raga. "Go on," she said.

"I'm always eating, not just in my dreams but all the time now. Though I've never been a health nut, I like to think I used to eat somewhat decent food. Now it's hard for me to walk by the kitchen without inhaling an entire box of Ho Hos and a two-liter Coke."

"Have you kept the charm close to you as instructed?"

"Umm. Not exactly."

"And why not?"

"I kind of chucked it."

Maya said nothing, coolly staring at me like I was touched in the head. Her silence and condescending gaze proved too much for me to handle.

"Look, it was a pain to lug around, okay? It was always warm, and I could even feel it through my clothes. Hell, I must've lost the damn thing in the washer three times. Besides, you were tracking me with it, weren't you?"

Another deep sigh came from Maya. "Not tracking, per se. If needed, I could call upon the stone's energy to locate you, but I have better things to do than watch your every move. Also, the warm sensation you felt meant the charm was working, helping to keep whatever was influencing you at bay. Without it you are vulnerable."

"So if you're not the one causing all this, who is?"

"Not so much who as what. Tell me again, what was the name you were called in your dreams?"

"Raga."

"I do not know it, but that doesn't mean much. There are countless spirits and powers that can trouble the living."

She was lying. Her initial reaction to the name was surprise. But why was she holding out on me now? Was she trying to protect me, or was she up to something bogus? Inquiring minds wanted to know.

"So you think there may be some kind of ghost haunting me?" I asked.

"Places are haunted, child, not people."

"Fine. So you think a spirit is trying to possess me?" I asked.

"Perhaps. From your description, it seems like it's trying to communicate with you, possibly through a connection you share from a time in your childhood."

"And the pooka? How is it linked to all of this?"

"I think I can help you with all of your questions, but first things first. I must find my book."

"What book? Is it a spell book?"

"I am a yaya, as was my mother and her mother before her and so on. Before the American Civil War, one

100

of my ancestors was sold to the Ogles from the plantation on which she and her family worked in Cuba. Entranced by her beauty, her new master fell in love with her, and within the year she had given birth to a light-skinned baby boy. The birth of the child was discovered by the master's wife, and suspecting her husband's infidelity, she flew into a jealous rage. As a result, the master banished the woman and her child from the plantation, and they were never heard from again. I am a descendant of the younger sister that remained in Cuba, and I am here to find the book my ancestor left behind. It contains all of the acquired knowledge of generations of yayas and is rightfully mine. For the longest time I thought the book was lost."

It finally clicked. "Ohhh," I said, glancing around my partially demolished surroundings, "so you think the book's stashed somewhere in this house, don't ya?"

"That is a conversation for another day."

Although I'm no Sherlock Holmes, I like to think my analytical skills are pretty good. "Uh-huh. So you wanna tell me what the Butcher of Bowie has to do with your book? Did he use it during his killing spree? I heard the cops found a bunch of bones and all kinds of satanic paraphernalia when they raided the place."

The fire returned to Maya's eyes as they met mine. "Careful, some doors are better left shut."

Bingo. "If that book can help me get rid of this Raga clown, then I'm willing to knock down any door in my way."

"All you need to know is that the one you call Edward Hutchinson took something that didn't belong to him and used it for evil purposes. When he left this world, some of the evil he sowed remained. I believe the darkness that surrounds you is linked to that."

Closing my eyes, I tried to recall the nightmare involving Mr. Hutchinson. It was surprisingly easy. "In one of my dreams, I was in this house. Mr. Hutchinson was shouting at me for some reason, but he wasn't calling me by my name. He was calling me Raga. Sweet Jesus!"

My eyes popped open but the haunting image of the old man's blood-filled eyes lingered.

Maya stared at me, a wary expression etched on her face. "What did you see?"

"Mr. Hutchinson changed. He turned into something else, something terrible."

"Visions are often misleading," Maya said. "Sometimes bad people manifest as things terrible to behold. This is simply an expression of the evil they represent. Can you remember where you were in the dream? Which room you stood in?"

The yaya seemed a little too dismissive of Mr. Hutchinson's hideous transformation to me, but I decided to let it go for now. "It's a little fuzzy, but there were a lot of books in the room." I stood and began walking around the kitchen table. "There was a desk in it too. It looked kind of like a home office."

Maya stood and opened a door to a small room that

looked out to the front yard. "I believe this used to be Edward Hutchinson's study, but I have found no residual energy lingering in it. It is interesting. It's one of the few rooms where there is no trace of evil. That's what has frustrated my search with the remaining parts of the house. There is so much latent darkness residing here; it is rife with the stains of evil deeds."

I entered the little room and tried to orient myself to where I would have been positioned in my dream. It was about the size of the kitchen, and empty bookshelves lined the surrounding walls from top to bottom. A chill crawled under my skin, stretching its icy fingers until it tickled my bones. I shivered. "This looks like the room except there was a desk in it, and the floors were wooden."

I stomped on the linoleum floor and listened to the echo. "Strange."

"What's strange?" Maya asked.

"All of the houses in this part of Bowie were built by Levitt and Sons."

"So?"

"Levitt didn't do basements or crawlspaces. All of their houses were built on cement slabs, and there's no cement beneath us. This room was added on, and I'd bet you a box of Twinkies there's something under us."

CHAPTER 13

At Maya's urging, I went on a scavenger hunt for the discarded charm the next day before school started. The bright red stone was hard to miss nestled beneath a row of hedges planted just outside of the cafeteria. Lucky me.

Mercifully, the next couple of days were uneventful, possibly due in part to the stone, and even though I would be stuck at home for the whole weekend serving out my prison sentence, at least I would have company. Chris and Steve had finally dropped by for a visit.

Our tête-à-tête had to wait until near midnight, after dinner and the inevitable Mom and Dad tag team interrogation that followed. The inquisition included such gems as, *"Have you two met any nice girls?"* and *"So what's new in the world of Tupperware sales?"* I had to hand it to my brothers. They flung the bullshit so thick but so persuasively I thought I was going to drown in it. Of course our parents bought it all.

I waited for Mom and Dad's bedroom door to shut

before saying, "If either of you goes on a rant about Tupperware's stay-fresh technology again, I swear I'll kick you in the nards."

Chris said nothing as he opened our parents' liquor cabinet and started rummaging through it.

Steve laughed. "I told you she wouldn't believe it. Kate's probably smarter than the two of us put together."

My brothers were opposites in almost every regard and had been for as long as I could remember. Steve stood just over six feet tall and sported a buzz cut that helped mask thinning hair, whereas Chris was a few inches shorter with a meticulously groomed shoulder-length mullet. Steve most often wore a smile on his chiseled face versus Chris's permanent smirk.

"Yahtzee," Chris said, pulling a bottle of Ancient Age out of the cabinet.

"So you wanna skip the BS and let me know what you guys have been up to? It's not drugs, is it? I can handle a lot of things, like if you were bounty hunters or worked for the CIA, but it would be a real disappointment if I found out you were smugglers."

Steve was quick to answer. "We're not smugglers."

Chris remained silent as he poured a couple of inches of bourbon into a glass and took a long sip.

"Then what the heck have you guys been doing since you left here?"

Steve gave Chris a pleading look as he said, "We've been searching for someone."

"A customer," Chris snapped, glaring at his older

brother.

"A customer," I said flatly.

Chris took another sip and winked at me. "Yep."

I grabbed the glass of bourbon out of my brother's hand and downed what remained in one throat-burning swallow. "You guys might want to think about another line of work. Seven years on the road and you still look like you don't have a nickel between the two of you. Maybe sales aren't your thing. You know, kind of like lying isn't. And Christ, that stuff is awful." I pushed the empty glass back in his hand.

"Since when did you start drinking bourbon?" Steve asked with a crooked smile.

"Since now," I wheezed out. The frustration of trying to squeeze the truth out of them was triggering the beast within me. At this rate there wouldn't be a box of Suzy Q's or Krimpets left in the house come morning. Though the liquor tasted like lighter fluid, there was something immensely satisfying about the warmth now running through my body.

Chris put the empty glass down. "Have you been having strange urges or cravings lately? Been boozing a lot or eating weird combinations of food?"

Nodding, I said, "For the past couple of weeks now, and it's been getting worse."

"And the dreams?" Steve asked.

"The same. I've had more of them since I talked to you guys last."

Closing my eyes, I recalled the dream where I was

standing at the foot of Chris's bed. When I opened them again, my brothers were staring at me.

"Shit," Chris mumbled.

"Have you told anyone else about this?" Steve asked.

"Only Maya. She moved into the Butcher's old house. She's a yaya."

"Seriously?" Chris blurted. "So you're going to some witch for advice? A witch who just happens to be living in the G –" Chris closed his eyes and shook his head before continuing, "– in the Butcher of Bowie's old house. Are you nuts?"

"Maybe. And since when do you know what a yaya is?" I asked with a thick tongue. "I doubt that's common knowledge. Also what's up with the hesitation? Did the Butcher of Bowie have a roommate I don't know about?"

"Maybe it's time to tell her," Steve said.

"That's not an option!" Chris shouted.

Steve raised a finger to his mouth. "Easy, bro. No need to get riled up. Mom and Dad just went to bed."

Steve was wavering. If I pushed a little, maybe the two of us could get Chris to crack. Scowling at both of them, I said, "I'll be right back."

I went upstairs and returned a minute later with Baby Jackie in my hand. "You remember her?"

"Of course," Steve said, smiling. "That's Baby Jackie. You got her when you were four or five. I can't remember which."

"So if that's the case, what the hell is this?" I asked, tossing Chris the mummified version of Baby Jackie that

I had been holding behind my back.

Catching it, he looked to what was in his hands. "Gah!" he shouted dropping the doll. "What the hell is that? Some kind of satanic *Evil Dead* zombie baby?"

Nodding to the doll, I said, "*That* is Baby Jackie too."

"Where did you get it?" Steve asked.

"I found it in the backyard," I said, not wanting to tell them the whole story for fear they might have me committed. "Now, would one of you mind explaining to me why I have two Baby Jackies?"

Chris said nothing, simply hunching his shoulders and playing dumb – as usual.

"Look, Kate," Steve said, "when you were young, you lost your doll. We looked everywhere for it but couldn't find it, so Mom and Dad replaced it with another. There's no big mystery behind it, no conspiracy. It's just one of those things parents do for their kids."

Steve's answer explained the reason for the two dolls but offered no insight into why the hell I had buried one of them in the first place. Frustrated, I blurted, "What aren't you guys telling me? If all the strange stuff going on has something to do with me, I have the right to know. Now's not the time for the overprotective brothers routine."

"Chris," Steve said, "Kate's already talking to some witch."

Chris pointed a full glass of bourbon in my direction. "You need to stay the hell away from that witch. Witches are nothing but trouble. And burn that doll," he said, nodding to zombie Baby Jackie. "It gives me the creeps."

Ignoring the doll comment, I said, "Meet a lot of witches in the Tupperware business? Difficult customers are they?"

"You don't get it, do you? You're just a kid," Chris said. "You should be out with your friends playing video games and going to sleepovers and crap like that."

"Sleepovers? Exactly how old do you think I am?"

"Look, leave the witch and that house down the road alone, and let Steve and me take care of things. Give us a week, and it will all be settled and back to normal. One week, that's all I ask."

"The stuff from my dreams, did it really happen? What's going on with me, and who is Raga?"

"Listen, Kate," Steve started, "when you were six we—"

"We screwed up," Chris interrupted. "And by we, I mean me."

Chris stared down his brother. "And dragging Kate into this shit show isn't going to help. What's done is done. There's no changing it, no going back in time. What we need to focus on is the here and now. You know I'm right." Chris downed the remains of his drink. "I'm hitting the sack. Tell her what you want, Steve. But then it's all on you, not me."

We watched Chris storm upstairs.

I was mad. Scratch that, I was *furious*. Who the hell did Chris think he was bossing Steve and me around, as if he was actually in charge of something? And who was he to keep stuff from me about my past, stuff that was now bleeding over into my dreams and influencing my behavior? "When exactly did Chris turn into such an asshole?" I asked.

"He's not an asshole," Steve said, sighing. "He just doesn't want to see you hurt."

I stood in front of my brother and locked eyes with him. "I don't get it. Why do you put up with his bullshit? I know you're tired and not just tonight but for some time now. I heard it in your voice when we talked on the phone. You clearly don't like...selling Tupperware. So why do you do it? Why did you quit college and throw away your life to play nursemaid to that ungrateful shit?"

Steve looked to the floor. "I don't expect you to understand. There's so much you don't know, but Chris believes it's for the best, and I have to respect that."

"Why, Steve? Why the hell do you have to respect anything he says? What am I missing?"

Steve glanced at me with the saddest eyes. "You don't see it, do you?"

"See what? What are you talking about?"

"Chris is slipping away."

"Slipping away? Away from what?"

Ignoring my questions, he muttered, "Chris wasn't always like this. When we were young he was as goofy and carefree as the next kid. He had a wicked imagination." Steve snickered. "Hell, I was the drama queen then. I was bossy, had a hair-trigger temper, and didn't have a lot of room in my life for an annoying kid brother."

"Get out of town. Chris was happy-go-lucky? *Our* Chris? I don't believe it."

Steve chuckled. "And boy did you used to follow him around like a lonesome puppy dog."

"I bet he loved that," I said as sarcastically as I could.

"Chris spent more time playing with you than I did, more than anyone else for that matter. He went out of his way to make sure you were included in the neighborhood fun and would frequently ditch his own friends to spend time with you."

I knew Chris and I had been closer when we were younger, but I had no idea he was so doting. "Really? He actually chose to hang out with me instead of his friends?"

"You two used to snuggle on the couch watching cartoons every Saturday morning. To be honest, there were times I was a little jealous of how close you were."

"This is mind blowing. So what hell happened to him? What turned him into an overbearing know-it-all?"

"I guess it all started around ten years ago, but it's getting worse. He's been getting worse."

After a moment, Steve gave me his best big-brother stare. "He's trying to protect you. That's the reason he is the way he is."

"From what though?"

"The past."

CHAPTER 14

Perhaps with a little help from Maya's charm, I was able to keep a low profile for the next week, which was a good thing considering my Raga-inspired booze fest at Belzer's party and the wiener portrait I drew of Mr. Evans had cost me ten days of freedom and two "strikes" with my parents. I had no idea what a third strike would get me, but I sure as heck didn't want to find out. I did still pick the desserts off Jake's lunch tray, but fortunately my midnight feeding frenzies had seemingly ended.

Like clockwork, Steve and Chris vanished each night after dinner to "work," often not retuning until long after I'd gone to bed. Mom and Dad never pried. I think they were just glad to have them home. In the news a decapitated body had been found in the woods near Old Pond Drive late on Wednesday evening. The incident occurred only a quarter mile from Glenn Dale and further stoked the fire fueling Mike's obsession with the hospital which, as it so happened, was our planned destination on Saturday. It wasn't exactly at the top of my list of things to do with my newfound freedom, but that was okay. I had a date with Jake on Friday. We caught *Halloween 4: The Return of Michael Myers* at the Marketplace Cineplex and ended up at Friendly's afterwards.

"So what did you *really* think of the movie?" Jake asked, fiddling with the napkin from the table dispenser.

Though I'd already answered his question several times in the car, Jake clearly sensed the lack of enthusiasm in my responses. His relentless interrogation was simultaneously adorable and frustrating. "Like I already said, it was definitely better than the third Halloween."

I wasn't lying. The latest installment in the Halloween franchise was a significant improvement over its predecessor. The problem was, that wasn't saying much. Fortunately, I was saved from elaborating on my opinion thanks to our waitress.

"That's one Peanut Butter Cup for you, hon," she said, placing a sundae in front of Jake, "and we have a Jim Dandy and strawberry Fribble for the hungry little lady."

Ugh. I would have been mortified if I wasn't starving. "Thanks for taking me here. I know it's a little out of the way, but I've been seriously jonesing for their ice cream." I took a quick slurp from my Fribble to keep from drooling. Even with Maya's magic rock in my pocket, my appetite was still amped up, just not all the way to ten. The only bright side was that I had yet to gain a pound. Maybe I was onto something. If there was just a way to loan Raga out to women looking to pig out and still fit in their jeans, I could make some serious moola.

A tiny burp slipped out as I opened my mouth to speak. "Oh God," I said, putting my hand over it and mumbling, "That's so embarrassing."

Jake couldn't stifle a chuckle. "I'm not laughing at you. I'm laughing near you."

"Thanks, that makes me feel so much better." I decided to switch back to the topic of spooky movies to avoid the possibility of a conversation centering on bodily functions. "So what are your favorite horror movies?"

Jake swallowed a mouthful of ice cream and then snickered. "Be warned, that's a dangerous question to pose to a true horror buff. I'm gonna have to ask you to be a tad more specific. See, there are your typical slasher-type movies. I would have to rate the original *Halloween* and maybe *A Nightmare on Elm Street* near the top of that list. Then there are the movies with less blood and guts and more psychological terror. *When a Stranger Calls* would be in my top five for that category. Oh, and so would *Rosemary's Baby*. That's a good one."

He was a nerd, but he was a cute nerd. "Okay, but what about your overall top pick for scariest movie of all time?"

Jake rested his chin on the palm of his hand and

frowned. "I'm not sure that I can choose just one," he said between his fingers.

"Then how about your top three?"

Tapping his cheek with his index finger, he said, "Top three. Top three. I suppose *The Exorcist* would be in there. That's a great one if you believe in the whole possession thing."

I wondered if Maya had something like that planned for me and Raga. If so would I puke up pea soup or Fribble when the exorcism began?

"*The Thing* had great special effects and tons of suspense, so I think that would also make the cut."

Since we started dating Jake had proven himself to be quite the riddle. He moved to Bowie from Poughkeepsie just over a year ago and didn't enjoy talking about his family or life prior to the move. Film, on the other hand, was something he couldn't shut up about once you got him started. He could quote cheesy movie lines verbatim. As such, the cinema was now my go-to subject when all other conversation had reached a dead end.

"The third would probably be *The Shining*. Even though King wasn't a big fan of it, Jack Nicholson played a perfect ax-wielding psycho." Jake cleared his throat and spoke in a pinched voice. "'Wendy? Darling? Light of my life. I'm not gonna hurt ya. You didn't let me finish my sentence. I said, I'm not gonna hurt ya. I'm just going to bash your brains in.' Classic."

Jake's nasally Nicholson impression was surprisingly good. "Not bad," I mumbled with a mouth full of banana and whipped cream. After washing it down with a swig from my Fribble, I added, "You should do stand up. Any other secret talents that I'm not aware of?"

Jake shrugged. "Nah. Movie quotes and bad impersonations are about all I have to offer."

"Oh, I don't know about that. You showed off some pretty sweet driving skills saving our butts from the redneck blockade at the Satan Church."

"What, that? There wasn't a whole lot to it. Just have to know how to handle a car off-road, I guess."

"Yeah, well the rest of us were pretty much freaking out. Come to think of it, you never even broke a sweat. Were you some kind of bootlegger in a previous life?"

"It was just instincts."

Whether due to modesty, shyness, or something else, he was shutting down on me again. It was time to turn the chatter back to safe ground. "Well, I would say *Mad Max* doesn't have anything on you."

"Now *that* was a great movie," Jake said. "Same with the second one. *Beyond Thunderdome* was okay, but not near as good as the first two, in my opinion."

We spent the rest of the night talking about movies and television and got into a heated debate over whether *Caddyshack* was funnier than *Revenge of the Nerds*. He was pro *Caddyshack* while I defended the comedic merits of nerds exacting their revenge on a bunch of jocks and bitchy cheerleaders. But if I was going to find out anything about his personal life, I obviously needed another approach. Maybe I'd do a little snooping of my own. Were private investigators expensive?

The conversation finally turned serious when we pulled up in front of my house. *As I Can Dream About You* played softly on the radio, Jake turned to me and asked, "So are you nervous about tomorrow?"

The question took me by surprise. "Huh?"

"Glenn Dale. Are you okay with going?" he asked. "Sometimes Mike can be a little pushy. If you're not cool with it, we don't have to go. There's plenty of other stupid things to do around here."

I had been so focused on stuffing my face with ice cream and pondering Jake's mysterious past that I completely forgot about our planned trip to the abandoned hospital. I wasn't ready to tell Jake the only reason I was interested in going was so I could spend more time with him. "No, I'm good with it…if you are."

Jake looked past the dashboard and out into the night. "Guess I am. I don't know. It's just, I've heard a few things about that place, and I'm wondering if it's smart idea to go poking around there."

From nowhere a giggle bubbled up out of me. The timing was queer and didn't at all reflect my mood. Could it have been from Raga? I tried to play it off. "You're not telling me the place has *you* spooked, are you?"

"It's not like that. It just seems a little, I don't know, stupid. First of all, I heard it's all rusted and riddled with asbestos. Second, they say it's patrolled by local police who can't wait to bust kids so they can feel like a bunch of big shots. And last, Alice Cook from my history class says a bunch of burnouts and thugs go there to get high. It just seems like we'd be pressing our luck against all of that, you know?"

It was strange to hear Jake arguing against a visit to Glenn Dale. Here we had spent the last hour talking about the most terrifying, sleep-with-the-lights-on horror movies, and Jake was suddenly hesitant about going to the abandoned hospital. The caution seemed out of character for him, almost like he was making up excuses for us to cancel the trip. But if so, why? He definitely didn't come across as the timid type. Could there be another reason he didn't want to go?

Thunk!

The sound of something heavy hitting the car roof made us jump in our seats.

Looking through the passenger window, I saw a familiar grinning face. "Chris, you butthead!"

"Hey there, Kate. I saw the car parked in front of the house and thought someone might be having some engine trouble. Figured I'd offer to lend a hand."

My brother leaned lower, looking past me to Jake. His smile grew as his eyes narrowed. "How you doin'? Let me guess. It's Jake, isn't it?"

"Fine, sir," Jake answered with a blank face.

"That's good. So it is car trouble, right amigo? Otherwise I figured you would have walked Kate to the door by now and been on your way. What's the problem? The starter? Or maybe you just ran out of gas."

Typical. Chris visits two to three times in a year and switches into overprotective brother mode the second he arrives. As if I needed his help. "That's my brother Chris. He's just mad because he has a crappy haircut. Don't let him bother you. He's full of nothing but hot air."

"She's right, Jake. You have nothing to worry about from me. Unless, of course, you get her shitfaced and drop her off after curfew. But that would *never* happen again. Would it, Jake?"

Jake's beautiful blue eyes were no match for my brother's glare. They dropped to the car floor. "Yeah, sorry about that whole thing."

Experience has taught me that few things in life were more embarrassing than an overprotective brother, and I'd had all of Chris's Clint Eastwood act that I could stomach. After giving Jake a kiss on the cheek, I said, "Feel free to ignore my brother. Everyone else does." I opened the car door with force, causing Chris to jump back. Stepping out, I turned around to my boyfriend. "I'll call you tomorrow, and thanks for a great time."

As Jake slowly drove away, I turned to Chris. The buffoon had the goofiest grin on his face, making me want to smash it with a frying pan. "If you screwed up my chances with Jake, I'm going to kill you, not figuratively, literally. I'll start by setting that mullet of yours on fire."

Chris was too busy laughing to acknowledge the threat. Pretending to wipe nonexistent tears from his eyes, he said, "Seems like a good kid. Knows how to respect his elders."

"Where's Steve?" I asked. "I need to talk to the one with a brain."

"He's inside. So listen," Chris said, losing his smile, "we need to talk, just the three of us."

CHAPTER 15

After reporting in with Mom and Dad to prove I wasn't plastered, I went upstairs to meet with my brothers. Dirty socks and T-shirts lay strewn on the floor beside Chris's unmade bed, surrounding a pair of jeans that still had underwear in them. Crumpled bags of potato chips and empty Budweiser cans sat on his nightstand, and the odor of stale beer and feet hung heavy in the air. Steve's side of the room was only slightly less disgusting, which was the reason I decided to remain there.

"So," I said, turning to Steve and smiling, "what's up, doc?"

The grave look on his face matched the tone of his voice. "We would like to ask a favor from you. It's not that big a deal, but you're not gonna like it."

As soon as I sat on the end of Steve's bed, the energy drained from my body. Though my date with Jake had been awesome, fighting the urges to get a second Jim Dandy at Friendly's and the family-sized popcorn with extra butter on it at the movies had left me totally wiped. For that reason, I was getting a little punchy. "Need me to kill Chris for ya? I'll do it for free. Just don't make me clean up his side of the room. My vaccinations aren't up to date, and Lord knows what's crawling around over there."

"Since when did you turn into Mom?" Chris huffed as he popped open a beer.

My throat suddenly felt parched. "Got another one of those?"

Chris smirked as he reached under his bed and grabbed what remained of a six pack. He pulled out one of the beers and lobbed it to me. "It's still cool, but not icy. Enjoy."

Closing my eyes, I chugged, losing focus on the world around me as the bubbly brew quenched my thirst. Next thing I knew, the can was empty. I opened my eyes to the dumbfounded looks on my brothers' faces, and before they could say anything, I let loose with an impressive five-second burp.

"Feel better?" Steve asked in a sarcastic tone.

"Yep. Please proceed."

"We need you to stay close to home for the next week or so," he said.

The request was almost as bad as cleaning up Chris's side of the room. Things were going really well with Jake and tomorrow night was supposed to be our Glenn Dale adventure. I knew Steve was doing what he thought was best for me by asking me to be a homebody, but I wasn't about to let my part-time brothers drop by for a week and start dictating my life to me.

"Oookay, why?"

Chris took a swig of beer and said, "Don't know if you've been watching the news lately, but over the last couple of months, they've been finding bodies all around PG County. The official count is up to five."

"And?"

"And," Steve added, "we believe the real number is at least double that. There's a killer out there somewhere."

"So how did you and mullet man figure out the *real* body count?" I asked Steve. "Is the killer one of your Tupperware clients? Does stay-fresh technology come in handy for storing chopped up bodies?"

Chris almost spewed out his beer. He pointed to Steve. "I told you we should have gone with Jehovah's Witnesses. Once you say you're one of them, people leave you alone. You also don't have to lug around all of that stupid Tupperware."

Steve glared at Chris before he turned back to me and said, "It doesn't matter how we know, just that it's the truth, and we want you to stay safe. Have any of your friends at school said anything about the string of killings?"

"It's come up, but nobody knows more than what's being said on television. Some people think it's the Bunnyman killing everybody."

"Ha! Bunnyman," Chris blurted.

"Others say it's the Goatman," I added.

My brothers exchanged a weird look before Steve said, "I suppose it was just a matter of time before someone blamed the murders on the Goatman. It is a Bowie tradition after all. Have you seen any strange characters hanging around the neighborhood or school lately?"

"You mean like the witch that moved into the Butcher of Bowie's old house?" I asked.

Steve nodded. "Just like her." He turned to Chris. "What do you think?"

Shaking his head, Chris said, "Too ballsy – even for you-know-who. If he's back, he'll keep a lower profile until the time is right."

"Time for what?" Steve and I asked at the same time.

Chris cocked his head as if our question was ridiculous. "To strike."

Looking back at me, Steve asked, "Anyone else?"

"Not really. All my friends are a little strange to begin with, so…"

"What about old blue eyes?" Chris asked, nodding to the window. "How long have you known him?"

Groaning, I said, "Not that it's any of your business, but we met at the beginning of the school year. He transferred in from out of state."

"Hmm. So that means you've known him for what, a couple of months?" Chris said.

"So what's your point?" I asked.

"And who moves for their senior year?"

Standing up, I said, "If you have a point to make, Chris, you better make it. It's been a long night, and I'd like to skip the whole overprotective brother thing, if you don't mind."

Steve raised his hands palms out. "Let's all chill for a minute. Kate, just please be careful these next few days and stick close to home. Can you at least promise that while we sort things out?"

Fighting the urge to light Chris's mullet on fire, I agreed to Steve's request. "Whatever you say."

Chris started mumbling something about taking care of family, but I split, shutting their door before he could get all the words out. Too irritated to go to bed, I decided to go for a walk outside to blow off some steam.

Closing my eyes, I breathed in the crisp night air and allowed it to clear my head. "What about old blue eyes?" I said in a pinched, mocking tone. Chris could be such an ass sometimes. I glanced up and down Spindle Lane. It was just shy of midnight and a slight breeze rustled the branches of the trees. A few lonely clouds glided across the black sky, occasionally blocking out an otherwise luminous full moon. I began walking with no particular destination in mind.

Why were my brothers so intent on ruining my life? First they go and ditch me to travel the country selling drugs, hunting down bail jumpers, or doing whatever the hell it was they did, and then they show up acting all concerned and bossing me around. What a bunch of bullshit. And when all's said and done, they'll hit the road again and disappear for the next year or two. Adios, Kate. Sayonara, Mom and Dad.

I stopped and looked up, not at all surprised to find myself standing in front of Maya's house. The lights were on, which meant the yaya was still up, probably tearing through the flooring in the study. For a fleeting moment, I thought about knocking on her door but reconsidered given the late hour.

Icy needles prickled down my spine. Shivering, I looked to the twisted crabapple tree that stood next to Maya's backyard fence. A pair of glowing embers hovered in the tree's branches like hellish Christmas ornaments. They blinked.

"Oh fuck."

Whatever was watching me had no doubt been spying on Maya, just as I had been a few weeks back. But I interrupted its late-night snooping, and those creepy-ass eyes were now locked on yours truly. We stood frozen for several seconds, staring at each other in the dead of the night in some sort of bizarre standoff. Then, with a sudden gust of wind, the eyes vanished.

Having second thoughts about my evening stroll, I slowly started toward home, but after just a half dozen steps, the prickly feeling returned. I swiveled back around, glancing up to the source of the sensation. Glowing eyes loomed from up above. Perched on the rooftop of the Bergstroms' colonial, silhouetted by the light cast from the moon, the creature stood, stretching its enormous frame up into the night sky. A pair of horns crowned its head.

"Fuck, fuck, fuck."

How a beast that big had managed to scale a two-story house in mere seconds was something I didn't care to find out. The problem was old red eyes had out-flanked me, effectively cutting me off from home. Out of instinct, I began backpedaling away from the creature and my house.

Hunched over like a gargoyle, its burning gaze took hold of me. A voice spoke in my head. It was both deep and powerful. *Awake, Raga. There is work to be done.*

From the recesses of my mind came another voice. It was barely a whisper. *Master?*

"No, no, no. This is *not* happening," I muttered while continuing in reverse. Whatever was up there was not only spying on Maya but was also Raga's boss – which was very uncool. Absent a better plan, I decided it was time to start running. If I could make it to Stonybrook Drive, I might be able to flag someone down for help. Pivoting right, I face-planted into something. "Gah!"

"Whoa, easy. That was my bad."

I knew the voice, but it had been years since I'd heard it. I looked up to the grinning face of Paul Perret. He was one of Chris's best friends from childhood and had lived close by on Stonybrook.

"Kate?"

"Paul?"

"In the flesh." Paul's brow furrowed. "You okay? You look a little...rattled."

I glanced back at the Bergstroms' and saw that red eyes was gone. Turning to Paul, I said, "No, I'm fine. Just went for a little walk. It's a nice night, and Lord knows I could use the fresh air." Eager to change the subject, I said, "What are you doing around these parts?"

Still frowning, Paul peered over my shoulder. "I'm visiting my parents for the weekend. After finishing at Duquesne, I got a job at a recording studio in D.C. It's not too far from here, so I come back every couple of months, get a home-cooked meal, and Mom tells me that I'm too skinny. So it works out well for everyone."

"Yeah, I remember my folks mentioning something about your job," I said. "I think it's cool that you decided to pursue a career in music."

The lines on Paul's face softened. "I suppose it is."

I watched as he stared out into the darkness as if searching for something. "Of course," I said, "it still doesn't explain why you're out and about at the witching hour."

Paul smiled as his eyes met mine. "Guess I just needed some fresh air too. So what do you say, want some company?"

The thought of getting a little quiet time to reflect had gone up in smoke with the arrival of the rooftop bogeyman. Now all I wanted to do was get home in one piece. "I think I've had enough of the night air, but you can walk me to my house if you'd like."

I'm not sure why I didn't tell Paul about the creature following me. Maybe I was worried he'd think I was nuts or, worse yet, that I was telling the truth. Then he would go investigate and end up on the evening news as the latest addition to the county's constantly growing body count.

"I know how you feel," he said as we began walking. "There's something about tonight that's making me a bit jumpy. Maybe it's just the chill in the air or the way the trees are swaying in the breeze almost as if they're talking to one another. I swear I wouldn't be surprised if we bumped into Freddy Kruger."

Desperate to keep the topic off things that could kill us, I said, "So what's Perry been up to?"

"Big bro? He's engaged now."

"No kidding?"

"Yep. She's a real sweetheart too." Paul grinned devilishly. "I don't know what she sees in him."

"Aw, Perry wasn't that bad. He was nice to me growing up."

"That's because you were Steve's kid sister. Sisters of best friends tend to get treated nice. It's different when you're brothers."

I snorted out a laugh. "Tell me about it. I still have no clue what the hell's going on between mine."

"It's strange. I was actually thinking about both of them a little earlier. For some reason I've been feeling oddly nostalgic these past few weeks. When was the last time you talked to them anyway?"

"About ten minutes ago. They're here visiting."

Paul stopped. "No shit?"

Turning back to him I said, "Scout's honor. Showed up a couple of days ago."

"Is everything okay? Are your parents all right?"

I stifled a chuckle. "Everyone is fine. But yes, it is weird for them to drop by out of the blue."

As we continued walking, I casually glanced over my shoulder in the event of a return visit from red eyes.

"Something wrong?" Paul asked.

Seeing nothing but darkened houses and a vacant street behind me, I released a long sigh. I opened my mouth to answer Paul when a brilliant idea struck me. Ignoring his question, I said, "I think you should give my brothers a call. Maybe you guys can go out for a few beers and catch up. You'd be doing me a favor by getting them out of my business for a while."

Paul shook his head. "It sounds nice, but it's been years since I talked to Chris or Steve. After high school Chris and I kind of drifted apart. Don't take this the wrong way, but he's changed from the kid I used to know."

"No offense taken. Trust me, I know Chris can be a total asshole sometimes."

Snickering, Paul said, "Your words, not mine. Listen, why don't you let Chris know that I'm staying at my folks for the next couple of days. If he really wants to get together, he can give me a call. I think it would be best that way."

As we neared my house, a blurry image of Paul entered my mind. He was much younger and was holding a large piece of wood in his hands as he stood above me with a look of smug satisfaction on his face. The image faded as a dull ache slowly spread from the back of my head toward my temples. Squinting, I started rubbing them. "I know this is going to sound a little strange, but when we were younger did we get into some kind of fight?"

Paul smiled and said, "I try not to make a habit out beating up little girls."

"I don't mean a fistfight. I mean a fight involving sticks maybe?"

The smile on Paul's face dropped for a split second before bouncing back into place. "Like I said, roughing up my friend's kid sister with fists, sticks, rocks, etcetera, is definitely a no-go for me. So that would be a negative, Ghostrider."

Okay, so he *definitely* knocked me out with a stick. Maybe I could pry something out of Steve later with this new tidbit of information. Trying to get anything out of Chris would be pointless. "Sorry, it was just some crazy image that popped into my head. Must have been from some game we used to play."

Looking up to my house, Paul said, "Guess we're here."

"Sure does. Thanks so much for the escort. It's been a strange night, but the company was nice."

"I enjoyed it too. Give my best to your brothers and your mom and dad."

"You bet."

Paul started back down Spindle but paused moments later and turned back. "Some advice for what it's worth.

See if you can crack that tough nut of a brother you have. I think a little heart-to-heart talk would do both you and Chris some good."

Waving, I said, "I'll do my best."

"Also, you may want to keep the midnight walks to a minimum, at least until they catch whatever is responsible for the murders."

Paul's odd choice of words stuck in my head. Why would he say whatever instead of whomever?

CHAPTER 16

I said a silent prayer of thanks that my brothers weren't home when the crew arrived. The last thing I needed was for Chris to read me the riot act for ignoring their request to stick close to home or, worse yet, give Jake a bunch of shit again. I still had no idea what my brothers' motive for visiting was. I only knew it had nothing to do with selling Tupperware or spending "quality time" with yours truly. So until they were willing to come clean with me, I felt no need to pay them any mind. Besides, I was with my homies.

They showed up a little after seven, as a pale blue moon climbed upward in the clear night sky. After Jake's stunt driving during our escape from the Satan Church hillbillies, we agreed he would be the designated driver for all future adventures, and since Jake and I were now officially a couple, I found myself riding shotgun.

"I'm telling you," Mike exclaimed from his wedged seat between Theresa and Jackie, "Glenn Dale is gonna make the Satan Church look like a trip to Disney World."

For the twenty minutes it took us to get there, Mike ranted and raved about stories he'd heard concerning the abandoned hospital. We only half-listened as he droned on about tales of botched genetic experiments, devil worshipping cults, and alien autopsies, all supposedly happening somewhere on the sprawling expanse of the former sanitarium.

"Okay, ladies and gents," Jake said, pulling onto Glenn Dale Drive, "the first parts of the hospital should show up on our right in a minute or so. I'm not sure how much of if we'll be able to see from the road though."

We had waited until just after dark to set out as the consensus of the group was we were less likely to get caught trespassing under the cover of night. Also, we figured it would be spookier, which was kind of the whole point. On a personal note, I was more excited than I was scared. Whether it stemmed from the prospect of being alone with Jake in some dark corner of the hospital or from something else, I wasn't quite sure.

As if on cue, the waxing moon revealed an enormous brick structure on the hill to our right. It was a ways off from the road but even from a distance, we saw half of the building's brick edifice was overrun with lush blankets of ivy.

"That's it!" Mike shouted.

"Is that all of it?" Theresa asked.

"No," Jackie answered in a monotone voice. "There's more, much more."

I was so stoked about hanging out with Jake that I failed to notice Jackie's sullen mood up until then. Looking back, it occurred to me that from the moment Mike first proposed the trip, she had been uncharacteristically quiet about the whole thing – which was so not her. Before I could ask if she was okay, Jake spoke.

"Turn right to that building or stay straight?"

"The Children's Hospital is to the right," Jackie muttered.

"Oh, hell yeah!" Mike blurted. "Nothing creepier than a place haunted by kids!"

When no one opposed Mike's suggestion, Jake said, "Children's Hospital it is."

He banked a hard right, driving into the heart of the abandoned campus. A large colonial-style building with dormers and a partially collapsed two-story balcony sat to our left, but the enormous red brick hospital looming on the opposite side of the road dwarfed it. Jake slowed the car as he pulled into the desolate parking lot and approached the front of the building.

"I haven't seen any guards yet," Jake said as he turned the car's lights off.

The rest of us sat and stared in awestruck silence. Broken glass caught the pale glow of the moon as dozens of windows shined like the glossy eyes of a monstrous spider. To our left and right the wings of the hospital flanked us, conjuring up images of furry legs ready to swoop in and stuff us through the main entrance – which was starting to look an awful lot like a mouth to me.

Theresa was the first to speak. "Umm, are we sure we want to do this?"

"You're kidding, right?" Mike said in a near manic tone.

"I heard this place was big," I said, "but I had no idea it was like big, big."

"This is just the beginning," Mike exclaimed. "The hospital grounds go on for acres, and there are at least another dozen buildings here. Word is that the worst of the government experiments, the really twisted stuff, goes on about a hundred feet below us in secret labs. That's where they did a bunch of crazy genetic experiments splicing alien genes with human ones. Heck, some people even say it's where the Goatman was created."

"Stop being such a dumbass for once in your life, Mike!" Jackie shouted. "This was a hospital, plain and simple. A lot of sick people were sent here, and a lot of them died. That's it."

"Whoa, take it easy, your highness," Mike said, placing his hand on his chest. "I'm just trying to build on the mood is all."

Jackie was getting tenser by the minute. I turned to face her. "We don't have to go in there if you don't want to."

She had a far-off look in her eyes. "It seems like such a long time ago, but it really wasn't," she whispered.

It took a minute for the words to sink in. Jackie's sour mood suddenly made sense, so did her knowledge of a place she had supposedly never been to before.

Theresa was the first one to speak. "Jackie, was someone in your family being treated here?"

If Jackie heard her, she didn't let on. "He would lay in his bed for days praying for the pain to end because the medicine they gave him didn't do crap. But his prayers went unanswered, and we all knew he would be checking out soon. Then one day the pain just stopped. They did some tests and found the cancer went into remission. They called it a miracle. Unprecedented, they said."

"So who was it?" I asked.

Jackie stared out the car window for several seconds before turning to me and flashing one of her picture-perfect smiles. "My pop-pop. He was here for about five years before he got better. He came back to live with us for the next seven years…until the heart attack."

"I'm sorry to hear that," I said.

"Don't be," Jackie answered. "He lived a long life, and when he finally did pass it was fast." She snapped her fingers. "Lickety-split. One minute he was dancing to some old-timey tune on the radio, and the next he was on the ground. They called it a widow-maker."

"I've heard of those," Jake said. "They're like a massive blockage of an artery. When it happens, odds are you're a dead duck."

"You know, it's totally cool if you want to sit this one out," Theresa said. "I can stay with you while these clowns go get arrested for trespassing. They're gonna need someone to bail them out, right?"

"Nah, I'm good," Jackie said. "Sorry for zoning out like that."

"You heard the little lady," Mike said. "She was just a bit freaked out is all. I can't say I blame her. This place is *freeaakay*. But we have a mission to accomplish, and we must venture into this massive, creepy, super-haunted place and live to tell the tale. So are we doing this?"

A strange stillness settled in the car. Jake, Theresa, Mike, and Jackie all seemed to be waiting for something or maybe someone to push them forward.

Let's do this.

The voice sounded like Kathleen Turner with strep throat. We had all been looking at one another when Mike posed the question, and I could have sworn nobody's lips moved. I was about to ask who had said it when…

I want to see what's in there.

There it was again. The words were coming from inside my head. It was Raga. It had to be. Panic ensued as I remembered the exact place I had left my magic charm: on the windowsill in the upstairs bathroom.

"Well, we're here. Might as well go inside so I can shut my boyfriend up," Theresa said.

The cold, damp air clung to us as we got out of the car. Ignoring the voice in my head, I tried to play it cool. Now was not the time to let my friends know that a Twinkie gobbling spirit had taken up residence in my body and was talking to me. Also, as much as I hated to admit it, I agreed with Raga. After coming all this way and making such a big deal out of the trip, it only made sense to go in and investigate. At least I'm pretty sure that's how I felt, unless Raga was somehow influencing me like she had with my recent dietary choices.

Mike took out a flashlight and looked at Jake. "This is gonna take crackerjack timing."

Jake pulled out his own flashlight and grinned at Mike. "Total concentration. You ready?"

They tapped them together as Mike said, "I was born ready."

The quotes from *Big Trouble in Little China* reminded Jackie, Theresa, and me that our escorts for the night were, in truth, morons. Cute and funny in a sad sort of way, but morons nonetheless.

"Do we really wanna follow these goons in there?" Theresa asked.

Follow the cute one named Jake.

Wonderful. Raga had a crush on Jake. I suppose it made sense. Raga loved food and booze, why not boys?

After confirming the main door was locked tight, we approached one of the first floor windows that had been nailed shut with plywood. The board was now silvery gray and half rotted. With a little tug from Mike, it groaned and fell to the ground.

Clearly pleased with himself, Mike smirked as he motioned toward the opening. "Voilà!"

Jake grabbed my hand and winked. "Step where I do, and watch your head."

The smell of wet earth and rust greeted us. Flashlights

flicked on, revealing paint-peeled walls that reminded me of skin flaking off sunburnt shoulders. To our left was a hall with a series of rooms on both sides of it. Some still had doors hinged to their entrances but most didn't. Patches of the black and gray terrazzo floor were still visible beneath the broken glass, grime, and mounds of powdered plaster that had settled against the walls like tiny sand dunes.

Mike and Theresa brushed by us and turned right to a pair of rust-splotched metal stairs. Spray-painted in red letters on the exposed terracotta wall next to the downward staircase were the words *Hell This Way* along with an arrow pointing down.

Illuminating his face with his flashlight, Mike turned to the rest of us wearing a creepy grin. "So whaddaya say, ladies and gents. Care to visit Hell?"

Been there.

Wonderful. Apparently, Raga wasn't the nicest of spirits. No surprise there.

Jackie was typically the first to egg Mike on, but she remained silent, leaving it up to Theresa to say, "Let's go for it."

With the boys in front, we crept down the stairs to what looked like a large storage room. Here chilly air mixed with the lingering moisture to create an invasive atmosphere which penetrated leather, denim, and polyester alike. The reek of ancient mold made me want to sneeze. Teeth chattering, I glanced at Jackie and Theresa and noticed they were shivering too.

"This place is wicked," Mike said. "I hope every-one's had their shots."

I felt Jake's grip tighten over my hand. "This may not be the smartest thing we've done. Stay close. It would be super easy to get lost here."

Flashlight beams scanned the graffiti-covered room. Pentagrams, peace symbols, and the names of prior adventurers decorated the cracked and crumbling walls, but one name stood out in particular. "Gerald Baskins" had been painted in large letters with the same scarlet color as the sign that had directed us down the stairs. Beneath the name was another arrow pointing to the right.

"Gerald Baskins. That name sounds familiar," Theresa said.

"It should," Jake responded. "That's the name of a kid that disappeared about a month ago."

Flashlights followed the arrow, casting their beams through plumes of excited breath, settling upon a series of metal doors affixed to the wall in a three by three arrangement. Two of the doors were open, one of them completely and the other just slightly. A metal rollout shelf extended from the mouth of the fully open door.

Theresa was the first to say something. "No, no, no. That's not—"

"Ohhh shit!" Mike interrupted. "That's a morgue! We're in a morgue!"

I watched the grin painted on Jake's face drop when it struck him. "We're in a *children's* morgue. Jesus."

"What kind of an asshole would write that kid's name in a children's morgue?" Theresa asked.

Approaching the open doors, Mike said, "That's messed up."

I was so creeped out from what I was witnessing that I had forgotten about Raga until…

Ghost.

Under the excited chattering of my friends, I whispered, "What?" to the voice in my head.

Ghosts actually. Behind you. They are watching from the shadows.

My skin broke out in goosebumps. As my friends examined the mortuary cabinets, I turned around and stared into the darkness. "I don't see anything."

Use my eyes.

The darkness suddenly shifted to a murky violet, and things that were hidden revealed themselves. Behind stacks of old rusty cots and moldy wooden desks stood several figures. Some were tall, most were not. They had no discernable features, as they themselves weren't much more than shadows.

"Why aren't they moving?" I whispered.

They are afraid.

"Afraid of what?"

Us.

"But why?"

Behind me the squeak of rusty hinges echoed as Mike opened the remaining mortuary cabinets. My friends continued to be preoccupied.

The dead fear infernal powers. At least most of them do.

"Infernal powers? What are you talking about?"

Scratchy laughter. *That's right. The witch didn't tell you.*

"Tell me what?"

I am Raga the Hungry. I am an ancient and powerful demon, and soon enough I will claim your body as my own and do as I wish.

Holy crap. It wasn't just a spirit trying to possess me but a frigging demon, and Maya had known all along. Just when I was starting to trust her, she had to go and do something like this.

A hand grabbed my shoulder, causing me to jump.

"Whoa, sorry," Jake said. "You okay? Is something out there?"

Turning to face him, I smiled. "Just some spiders and dusty old furniture."

Jake shined his flashlight into the darkness. The light traveled through the ghosts, shining on the cracked and moldy plaster wall behind them. "Wow, you have a good pair of peepers. Those cots were hard to spot without a light. You sure you're not part vampire?"

Part vampire? There's no such thing. You are either a vampire or you're not. Jake is nothing more than a pretty fool.

"Will you shut up?" I whispered slightly louder than intended.

Jake's hand dropped from my shoulder. "Sorry, didn't mean to offend you."

"No," I said clutching his arm. "I was talking to

myself. This place just has me spooked."

He placed his hand over mine and squeezed it. "No worries. It has me spooked too. There's also something really sad about it. I don't know. Maybe we should –"

"Hey, lovebirds!" Theresa shouted. "Mike's heading upstairs. He wants to check out the building we passed on the way here. He mumbled something about tunnels."

CHAPTER 17

With my enhanced perception, compliments of Raga the Hungry, the nightscape of Glenn Dale took on surreal qualities. The shadows cast by the waxing moon ebbed and flowed like a black tide while the trees whispered secrets to one another as they swayed to and fro. The hospital ruins were teeming with otherworldly activity that was concealed from the world of the living, except for me – and Raga. Across the parking lot a couple hundred yards off stood a large brick building that looked like it could have belonged in colonial Williamsburg if not for its dilapidated condition.

"Target acquired," Mike said. "Rumor has it there are tunnels connecting most of the buildings in this place, and Brandon Schumacher told me one of them is in that building."

Thanks to my newfound ability, the hospital had become far more interesting. These were no longer just a bunch of ivy-covered, boarded-up buildings and crumbling dormitories. The place was a cauldron simmering with supernatural activity.

With the moon lighting the way, I started off across the weed-ridden parking lot shouting, "What are we waiting for then?"

Catching up to me, Jake said, "You sure are pumped up. Figured it would've been Mike running around and acting like a lunatic."

I gave him a twisted smile. "So I'm a lunatic now?"

Jake scratched the back of his head. "That's not what I meant. It's just –"

I stifled a giggle. "I was just messing with you."

"I don't like this," Theresa said from behind us. "I'm getting this creepy vibe like we're being watched."

Above the murmurs of the trees, a sound echoed. Someone was crying. It sounded like it was coming from one of the upstairs rooms in the building we were approaching. My mind began to race. Maybe some kid had gotten lost or even trapped somewhere within it.

"What's this place?" I asked.

Mike opened his mouth to speak, but was interrupted by Jackie. "I think it was a dormitory for the nurses that worked in the Children's Hospital."

I needed to know whether the sound I heard was coming from the living or the dead. "Does anyone else hear that?" I asked. "I swear it sounds like someone is crying."

My friends' blank expressions gave me my answer.

"Are you okay, Kate?" Theresa asked. "You're

starting to freak me out a little."

The only one smiling was Mike. "Good one. I didn't have you pegged for a prankster. But I have to say, your technique is a tad amateurish. Might I recommend throwing a rock or causing some kind of commotion next time before asking if someone heard something? It helps set the mood."

Ignoring Mike, I crept to the back of the dormitory where a thick wooden door stood next to an enormous tiered balcony that was nearing collapse. With one push the entrance swung open, its lock having been rendered useless in its rotted wood frame. A musty smell of neglect met us.

Jake took hold of my arm as I stepped across the threshold. "How about you let someone with a flashlight go first?"

Telling Jake that I had night vision thanks to the demon attempting to take control of my body wasn't the kind of thing that just rolled off the tongue, so I smiled and said, "Duh. Guess I'm getting a little too into our ghost hunting adventure."

He slipped past me and winked. "That's cool. Just be careful around this place. Ghosts may be dangerous, but so are rotted floors and tetanus."

The weeping was louder now, sounding more like a woman's than a child's. It was coming from one or maybe two stories above us. Grabbing Jake's hand, I gave it a tug and said, "We need to go up."

We maneuvered through a maze of rusty bedframes

and moldy mattresses and bolted upstairs, leaving a room of confused friends behind us.

"Looks like the crazy train has left the station!" Mike shouted from below.

Glass crunched and clouds of decayed plaster rose in our wake as we stomped up two flights of stairs. A checker-tiled hall lay before us, stretching thirty feet until dead ending in a pool of blue light cast from the window opposite us. There were three rooms on each side of the hall. Up and to our left, the crying was coming from two doors down.

"Remind me," Jake wheezed between breaths, "what exactly are we looking for?"

"Shh, listen," I whispered. "They're just ahead. Follow me, and be quiet. We don't want to startle them."

Approaching the partially closed door, I hesitated. *Careful.*

Raga's word of caution wouldn't dissuade me. I pushed the door open. Cobwebs broke apart and floated toward my face and hair. Shuddering, I brushed them away.

Beyond was a small bedroom, probably meant for the hospital staff. In the far corner the figure of a woman sat on a stained mattress. She was hunched over, and something dark and thick was dripping from her wrists onto the floor and bed. I watched in horror, knowing in my gut I was intruding on something immensely sad and terrible.

The phantom rose, standing before us as black

droplets trickled from her fingertips. She stretched an arm to the wall next to her and began scrawling a message in her own blood.

Jake started to speak, but I shushed him again. The note read:

Let us go.

With her strange message written, the ghost turned to face me, and for a few fleeting seconds, the image of a nurse in her mid-twenties came into focus. A burning hatred shot from her black eyes as she glided across the room and reached a gnarled hand out.

Before I had a chance to scream, she paused with a puzzled expression on her pale face. Seconds later she smiled softly and then vanished into the inky darkness surrounding us.

What the hell was all that about? The thought that I had witnessed the final moments of a person's life, perhaps a nurse falling into despair after being overwhelmed by the suffering around her, left me speechless. And what did the message mean? Was she a prisoner in this place and were there others trapped here too?

"Sorry to break the mood, but what exactly are we looking at?" Jake whispered.

Coming back to my senses, I turned to him. "Huh? Oh...nothing. I thought I saw something, but my eyes must have been playing tricks on me."

Jake frowned. "Uh-huh. And what about your ears?

Were they playing tricks on you too? You said you heard someone crying up here."

"Oh yeah, that. Guess I was mistaken. It must have been some animal creeping around up here. Maybe a cat. A cat can sound like a person crying, right?"

The frown on Jake's face faded, but something told me he wasn't buying my BS.

"You guys still alive?" Mike's voice echoed down the hall. "Or are we going to have to hitchhike home seeing as Jake's the one with the keys?"

Before Jake had a chance to interrogate me further, I snuck past him and back into the hallway where the rest of the crew was.

"So what happened?" Mike asked, barely able to contain himself.

I had to think up a lie fast. I didn't want the whole gang to know I was off my rocker. "It was nothing. Just a stupid old cat, I think. It bolted as soon as we went in the room."

I looked into Jake's cool blue eyes hoping he would be merciful and back me up.

He grinned for a couple of seconds before nodding and saying, "Yep, just some dumb cat."

I mouthed the words *thank you* to him when no one was looking.

"Rumor has it there's a demonic dog with red eyes that prowls the halls of this place," Mike said. "Are you sure it was a cat you saw and not a dog? Were its eyes red?"

"Stop being a dumbass," Theresa said.

Raising his hands above his head, Jake opened his mouth wide and yawned. "Well, this has been fun y'all, but what do you say we call it a night? Personally, I think we're pressing our luck. It's just a matter of time before some security guard stumbles across our car."

Mike seemed ready to protest, but Theresa elbowed him in the ribcage before he could speak. "Good idea," she said. "Let's head back to my place and chill. I just got *Beetlejuice* on VHS."

With no further objections, we slowly made our way back downstairs.

That ghost was pissed.

I decided it would probably be in my best interests to ignore Raga until I was back home and in possession of Maya's charm, so the silent treatment it was.

As we neared the exit to the dormitory a jolt of energy shot through me from head to toe.

"Yow!" Jake yelled, yanking his hand from mine. "What the heck?"

The buzzing I had heard in my head at Governor's Bridge had returned but was louder this time, like an entire hive was stuffed between my ears. I stared into a dark corner of the room. "Sorry," I mumbled absent-mindedly as I walked toward the source of the noise. "Something's there," I said, pointing into the blackness.

CHAPTER 18

Tucked in the far corner of the dormitory lobby, a door clung to its frame by a single hinge. "There's a tunnel there," I said.

Mike peeked over my shoulder. "That's it! That's one of the tunnels I told you about. They connect all of the main buildings. Andy Farrow and his brother found one in the basement of the Adult Hospital, but they didn't have the cojones to explore it."

"Maybe their decision had something to do with that," Theresa said, pointing to a spray-painted warning that read *Beware of the Bunnyman.*

"Oh damn," Mike blurted. "Who's up for a visit to see the Bunnyman?"

Stepping away from the tunnel entrance, Jackie said, "So this is where I call it quits. Think I'll go wait in the car for the survivors."

The buzzing in my head dulled as I acclimated to it. I took a step toward the tunnel but stopped. As much as I wanted to see what lay beyond, deep down I knew Glenn Dale was no place to leave someone alone.

Jake must have sensed my apprehension. As if on cue, he said, "Think I've had enough adventure for one night too. I'll keep Jackie company while the rest of you knuckleheads go piss off the ghosts of Glenn Dale."

"Dude, really?" Mike exclaimed. "Just when it's starting to get good, you—"

Theresa's shot to Mike's ribcage was harder this time, but it had the desired effect, both shutting him up and making him glare at her. Saying nothing, she nodded to Jackie.

Mike sighed before taking a swig from his flask. Clearing his throat, he turned to Jake and Jackie. "Okay, you people sit tight, hold the fort, and keep the home fires burning, and if we're not back by dawn…call the President."

"Hope your mind and spirit are one," Jake replied.

Theresa, Jackie, and I let out a collective groan as we endured yet another round of quotes from *Big Trouble in Little China*. What was it about that movie that turned otherwise normal guys into complete dorks?

Theresa and I followed Mike into the tunnel as Jake called from behind. "If you see the Bunnyman, say hi to him for us!"

If any of us were claustrophobic it would have been a short adventure. We had to hunch down as the ceiling couldn't have been more than five feet high, and to make matters worse, two large pipes ran along the bottom and top left side of the passage making footing tricky. The conversation died off shortly after we entered, replaced by the sounds of our steps echoing off the tunnel walls. The buzzing in my noggin grew louder the deeper we went into the unknown.

Our feet began making squishy sounds.

We stopped as Mike shined his flashlight on the tunnel floor, revealing an inch of standing water. "Well, isn't that special. Can anyone say E. coli?"

"Yuck, maybe we should turn back," Theresa said.

For the last several minutes, I had been waiting for one of them to call it quits and was frankly a little surprised it had taken so long. But we were getting close to something important. I sensed it, or more accurately, I heard it. "Just a little farther," I whispered.

The lack of a snarky response from Mike was unusual, telling me he was having second thoughts as well. We sloshed on for a little while longer before coming to an underground junction. Though the tunnel continued straight, it also split into three additional passages, two to our left and one to the right. Painted placards were affixed to the walls for each tunnel with corresponding arrows pointing to their destinations. Mike shined his flashlight on the moldy sign directly opposite us showing the words *Adult Hospital* painted in black letters. The signs on the passages to our left said *Finucane Hall* and *Children's Hospital* respectively. The one to the right said *Power Plant*. Reaching out, I touched it.

Sparks leapt from the sign to my fingertips.

"Whoa!" I shouted, yanking my hand back. Rubbing it, I noticed there was no pain, just a slight tingling sensation. A burning stench of ozone permeated the air.

"Oh my God! Kate, are you okay?" Theresa asked.

"I—I think so," I said, looking for scorch marks on my hand.

"That was awesome! Can you do it again?" Mike asked.

"There's something there," I said, touching the sign again. This time there were no sparks, but I felt the prickly current of energy flowing from my hand and into the rest of my body. Wedging my fingertips into the crack between the wood sign and brick wall, I pulled down.

The sign fell along with bits of crumbled mortar. Behind it was a strange symbol painted on the wall in red:

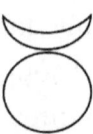

"What is it?" Theresa asked, her voice squeaking.

That is the sign of the master.

Raga didn't sound particularly psyched.

Mike whistled and said, "There is definitely some kind of satanic juju going on here."

We should leave.

For once I agreed with Raga, but before I could say anything, a splash echoed down the narrow tunnel to our right. Something heavy had dropped into the water.

"Oh shit!" Theresa shouted

"Who's there?" Mike demanded.

An eerie stillness followed. It lasted for a few seconds before…

Splash, splash, splash.

Something large was barreling toward us. Using Raga's vision, I gazed into the tunnel beyond the reach of Mike's flashlight. Slouched over due to its tremendous height, a shadowy humanlike figure sloshed through the muck. A murky green aura surrounded it.

Definitely time to go.

Pointing back the way we came, I looked at my friends and shouted, "Run!"

Mike opened his mouth to protest, but I cut him off. "I'm right behind you. Just watch out for Theresa. Now move it!"

I must have hit the right tone because my friends broke into a mad dash.

Looking back into the darkness, I guessed the creature to be about a dozen yards away and closing fast, but it was hard to tell for sure. A pair of green eyes flashed as it narrowed the distance. I had seen them before.

Run now or you will die.

Raga's words snapped me back to reality. I took off after Mike and Theresa and was close behind them a moment later. Frantically clambering through the low, narrow tunnel as Mike's flashlight strobed every which way, we made surprisingly good time and were almost out of the tunnel when…

A couple of steps shy of freedom, Mike lost his footing on a pipe and went down hard. "Faaa!"

Theresa was close behind him, but being the jock that she was, she hurdled over his prone body like a frigging gazelle and cleared the tunnel. I tried mimicking Theresa's actions, but lacking her athletic prowess and long legs, I ended up smacking the side of poor Mike's head with my foot while jumping over him.

"Jesus! Sorry, Mike!" I shouted.

Grabbing his hands, Theresa and I dragged Mike a couple of yards away from the tunnel entrance.

This is good. Leave the boy for the creature, and let us be on our way.

Raga was so damn annoying.

A high-pitched shriek echoed down the passageway.

Theresa crouched beside her boyfriend. "Mike, we have to go! You need to get up now!"

It was too late. A clawed hand reached out from the entrance and grabbed the door frame. Covered from head to toe in coarse black fur, some of it singed, a pooka emerged. I could tell from the burns it was the same one Maya had saved me from at Governor's Bridge. Pulling itself through the doorway, it stretched its massive frame up and outward, its pointed ears brushing against the ceiling. Without the cover of the forest to hide it, I could now see the pooka for what it truly was.

Mike stared in disbelief. "Am I dead or does that thing look like a—"

"Giant bunny," I said. "It looks like a giant Bunnyman."

CHAPTER 19

The Bunnyman's hellish gaze fell on me.

Last chance. If you surrender your body to me now, I can still save us.

Apparently, my only choices were to be served up as an entrée to the Bunnyman or let a gluttonous demon named Raga possess me. Before I had a chance to answer, a series of loud cracks erupted from behind me. I watched the Bunnyman stumble and then fall backward into the tunnel. A pained howl followed.

Steve appeared out of nowhere, grabbing Mike by the arm and heaving him up like he was made of straw. "C'mon!" he shouted to Theresa and me. "Let's get you out of here!"

From a haze of gunpowder Chris emerged with a shotgun in his hands. "Three slugs of blessed lead and I barely slowed it down. It's not a revenant or ghoul. Hell, it's not undead at all."

"Did you spot its ears?" Steve asked.

Chris frowned. "Sure. Long and pointed. Kind of like a fae. But this ain't exactly Ireland."

"True, but it wouldn't be the first time we've encountered one of them, would it? Could have stowed away on some freighter inward bound from the old country."

A bone-rattling screech tore through the air as the Bunnyman emerged once more from the tunnel.

"So what are we thinking? Pooka?" Chris asked.

Steve hunched his shoulders. "Wouldn't be that far-fetched."

"I suppose. But since when do wood spirits hang out in abandoned hospitals?"

"I guess since now," Steve answered.

A crooked smile crept across Chris's face as he reached for a metal spike that was tucked in his waistline. With a flick of his wrist, it disappeared from his hand.

Staggering forward, the creature placed a hand over the smoking wound left by the spike and unleashed a gut-wrenching wail.

"Looks like our friend's allergic to iron," Steve quipped.

"Sure does," Chris said, pulling two hatchets out from beneath the long coat he wore. "I think it's time to skin us a wascally wabbit!"

What the hell was I watching? As Steve pulled us farther away from the chaos, Chris moved in, placing himself between us and the Bunnyman. Before the creature had a chance to attack, Chris had buried a hatchet deep in its left shoulder. Gliding effortlessly under the pooka's right arm as it swiped at him, he sank a second hatchet in its other shoulder, taking out its ability to use its arms. Enraged, the Bunnyman lunged at Chris with gnashing teeth.

Chris dove out of the way at the last second. "Yikes! This guy's got some real fight in him. Say, do you think I could save his foot and use it as a good luck charm? It would make one hell of a keychain, don't you think?"

"Enough already, Chris!" Steve barked. "Quit dicking around, and put the thing out of its misery!"

Dusting himself off as he rose to his feet, Chris stuck his tongue out at his older brother before saying, "All right! All right, you party pooper." With a jump to the right, my brother ducked behind the Bunnyman and clambered onto its back like a ninja. He pulled out a black dagger and drove it deep into the creature's neck. Smirking, Chris slid the blade through the creature's throat, unleashing a torrent of black blood.

Theresa screamed.

Mike looked like he was about to hurl.

Your brother has serious issues.

I found myself agreeing with Raga again.

Steve gently placed his hand on my shoulder. "Show's over. Let's get you back to your car and the hell out of here."

As we turned to leave the carnage, Chris shouted, "Don't worry about me! Guess I'll take care of the cleanup…again!"

Steve fell behind as my friends and I hustled to Mike's car in stunned silence. I was prepared to accept that my brothers were many things. Bounty hunters, bank robbers – even spies would have been in the realm of believable. But never in a thousand years would I have guessed they were monster hunters. The savage and almost joyful way Chris took out the Bunnyman even left Raga disturbed.

When we got back to the car, we found Jackie alone in the back seat with her eyes closed. She screamed and jerked away from the window when Mike rapped on it. After seeing it was us, Jackie unlocked her door and got out. Punching Mike in the arm, she shouted, "You almost gave me a heart attack!"

"Where's Jake?" I asked.

Jackie pointed to the entrance to the hospital. "Jake told me to wait in the car with the doors locked while he checked some stuff out at the Children's Hospital. He said he would stay within earshot if I needed him."

"I'll go check on my boy," Mike said, heading in the direction of the hospital. "Be back in a jiff."

So who's that with you?" Jackie gestured at Steve.

"That's my brother Steve."

Like a switch had been flipped, Jackie's face went from sour to all smiles. "Oh, hi. I've heard so much about you from Kate."

"Yeah well, don't believe everything you hear," Steve said. "Only most of it is true."

Jackie's giggle was loud and pitchy.

"Wouldn't you know it!" Chris shouted as he jogged up from behind us. "I turned my back on the fucker for one second and the pooka's up and hauling butt back through the tunnels. I knew they were hard to take out, but I was positive I'd bled him dry. Lesson learned. Next time the head's *gotta* come off."

I noticed the deranged smile was still on Chris's face. Following a heavy sigh, I said, "This is my other brother."

"Chris?" Jackie asked.

Chris nodded while mustering up a cheesy John Wayne accent. "In the flesh, little lady."

Jackie brushed a finger against her cheek. "You have a little something on your…"

"Oh, thanks," Chris said, wiping a smear of the black blood from his face.

Jackie's ear-to-ear smile seemed to actually grow if that was possible. "You're welcome."

Looking at his older brother, Chris said, "Did anything strike you as weird about that?"

Steve nodded. "You mean like why is a typically harmless woodland fairy skulking around a maze of underground tunnels trying to kill trespassers?"

"Exactamundo."

"Of course. But…"

Chris rolled his eyes. "Here we go again. But what, brother dear?"

"But you didn't even try communicating with it. You just went in for the kill, like always."

"Excuse me for wanting to protect our sister and her friends. Did Bugs look like he was in a chatty mood to you?"

Steve shrugged. "I suppose not."

As my brothers bickered about the proper etiquette for killing pookas, Mike returned with Jake in tow.

"Hey, guys," Jake said. "So Mike claims some serious stuff went down in the tunnels but wouldn't share the details. Guess I missed all the fun."

Chris's eyes homed in on Jake. "Missed all the fun?"

"Easy, Chris," Steve said, resting a hand on his brother's shoulder.

"I'm easy. I'd just like to know where pretty boy was when my sister almost got killed."

Jake turned to me. "Almost killed?"

"It's not exactly like that," I said.

"Actually, it *was* kind of like that," Theresa countered.

"Abso-freaking-lutely," Mike added.

"So back to my question, *Jake*," Chris continued. "Where did you wander off to while the rest of your friends were seconds away from becoming rabbit food?"

It was like the night Chris first met Jake all over again. Once more he was being overprotective and just plain nasty. It was almost as if there was some kind of grudge between the two of them.

Unable to meet Chris's glare, Jake glanced back at the Children's Hospital. "I was just poking around a little. Thought I heard something coming from the hospital."

"Really?" Chris said as he squared off in front of

Jake. "Aren't you just a freaking godsend. I—"

Steve shoved his arm between Chris and Jake and separated them. "Okay, kiddos. Think it's time to call this night a wrap. Kate, why don't you and your friends get in your car and split. Chris and I will catch up with you back at home a little later."

Chris was mumbling something about needing a drink as Steve coaxed him to their Monte Carlo, which was parked a couple dozen yards away. Before peeling off, Chris shouted out the window, "You're welcome by the way!"

We watched in silence as the car sped away before Jackie blurted, "Your brothers are awesome!"

On the way home Mike and Theresa took turns filling Jackie and Jake in on our near death experience beneath the abandoned hospital. As Mike recounted our underground adventures with his unique dramatic flair, Jackie leaned over and whispered in my ear, "Something's up with Jake. I got tired of waiting for everyone at the car, so I went back in the hospital entrance to see what he was doing. I couldn't find him."

I waited until Mike was at full steam before whispering back, "Maybe he just got bored and explored a little."

"Doesn't that seem a little creepy to you? I mean, would you go off on your own in this place?"

Raga echoed Jackie's concerns. *Watch out for the one called Jake.*

CHAPTER 20

By the time I got home, my brothers were still out, probably hunting down Dracula or the Wolfman, if I had to guess. Emotionally spent and physically exhausted, I plopped face down in bed and didn't move for the following eleven hours. The next morning, I decided it was high time to pay Maya a visit.

She was wearing a huge smile on her beautiful dust-covered face when she answered the door. "I've found it," she said before I could get a word out. "I've found my ancestor's book thanks to you. It was hidden under the study and camouflaged by a spell."

"That's awesome. The timing couldn't be better. I am so ready to get Raga out of my head."

That's not nice.

From the last time I'd seen her, the house had graduated from renovation project gone south to a full-on *Money Pit* scenario. In addition to the gaping holes in the walls and countless piles of rubble, there was now a three-foot-wide ditch in the center of the study.

I gave her the *Reader's Digest* version of the prior night's events. To her credit, she listened intently and asked no questions until I was done talking.

"So the demon is talking to you?" she asked.

"Yep. By the way, thanks for telling me Raga was a spirit. Any other secrets you're keeping from me?"

The yaya's smile twisted into a smirk. "Quite a few as a matter of fact. But you need to understand, what I did was for your protection, Kate. I didn't want you to overreact and do something rash."

"What, like pay my parish priest a visit and vomit pea soup all over him?"

"Something like that. Now back to the subject. You also say that Raga has shared some of her power with you? Preternatural vision, was it?"

"That's a roger. Even in pitch black, I could see like it was midday. And the ghosts, whew. There were tons of them. Also, did you say her? Do demons have genders?"

"Most assuredly. And Raga is of the feminine variety. Beware, she is as insatiable as she is evil."

That explained Raga's infatuation with Jake.

"And the pooka made another appearance?" Maya asked changing subjects.

"Yep. Only we're calling him the Bunnyman now seeing as that's what he looks like. I'm not sure if he's dead or alive. Chris did a real number on him. It was… brutal."

Maya remained stone-faced, as if I was telling her

about a recent insurance seminar I attended or about the time I got my braces off. "I see. I suppose we are fortunate your brothers intervened."

"That's exactly what I was thinking. Stalked by ghosts, harassed by demons, and chased by a giant Bunnyman, how fortunate I am. What a *fortunate* night it was."

Maya's eyes tightened.

"Look, sorry if I'm being a bit bitchy," I said. "It's just that I'd like my own body back, and I'm pretty sure we reached an agreement the last time I was here. I help you find the book and you use it to boot my new roommate out of my body."

Maya's face softened. "That was our arrangement, wasn't it? I have already prepared what is needed. Wait here."

The yaya disappeared into the kitchen.

Won't work.

"Scared, are we?" I replied. "Don't worry. This should all be over soon. It won't hurt – at least I don't think it will."

Maya returned. She had an iron cauldron cradled in the crook of one arm and a tiny satchel over her shoulder. Unslinging the satchel, Maya laid it and the heavy-looking pot on the table. It was a wicked thing, filled with charred sticks and metal spikes jutting out from something dark and round in the center of it. I leaned in for a closer look and found I was face-to-face with a grinning skull.

Pushing back from the table, I blurted, "Nope, nope, nope! Uh-uh. Where did you get that?"

"Easy, child," Maya said. "This is my nganga. It's the source of my power and will help free you of the demon."

"Yeah, well," I said, pointing at the cauldron, "whose skull is that?"

"It is my grandmother's. She is still with me, and I talk to her all the time. This is the way of Palo Mayombe, Kate. I don't expect you to understand, but you do need to believe in its power."

The sight of the skull was messing with me, and when nervous, I tend to rant. "So where's the rest of your grandmother? In the pantry? Any other relatives around here I should be aware of?"

Ignoring my comments, Maya continued. "Raga is a demon of lust and voraciousness. I was able to find her in my research. She is ever hungry, which is why you find yourself filled with such strong desires. But now that we know who she is and I have my book, we will send her back to the abyss."

Not going to work.

"Will you *please* shut up already," I said.

Maya frowned. "Come again?"

I shook my head. "Not you. Raga. She's being really annoying right now."

"Your ability to converse freely with the demon indicates the possession has progressed to its final stages. It is good you came to see me today. We must free you of this creature immediately."

Raga said nothing, but I could hear her dark laughter in the corners of my mind.

One by one Maya emptied the contents of her satchel onto the table. The spell components seemed harmless enough at first, starting with a salt shaker, green candle, cigar, and a jar of what looked like dirt. But they gradually progressed to more ominous items like a cotton ball, bottle of rum, and a vial filled with an evil-looking black liquid. It was the final magical accessory, however, that caused my pooper to pucker. The bone handled dagger the witch held looked like it was razor-sharp.

Laughing nervously, I said, "So, we gonna do some shots and smoke stogies?"

"*We* are not," Maya said as she sprinkled salt into the nganga. "Now hush while I prepare."

Like a scolded child, I watched in silence as Maya got her witch on.

Opening the jar of dirt, she dumped its contents into the cauldron while whispering, "Earth from hallowed ground." Next she tilted the vial with great care and said, "The teardrops of Zarabanda." Maya took the cigar, bit off the stub, and spat it on the floor. She lit it and took a puff, filling the room with its pungent smell.

"What about the rum?" I asked.

"The rum is for me," Maya said, lifting the bottle to her mouth. After taking a long swig, she picked up the dagger. "This is for you. The last ingredient is your blood."

I hated pointy things, especially those that made me bleed. The look on my face must have been a sight to see.

"Don't worry, *mija*. I only need a drop or too. We'll just prick your thumb."

"Can I have a taste of that first?" I asked, pointing to the bottle.

Maya hesitated before passing the rum to me. "Don't tell your parents."

Between the witchcraft, demonic possession, and bloodletting, I sincerely doubted the drinking would have made my parents' top three list of objectionable things. Before I knew it I was chugging from the bottle.

"Easy, Kate," Maya said, snatching it from my grip. "Raga would have you empty the whole bottle if she could."

Wiping my mouth, I burped out a rum-scented, "Sorry."

"Come, we must move fast," Maya said, offering her hand palm up.

I took a deep breath and gave her mine.

Placing it over the cauldron, Maya said, "Don't worry. This will be over quick."

A few seconds later came a sharp prick. "Ow!"

Drops of crimson painted the skull.

"That's it," she said, putting the knife on the table. Maya picked up the cotton ball and placed it over the red dot on my thumb. "Put your hand over this and keep some pressure on it."

I did as instructed.

"Now I want you to close your eyes and focus on my words. You need to believe in order for the exorcism to work."

Maya lit the candle. "Almighty and wise Zarabanda, please accept this offering of rum, cigars, and blood, and give this girl the strength to reclaim her body. Take your wayward child Raga and send her home to the eternal darkness from where she came."

My body felt lighter for a moment, as if a heavy weight was departing it. But as quickly as the sensation arrived, it vanished, replaced by a tightness in my chest.

Not going anywhere. My master is here. I must stay.

Maya took hold of my hand. She was speaking in Spanish now, repeating the same phrase over and over. The only word I understood was Raga. Pausing for a moment, she looked into my eyes. "The demon is being stubborn. Concentrate, Kate. Think of Raga like a splinter under your skin; you want to dislodge it, pluck it out."

I felt Raga being pulled from me, but every time the demon seemed hell bound, something would yank her back, almost like an invisible bungee cord was connecting us. The strain on my body was insane. Each time she was pulled away, fire burned through every muscle fiber, and when she inevitably snapped back into me, it felt like I was getting run over by a freight train. Rocking back and forth in my chair, I shouted, "You need to stop! This isn't working. I feel like I'm being torn apart."

Maya squeezed my hand. "You have to believe for

the magic to work. You must—"

"I said *stop!*"

The table shook, and the candle blew out.

Maya yanked her hand back as if she had been burned. Her beautiful brown eyes grew wide. "This shouldn't be possible. The offering was good and the power of Zarabanda is formidable. A demon such as Raga does not possess the strength to resist."

Breathing out, I waited for the pain to leave my body before speaking. "Well, what if Raga was getting help? She told me that her master is here."

Maya massaged her hand as she spoke. "What master? Can you get a name from Raga?"

More laughter croaked in my head. *Not telling. You'll find out soon enough, as will the witch.*

"No dice. She says we'll find out soon."

Maya sighed and took a swig of rum. "This master, is it hiding at the hospital?"

Could be.

"Raga says it might be, but I'm pretty sure it is. There was a ton of weird energy in that place. Also, there was a symbol painted in the tunnels. It was hidden behind a sign for one of the buildings, and when I touched it, it shocked me."

Maya grabbed a pen and sheet of paper from a kitchen drawer and handed them to me. "Draw for me exactly what you saw."

I drew the image of a circle crowned with a crescent moon laying on its back and pushed the paper to the yaya.

Maya stared at the symbol. "*That* is the sign of the horned god. In truth, he is a demon that haunted this place many years ago. You might know him by another name."

Though I never considered myself an Einstein, the puzzle pieces were coming together to form a pretty clear pattern. "Wait. You're not saying that this thing, this horned god is

actually—"

"The Goatman," Maya said. "He has gone by many names over the centuries, but that is what he was last called before being exiled over decade ago. The demon's true name is Corabas."

He is my master.

"Holy crap! You're saying that the Goatman is real?"

"Most definitely. And it appears his banishment may have been temporary."

"I think you're right. Raga just said that's her master."

Maya chewed on her fingernails as she thought aloud. "It could be that Raga is bound to him. As long as he is walking the Earth, Raga is anchored here. That's why the exorcism didn't work. To free you of Raga, I must confront the power keeping her here."

"Unless you have an Uzi or rocket launcher at your disposal, I wouldn't recommend a trip to Glenn Dale. I get the feeling the Goatman has more than one wounded pooka guarding the place."

Maya stood and smiled. "Such things won't be of

much use against Corabas. My guess is you and your friends were getting too close to his lair. You must have triggered an alarm when you touched his anchor. That is why the pooka attacked you. It was under his control."

She closed her spell book and picked it up. "All I need is in here; however, I must get close enough to use it."

"Are you saying you're going to Glenn Dale?"

"In time. First, I must arm myself properly."

"Then let me go too. I can help."

"In your current state that's not a good idea. You are too closely connected to Corabas. Raga may not be able to act on her own yet, but the closer you get to her master, the more you risk succumbing to the demon's will."

I stood and faced the yaya. "But I want to help. After all, this is my life we're talking about. If you won't let me go, maybe my brothers—"

"No! Those two have been through enough. I will not drag them into this. This is for me alone to fix."

Her mood swing caught me off guard as did her words. "Wait, what does that mean? Do you know Chris and Steve?"

Maya lips pursed before she spoke. "That is a question better answered by your brothers."

Motioning to the door, she said, "For now go home and sit tight. Keep a low profile and try not to do anything stupid. I have much to do and little time to do it in. Pray that I am successful; otherwise, the infernal power inside you will assume control."

CHAPTER 21

Frustrated by the failed exorcism attempt and with the rest of the morning to kill, I decided to spend some "quality" time with my brothers. Since they had come home, the knuckleheads were out most nights until the wee hours of the morning, typically sleeping in until well past noon. Knowing what I now did, their odd schedules made a lot more sense. After all, monster hunting wasn't something one tended to do during normal daylight hours.

With Dad out golfing and Mom running errands, the house was as still as the grave. I crept to my brothers' bedroom door and opened it with feline stealth. Chris had fallen asleep in his clothes and was drooling on his pillow while Steve was sawing away like a lumberjack. Putting a hand over my mouth to stifle a giggle, I squeezed the air horn I used for football games. It was much louder than I remembered.

Jumping to his feet like he had been zapped in the

butt by a cattle prod, Steve made it a couple of steps before tripping over his shoes and face-planting on the carpet. Chris was just as entertaining, flipping over from his prone position and launching a spastic karate kick into the air while shouting, "Fuck you clowns!"

I almost peed myself laughing.

"What the hell?" Steve barked as he spat out carpet fibers.

With wild eyes Chris searched the room for hidden clowns.

"Sorry. Did I wake you guys?" I asked. "Must have been a long night."

After finding no trace of Pennywise or Ronald McDonald, Chris glared at me. "You're five seconds away from certain death."

"Uh-huh. Look, apologies for waking you dorks before noon. But given my near death experience last night, I'd say it's well past the time for you two to quit bullshitting me and come clean. And I swear if the next words out of your mouths have anything to do with selling Tupperware, I will end both of you here and now."

Rubbing the dirt from the corners of his eyes, Chris said, "You got this one, bro."

"It's kind of hard to explain and even harder for most people to believe," Steve said between yawns.

"Considering the show you put on at Glenn Dale, I doubt there's anything you could say that would surprise me."

"Before we get too far into this," Steve said,

"understand the reason we haven't opened up to you earlier was because we wanted to protect you. We didn't want to get you involved."

"Involved? Ha! Last night my friends and I almost got killed by the freaking *Bunnyman,* and I spent the better part of the morning hanging out with a witch that tried to exorcise a demon from me. Didn't work, by the way. So I'd say it's a tad late to keep me from being involved!"

"Sorry," Steve said. "Chris and I really are worried about you. That's the reason we're here. Well, one of the reasons. We're searching for something too. We've been doing it for the past six or so years – ever since Chris graduated high school."

"So all the traveling salesmen stories were—"

"A load of crap," Steve said with a smile. "But you knew that. You've been able to see through our stories for a while now."

"It hasn't exactly been hard. What was the one you guys used before Tupperware salesmen? Hawking vacuum cleaners? That was lame. If you're gonna be doing this for much longer, you'll need to think up better lies, like you're hit men or maybe smugglers. What are you looking for anyway? Vampires, ghosts...maybe the Goatman?"

"The Goatman's been taken care of. And even though we've stumbled across a vampire or two, they're not what we've been looking for either."

"You might want to uncheck that box next to the

Goatman. According to Maya and my new roommate, he's back."

"That's the witch?" Chris asked.

"Yep. Except she called him by another name. Something like Crapabus."

My brothers' eyes met for a split second before Steve grabbed me by the shoulders. "Do you mean Corabas? Is that what she said?"

For someone usually very chill, Steve's sudden drama took me by surprise. "Whoa, easy. Yeah, Corabas sounds right. She said he was back and that the Bunnyman Chris mauled might have been guarding his hideout."

I watched the color drain from Chris's face.

"Shit," Steve muttered.

With a hint of snarkiness, I asked, "This guy a friend of yours?"

"This has gone far enough," Steve said, looking at Chris. "Kate needs to know for her own protection."

"Yeah," I said. "Kate *does* need to know. So out with it."

After a few seconds, Chris looked up at Steve and said in a flat voice, "I need some coffee. Tell her whatever you want to."

Steve patted the end of his bed. "You're gonna want to have a seat for this one, sis."

"I think I'll stand for now, thank you very much."

Hunching his shoulders, Steve said, "Suit yourself. I want you to think back as best you can to around ten years ago. It was the summer. You used to carry that grungy doll around with you everywhere."

"Was this first edition Baby Jackie or second?"

Steve grinned. "Don't know. Both I guess. Anyway, do you remember Mr. Hutchinson? The old man whose lawn Chris used to mow?"

"You mean the Butcher of Bowie? Duh, everyone in PG County knows him."

"So there was a little more to the story. It turns out Edward Hutchinson wasn't your typical serial killer. He was actually possessed by a powerful demon named Corabas. The demon had been around Bowie since the nineteenth century killing at will and swapping out bodies when his host got too old."

The pieces were falling into place. "Let me see if I have this right. Mr. Hutchinson is the Goatman, the Goatman is Corabas, and Raga works for Corabas."

Steve put a finger to his nose. "Bingo. But how did you know that last part?"

"Raga told me so. She called him her master. But why would the Goatman choose Glenn Dale as his hangout? Because it's abandoned and creepy?"

"That's the question," Steve said. "Ten years ago we thought we got rid of him for good but apparently not. What did we forget to do? The spells worked and the anchors were cut. How the *hell* did he come back?"

"What's an anchor?" I asked.

"Anchors are symbols made by Corabas that keep him tethered to our world. He makes them all around the place he lives and where he hunts. In order to send him back to Hell, we had to remove them."

"How did you do that?"

"See, the symbols were carved into trees. To destroy one, you needed to hack it off the tree and burn the wood chips."

I knelt down and drew a pattern in the carpet with my index finger. "Any chance the symbol looks like this?"

"How did you know that?" Steve asked.

"One was painted on a tunnel wall at Glenn Dale."

"Fucknuts!" Chris shouted.

Steve and I turned to see him standing in the doorway.

"Of all the stupid-ass things," Chris continued. "We should have swept the area better. Looked for any traces of that son of a bitch!"

Steve walked over to his brother and grabbed his shoulders. "It's not your fault. You had no way of knowing there were more of them. *We* had no way of knowing. Hell, we saw the demon disappear in front of our eyes."

"Yeah, I know, but don't you remember his last words? 'Your cut is too shallow, and my roots run deep.' It was right in front of our faces. Dammit!"

Turns out our morning chat was evolving into quite the show. I decided to zip it and let the drama unfold.

"We were all there, Chris, and none of us picked up

on it," Steve said. "Sooner or later you have to let go of all that guilt. It's slowly burning you up inside. I want my little brother back. I miss the kid who loved nothing more than playing Dungeons and Dragons with his dorky friends and riding around all of Bowie on his beat-up dirt bike."

A tiny smile split on Chris's face. "The beast."

Steve gently shook his brother. "That's right. The *blue* beast."

The smile vanished as Chris brushed his brother's hands off. "How can you say that? You lost so much because of me, and you expect me to be okay with that?"

Steve's frustrated grimace led me to believe the two must have had this conversation many times before. As the room fell silent, I decided to take advantage of the lull in conversation. "So what's the plan? Storm Glenn Dale?"

Chris closed his eyes and began massaging his temples. "All I wanted was some damn coffee," he mumbled.

"Did he kill any people at the hospital back then?" I asked.

"I don't think so," Steve said. "All the murders we heard about happened in Bowie, but that's not to say we knew about all of them. I suppose it's possible."

Chris opened his eyes and dropped his hands. "TB."

"Come again?" Steve said.

"Tuberculosis. I remember Corabas telling me about how he possessed Edward Hutchinson. He said he cured him of tuberculosis. Glenn Dale started off as a sanitarium."

"So that's where Corabas found a host. Makes sense to go to a place where people are sick or dying to make a deal," I said.

"I think we found what we were looking for. Kate just happened to stumble across it before we did," Steve said.

There was still something they were not telling me. "I'm confused. What did *we* find?" I asked.

"A second chance, sis," Chris said. "We found a second chance."

Their cryptic double talk was grating on my nerves. "Will one of you two knuckleheads *pleeease* tell me what heck is going on? What did Chris screw up, and why the hell is Raga bothering with me?"

"Time to show her the trunk?" Steve asked Chris.

The smile on Chris's face almost touched his ears. "It's definitely time to show her the trunk. You do that while I get us some coffee."

CHAPTER 22

Steve popped open the trunk of their silver and black Monte Carlo SS he and his brother arrived in. Boxes of Tupperware were everywhere.

"If you're trying to sell me some of that junk, don't waste your time. There's no more leftovers in this house thanks to Raga."

"Hold on," Steve said, tossing the plastic containers out until the trunk was empty. Reaching down, he pulled up a false bottom. "Dig this."

Guns. Lots and lots of guns. The hidden compartment held a pair of shotguns, several handguns and revolvers, and a mean-looking rifle with a scope. There was also a sword, machete, crossbow, some wooden stakes, a bible, several tiny vials of what I guessed were holy water, and one baseball bat with a lot of nicks on it.

"Whoa. So, what do you guys do? Travel around the country killing monsters?"

"There's a little more to it, but you're not far-off."

"Enlighten me then. You two on some kind of mission to protect the innocent from the forces of evil? Kind of like Batman and Robin?"

Steve laughed. "Nah, nothing so noble."

"That's right. You're searching for something. So what's proving to be so elusive for the dynamic duo? The fountain of youth? The Ark of the Covenant? A low-fat diet that still leaves you feeling satisfied?"

The grin dropped from Steve's face. "Time."

"Think you could be a tad more specific?"

"You'll need to talk to Chris if you want more than that. I promised him I'd never discuss it with anyone without talking to him first. All I can tell you is that I'm tired, and my searching days are just about up. Life's too short to run around chasing shadows and pipe dreams. It will be hard for Chris to hear this, but I suspect he already knows it's coming."

I wouldn't get any more out of Steve on the matter. If he made a promise to Chris there was no way he was going to break it, so I decided to switch subjects. "So what about Raga? Why is she so interested in me?"

Steve slid the cover over the arsenal and began loading the Tupperware back in. "Raga possessed you a long time ago, Kate. You were young, about six. It was freaky as all hell. Understand, Raga is Corabas's servant, and he initially summoned her to spy on Chris and me. The best way to do that was to possess a family member."

"Guess I drew the short straw on that."

"You were an easy target. Also, you and Chris were

pretty tight, so it made your possession all that much the worse for him. Corabas informed Chris that if he did as he was told, you would be fine and he would send Raga back when he got what he wanted."

"Which was what, time?"

"No, smartass. He wanted Chris."

"Come again."

"Corabas had possessed Edward Hutchinson, but the guy was like eighty years old. It was time for the demon to choose a new host, and he had his sights set on Chris."

"Why Chris? What made him so special?"

Steve scratched the back of his neck. "Don't know. Maybe he was just looking for some healthy kid to possess and Chris happened to be the closest target, or maybe it was Chris's personality that drew the demon's attention. Chris had a wild imagination and was full of fire when he was young. He was into swords and sorcery and that kind of stuff. As a matter of fact, he was pretty close to discovering Mr. Hutchinson was the Goatman when the demon cornered him and made him an offer he couldn't refuse."

This was totally insane but fascinating. I was learning things about my brothers that I could never have dreamt of in my wildest dreams. "I'm still having trouble picturing Chris as some creative, easygoing kid."

"Trust me, I get it."

"So what was the Goatman's offer?" I asked.

"Your life for Chris's."

"Really?"

"Actually, it was your life and then mine, then Mom's and Dad's, etcetera. You would be his first victim if Chris didn't agree to become Corabas's vessel."

It was information overload. Up until a few minutes ago, I thought my brothers had bailed on the rest of the family in search of a fast buck. Although I loved them and deep down I believed they loved me, I resented them for turning their backs on us. As it turned out, they were doing what they felt they had to in order to protect our family. The revelation left me almost speechless. "Wow."

"So now you know the story, most of it anyway. I just hope to God that we're nearing the end of this. If we can stop the Goatman once and for all, maybe Chris can finally put the past behind him. If not…"

"If not what?" I asked.

Steve gazed into my eyes. "You saw how he was last night when he killed the pooka."

"Yeah, he was like Rambo, so fast and…"

"Violent? Bloodthirsty?"

"Now that you mention it…"

"Kate, you saw the same thing that I did. He was *smiling* when he sliced that creature's throat open."

The image of Chris's bloodied face flashed in front of me. The grin was there along with an emptiness in his eyes, almost like he wasn't Chris at all but something else, something horrible. I shuddered.

"We're losing him," Steve continued. "At first I

figured if I joined Chris on his hunts maybe it would be helpful, therapeutic even. But instead of getting better, he's been getting worse. He hardly sleeps anymore and his desire to kill all things evil is insatiable. He's blind to it though. He can't see he's becoming one of *them*."

"A little java juice to the rescue," Chris said, standing a few feet behind us with a cup of coffee in each hand. If he had heard what we were talking about, he failed to acknowledge it. "Get it while it's hot."

Steve cleared his throat. "Just giving sis a recap of our adventures with the Goatman and the last six years of our lives."

Chris handed one of the mugs to Steve. "Ah, good times, good times. Did you tell her about the vampires?"

"We didn't get into the nitty gritty of things. I just said that we've done what we've done to protect the family."

"And that you guys are searching for time," I said.

Wrinkles formed on Chris's brow. "You told her that?"

"That's *all* I said. Nothing more."

Steve took a sip of coffee and then spit it out. "Ugh, what the hell! That stuff is like half whiskey."

"My bad," Chris said exchanging mugs, "gave you the leaded one by mistake."

"Dude, it's not even noon," Steve muttered, shaking his head.

A devilish grin sprouted on Chris's face. "So now that we've let you in on our little secret, you have to promise not to tell anyone, especially our parents. It's for their safety."

"Scout's honor." I put my thumb and index finger on my lips and twisted an imaginary key.

Chris sniffed his Irish coffee before taking a sip. "Also, for the next couple days you and your friends need to play it cool. That means no returning to Glenn Dale and no blabbing about what you've found to anyone. Give us time to do our work. *Comprendez?*"

Maya's words resonated in my mind. *To free you of Raga I must confront and banish her master.* "Yeah, that might be a problem."

"What did you do?" Steve asked.

"Funny story. After Maya tried to exorcise Raga and failed, she said she needed to go to Glenn Dale to take out the Goatman."

"Ha!" Chris huffed. "That witch is going to get herself killed."

"We're going to have to do some serious prep work for this," Steve said. "How are we on our Hecate shells and devil's bane?"

"We're down to three shells," Chris said, "but we have tons of bane."

Steve grunted. "That's not good. We'll need to make more ammo."

"Anything I can do?" I asked. "Maybe whip up some ghost poppers or zombie grenades."

My brothers stopped their bizarre conversation and looked at me with blank faces.

"Do you actually have any ghost poppers?" Chris asked.

"Kate, we know this whole thing is kind of hard to swallow, but for now you're just going to have to trust us," Steve said.

Just when I thought I was finally connecting with my brothers, I was being pushed away again. "But I can help. I've been to Glenn Dale and know the layout. I can show you the tunnel where I found the horned god anchor, and I can—"

"You heard Steve," Chris interrupted. "There is no chance you're coming with us, and that's final."

Typical Chris. Pretending to be some big shot in charge of everything. I turned to Steve to see if he might argue my case. He had the saddest look in his eyes but remained silent. Having been once more shoved aside by my brothers, something inside me snapped. "Well, this is fucking great!"

Steve put his hands up as if to calm me. "Kate, I—"

"No! Uh-uh. You need to stop covering for your dickhead brother. I'm sick and tired of him bullying you and me, as if he's the only one who's been hurt in all of this. And as for you," I said, stabbing a finger at Chris, "the whole overbearing, obnoxious, psycho killer routine is getting old. You don't have a monopoly on pain and regret you know."

Chris held his mug up to his mouth and nodded the entire time I was talking. All it did was piss me off even more.

"Know what I think?" I said. "I think you're really nothing but a scared little kid on the inside and the whole whiskey for breakfast and chopping up giant bunnies thing is an act, and a poor one at that. That's why you're standing there pretending to sip on your coffee. You have nothing to say because you know I'm right."

Chris tilted the mug in my direction to show it was empty. "Bourbon not whiskey." Looking at Steve he said, "We don't have time for this. I'm gonna go wash up before we head out."

As Chris turned his back on me once more, I blurted out the only thing I could think of. "You're nothing but a coward!"

CHAPTER 23

As Tweedle Dee and Tweedle Dumbass prepared to take out the Goatman, I fussed and fumed in my room before finally calling Jake to vent. He picked up on the third ring.

"Hello?"

"Got time to listen to me bitch?" I asked.

"For you, sure. Don't want you to sic your brothers on me, do I?"

"They're the reason I'm calling. Those jerks are *so* annoying and *so* condescending; it drives me crazy."

"Well..."

Jake's lingering *well* was one of the last things I expected or wanted to hear from him. "Wait. You're not taking their side in all of this, are you?"

"It's not like that. All I'm saying is whatever they're doing is probably just to protect you. That's what big brothers do. I know it can be as irritating as hell."

Tapping the phone on my forehead, I sighed and

said, "I can't believe you're on their side."

"I'm not on their side. I can just see their point of view is all."

"Well, how about you be a good boyfriend and look at it from *my* point of view."

"Think about it this way," Jake said. "At least your family cares about you and is trying to protect you. I'd kill for an overprotective big brother or sister."

As unsympathetic as Jake was being, he was making a lot of sense. It was so annoying. "Want one of mine? You can have Chris for free. You two seem to have hit it off."

Chuckling traveled over the line. "Man, I thought for sure he was gonna beat my ass last night. Guess I missed the real show. Mike said your brothers were wicked the way they took out that creepoid in the tunnels."

An image of Chris's bloodied face flashed in my mind as Steve's words came back to haunt me. *He's becoming one of them.*

"Hey, you okay?" Jake asked.

Shaking my head to clear it, I said, "Nothing ten years of therapy and some good pizza won't fix. Which brings me to my point. What are you doing tonight?"

More laughter over the phone. "Figured your brothers would have you on lockdown given what happened."

"Meh. Believe it or not, those two nut jobs are headed back to Glenn Dale. They actually plan to hunt down the Goatman."

The laughter that I expected was replaced with

silence. For a few seconds I thought the line had gone dead. "Are you still there? Earth to Jake. Come in Jake."

"Yeah, sure," he said in a wavering voice. "So they're going to Glenn Dale tonight to get the Goatman? That's crazy."

Ignoring his out of tune response, I said, "I know, right? Turns out they've been doing this kind of thing for years, hunting down ghosts and vampires. It's a trip."

"Wow, sure is. Totally nuts."

Jake suddenly sounded distracted. Maybe Chris had rattled his cage more than I thought. "So whaddaya say we take a break from all of this freaky stuff and grab a couple of slices at Angelina's tonight?"

"Huh? Oh…that sounds great, but my mom's not feeling well, and I promised I'd help out with the chores and dinner. Maybe next time though."

Something didn't seem right. Jake mentioned that it was just him and his mom living together, but he rarely talked about her otherwise, and I got the impression their relationship wasn't exactly the best. "Oh, sure. You gotta take care of the one who takes care of you."

"Exactly. Look, I feel bad about this, but I promise I'll make it up to you. Deal?"

The words came out rushed, like he was dying to get rid of me.

"Yeah. Tell your mom I hope she feels better."

"Huh? Oh, absolutely. I'm sure she'll be up and at 'em in no time. Listen, gotta run. Mom can be high maintenance when she's under the weather. Call you tomorrow, okay?"

"Sure. Goodnight."

The line went dead.

I told you not to trust the cute one.

It was the first time I'd heard from Raga since Maya had tried to exorcise her. I got the feeling that the witch's attempt to send her back to Hell had taken its toll on the demon. Of course her timing now couldn't have been more perfect. "Would you please zip it?"

CHAPTER 24

I was on my third slice of pepperoni before I got up the nerve to ask Mike and Theresa if they would be up for a little recon. The weird way my conversation ended with Jake did nothing but stoke the suspicion already smoldering in my brain thanks to Raga. I was now sufficiently paranoid enough to take things to the next level.

"Excuse me, Kate," Mike said doing his best Peter Venkman impression. "I thought your brothers said that going to Glenn Dale was *bad*. You're gonna endanger us. You're gonna endanger my girlfriend, which means I might have to find another one."

"As much as I hate to admit it, Mike's right," Theresa said. "I used to think our adventures were fun and, truth be told, a little stupid. But knowing that this crap is real and there are actual ghosts and monsters out there," Theresa paused and shook her head, "that shit's just crazy."

"Plus," Mike said, raising a finger, "your brothers

scare the hell out of me, especially the one with the mullet."

Dumping half of the shaker of parmesan on a slice of pizza, I said, "I'm not talking about spying on my brothers at Glenn Dale. They're not the target. Jake is."

Mike scowled. "What's up with that?"

I took a big bite and spoke with a mouthful of gooey cheese and peperoni. "Maybe you two haven't noticed it, but Jake's been acting a little strange lately, and I just want to make sure everything's cool."

Mike started snickering. "I get it. You think Jake is messing around on you, don't you?"

Although the thought may have crossed my mind, I didn't really believe that was the case. Jake didn't strike me as the cheating type, even though I wasn't exactly sure what the cheating type was. But regardless, the accusation stung a little. I swallowed hard and said, "No, you boob. It's not that."

"Then what is it?" Theresa asked.

Ignoring her, I posed the following question. "Have either of you ever met Jake's mom?"

My friends looked at each for a moment before answering in the negative.

"Do either of you know if Jackie has?"

"Don't think so," Theresa answered.

"How's she doing anyway?" I asked.

Theresa took a sip of Coke and said, "She sounded okay, but a little tired. I think going to Glenn Dale really messed with her. I'm sure it had something to do with her grandpa being a patient there."

"Were they close?" I asked.

Theresa shrugged. "Don't know. She doesn't talk about him that much, at least not to me."

As worried as I was about Jackie, I had to stay focused on the mission. "Back to the question at hand. Have you guys ever been to Jake's home?"

Theresa shook her head while Mike quipped, "Darn tootin'."

"When was that?" I asked.

"A couple weeks ago. I dropped by his place to pick him up before we went to the Satan Church. He lives in those new apartments they built off 197 across from the H Section."

"So what was it like?" I asked before stuffing a wad of the pizza crust in my mouth.

Mike's nose scrunched up in disgust. "I think you need a bigger mouth. Human bites, Kate."

Stuffing my face was the only thing keeping Raga quiet during this whole exchange, and I wanted to keep it that way. With a full mouth I mumbled, "Shut up."

"Aaanyway," Mike continued. "By the time I got there, he was already outside waiting for me. He jumped in, and we split."

"So you haven't actually been *in* his apartment," Theresa said.

"No, but—"

"That's what Kate was getting at, doofus."

"Would you remember his place if you saw it?" I

asked.

"I guess. Pretty sure it was a ground unit. So what did you have in mind? A drive-by to make sure Jake's behaving?"

I put my hand over my mouth to try and stifle a burp that must have lasted at least five seconds. "More or less."

"Kate, are you feeling okay?" Theresa asked.

Up until this point I had been embarrassed by the impulses and urges I was feeling thanks to Raga, and though a part of me wanted to come clean with Theresa and Mike, I had already spent the better part of an hour explaining what my brothers had actually been up to for the past several years. Simply put, I didn't have the strength to open up another can of worms.

"I'm fine," I said. "Just a bit hungry is all."

"Like a hippo," Mike muttered.

Theresa landed an elbow in his ribs. "Is it possible for you to stop being an ass for a minute?"

Want me to snap his neck?

And there was Raga right on cue.

Grimacing as he clutched his side, Mike blurted, "Geez, that really hurt. She knows I'm only playing."

"We're here for you, Kate," Theresa said. "We'll go with you to Jake's, and if he's not there, the next time we see his lying butt, I'll hold him down for you while you cut off his nards."

What are nards?

Grabbing Theresa's hand, I said, "You're the best,

but I don't think it will come to that."

Theresa and I looked at Mike, who had fallen silent.

Still rubbing his side, he turned to Theresa and said, "Look, Jake is my boy and all, but if he's messing around on Kate, that's not cool. I'll take you two by his place, and you'll see he's home and there's nothing to worry about. And after that," he said, pointing to the arcade across from the pizzeria, "we're coming back to Quicksilver so I can open a can of Double Dragon whoop ass on both of you."

CHAPTER 25

"You two are going to feel really silly when you see my homeboy's taking care of his mom," Mike teased as we rounded a bend and turned into the apartment complex Jake lived in.

My heart switched to hummingbird speed. "What will we do if he spots us? What will I say?"

"Should have thought about that back at Angelina's," Mike said.

"Slow down and tell us where to look," Theresa barked at her boyfriend.

"Up there on the right, just past the red Citation. It's the bottom unit on the left side of the entrance."

"You mean the one with no lights on?" Theresa asked.

Mike sighed. "I don't see Jake's car parked around here either. Dang, this doesn't look good."

"It doesn't necessarily mean he isn't taking care of his mother," Theresa said in a desperate attempt to keep me from freaking out. "Maybe he went to get some food or medicine for her."

As plausible as Theresa's theory was, I knew in my gut it wasn't true. But then why the hell was he lying to me? What was he hiding?

Told you. Too cute to trust.

Pointing to an empty parking spot, I said, "There. Pull in and wait for me. I'm going to check on some things."

Mike slowed to a stop but didn't turn in to park. "Seriously? What are you going to do? Break in?"

"Just do what she's asking," Theresa said. "Can't you see she's upset?"

"All right. All right. Keep your shirt on."

Mike did as instructed, pulling into the parking spot. After putting the car in park, he said, "I'll keep it running and honk if I see Jake coming. We can tell him we dropped by to see how he and his mom were doing."

Leaving Mike behind as our early warning system, Theresa and I hopped out of the car and ran across the parking lot with all the grace and stealth of a couple of pissed off geese. Once in front of Jake's apartment, we clambered over a hedge of laurel bushes onto a small patio where we crouched low.

Excellent plan. Wait in the dark for Jake's return and then kill him. This is fun.

Ignoring Raga, I crept over to the sliding glass door. Vertical blinds blocked the inside of the apartment from prying eyes save for a foot-wide gap near the door's handle. Though it was dark inside, I made out a couch to my left and a television sitting on top of a milk crate to the right. Aside from the sparse furnishings and a mound of clothes piled in the far corner, the room was empty. Did Jake actually live alone? If so, why would he lie about it? Reaching up, I grabbed the handle and gave a tug. Locked.

"What is it? What do you see?" Theresa asked as she kept a lookout from her nest between a pair of laurel bushes.

"His place looks pretty barren…kind of like a bachelor pad."

Let's go in. I could lend you my strength to open the door.

"Why would you do that?" I whispered.

We need to know what your boyfriend is up to. So do you want it or not?

Deep down I knew breaking into Jake's place wasn't cool, but with my brothers out hunting down the Goatman and me days or possibly even hours away from being possessed by a demon, my moral compass might have been a bit off-kilter. "Okay, let's do it," I muttered.

"What did you say?" Theresa asked.

My body quivered as adrenaline shot through my veins. "Nothing. Just talking to myself." This time I pulled slowly, listening to the moan of metal as the door's lock fought a losing battle.

Ping.

"Did you hear that? What was that sound?" Theresa asked.

"Waddaya know? The patio door isn't locked."

Theresa turned around. "Wow. Are you actually going in?"

We are definitely going in.

With a sheepish grin, I looked at Theresa. "Well, he did leave the door unlocked, and it looks like no one's home. So..."

In response to my grin, a mischievous smile spread on Theresa's face. "I can't believe we're doing this."

I like the tall girl.

The place smelled like a musty mix of dirty laundry and air freshener. Once inside we opened the blinds, which gave us enough light from the outside streetlamp to search through the front living room and adjoining dining room and kitchen, not that there was much to see.

Pointing to the television, Theresa asked, "Is that thing sitting on a milk crate?"

Not bothering to look, I said, "Yep."

I stepped over a pile of Jake's clothes and entered a back hallway that led to the bedrooms. It was darker here, so I took the risk of switching a light on. "Theresa, why don't you check out the kitchen while I snoop around the back here?"

"Why do I have to search the lame kitchen while you get the bedrooms?"

"Because Jake's my boyfriend and if there's anything back here that shouldn't be, I want to be the one to find it."

Theresa frowned. "Fine. I guess I'll go search the

boring kitchen."

A box spring mattress and beat-up dresser occupied the bedroom on the left. After a brief inspection of the dresser and adjoining closet to make sure no bras, panties, or other women's garments were present, I moved on with my search.

A large map of Bowie was pinned to the far wall of the second bedroom. Moving in to get a better look, I noticed dozens of red circles spread around the town with dates written next to them. The most recent was on Old Pond Drive and was dated October 27, 1988 – just three days ago. It was the day the police discovered the last body – the one missing its head. Looking closer, I discovered several of the dates were older, going back ten years ago. There were circles at Whitemarsh, near J-Mart, and even at Crybaby Bridge. "What the hell?"

A desk sat below the map and on it was a leather-bound scrapbook. Opening it, I found clippings from The *Bowie Blade* newspaper dated from a decade back. All of the headlines and articles had to do with missing persons or with bodies that were found. The last one in the book was from August 16, 1978. The headline read *Human Remains Discovered in Home of Bowie Resident* and was accompanied by the picture of a ranch-style house with a beautifully manicured lawn. I knew it in an instant as I'd been in the house just this morning. It was Maya's now, but its prior owner had been the Butcher of Bowie. "What are you up to, Jake?"

I reached for the desk's sliding drawer but hesitated,

afraid of what might be within.

Do it. We have to know.

Jaws clenched, I grasped the handle and pulled. Inside was a bowl full of tiny bleached bones along with a bird's claw with a bunch of beads wrapped around it.

That's weird.

They looked like magic charms, similar to the stuff Maya used in her spells. But why did Jake have them, and why the hell did he have a map and scrapbook of all the murders in Bowie going back ten years? Shaking my head, I mumbled, "Why do all the cute ones have to be crazy?"

Good question.

CHAPTER 26

It took a tag team effort from Theresa and Mike to convince me to go home instead of stay and confront Jake. I was pissed, too pissed to realize that he might actually pose a threat until Theresa brought it up. When I finally got to my house I was still riled, so I flipped on the television and figured I'd wait up for my brothers. I made it until near midnight rehearsing in my head what I'd say to Jake when I saw him at school and ended up dozing off to an image of my soon-to-be ex-boyfriend wearing a tray of cafeteria food on his head, compliments of yours truly. Raga let it be known she thought it was a terrible waste of spaghetti.

Since their arrival Steve and Chris had always managed to make it back home before sunup, so when there was still no sign of them the next morning, I got a little worried. I wanted to check in on Maya to see if she had returned safely and had any info on my brothers, but that would have to wait until after I kicked Jake's ass at school. I mean, a girl has to have her priorities, right?

Unfortunately, the much anticipated butt whooping turned out to be a bust because Jake was a no show. That was a bit odd as it wasn't his style to play hooky, but when Jackie also turned up absent, I got even more worried. Theresa was quick to point out that Jackie hadn't been feeling well when she spoke to her the day before and promised to drop by Jackie's after school to make sure she was okay.

When I got home the first thing I noticed was no Monte Carlo parked in front of our house. Though I felt a bit guilty about heading inside for a quick bathroom break and snack before dropping by Maya's, I knew there would be hell to pay if I didn't placate Raga with an offering of empty calories.

I think your brothers are dead.

Raga's timing sucked as usual. "They're not dead, you butt wipe."

How do you know?

"Because they're tough," I said. "They handle this kind of thing all the time. That's how."

They have defeated other demons?

It was time to change the subject. "Would you just zip it? I'm tired and not in the mood. I'll get us a Twinkie if that will shut you up."

Make it two.

"Fine."

And some salt and vinegar potato chips.

Blech. "Okay, but then that's it until dinner. Got it?"

For now, but soon I'll be the one calling the shots and you'll be the voice begging for scraps. "Got it?"

The words weren't in my head; they were uttered by *my* mouth. I watched Raga speak to me in the bathroom mirror using my mouth. The demon was getting stronger and was now taunting me.

"Don't push it, Raga. I've had a rough day."

My face snarled as the demon spoke. "While you've been stuffing your face and chasing around your lying, stupid boyfriend, I've been getting stronger. I give you another day or two before I'm in charge, so you better start showing me a little respect."

I didn't have time for this. My brothers were missing, the Goatman was back in business, and my boyfriend might be a murderous psycho. I pointed at my reflection. "One more peep out of you and I swear to God I'll go vegetarian. There'll be nothing going in this body but salads and tofu."

My mouth fell agape in horror. "You wouldn't *dare*."

"I would and I will if you don't shut up. Be quiet and play nice and I'll throw a pop tart on top of that Twinkie; otherwise, we're having a fruit smoothie."

My challenge was met with silence. Deep down it was all a bluff, which I was desperately trying to hide from Raga. The demon's appetites were now so strong there was no way I could live up to my threats.

After a few seconds, Raga spoke. "Make it blueberry and you have a deal."

Kate one. Raga zero. "Okay. Now zip it."

After our snack I made my way over to Maya's. She opened the door after the first knock. A bandage was slapped across one of her perfect cheekbones, and there were dark circles under her piercing eyes. "You are alone?"

"Just me and my shadow."

Maya stepped back. "Come. We have much to talk about, and time is precious."

I entered the trashed house and followed Maya, taking a seat opposite her at the kitchen table.

"As you have no doubt guessed, I was unsuccessful in my mission," Maya said. "If it wasn't for your brothers, I wouldn't be here now."

"Are they safe? Are Chris and Steve okay?"

"They are but not for long. The new moon comes tonight and with it the enemy's powers grow stronger. He will wait until then to finish what was started ten years ago."

"And what was that?"

Maya tilted her head and scowled. "Your brothers didn't tell you?"

"Tell me what?"

"It was just over a decade ago Corabas tried to possess Chris. The demon believed your brother would be the perfect vessel, making him stronger and more powerful than he'd ever been. If it wasn't for Steve's sacrifice, Corabas's plan would have worked."

"What sacrifice?"

Maya's voice went cold. "He made a blood trade."

"Can you translate for those of us that aren't witches?"

"You can't get something for nothing in Palo Mayombe. In order to free Chris from the demon's power, a price had to be paid equal to the boy's life. In his case that was fifteen years."

"So what are you saying? Steve had to give up fifteen years of his own life in order to free Chris?"

"It was a steep price to pay, but he did so without a second thought. Such sacrifices are rare these days, even between kin."

It all made sense. Chris's obsession with the supernatural was fueled by his desire to find a way to get those bartered years back for his brother. The guilt he felt changed him over the years from a happy-go-lucky kid to a monster-killing machine obsessed with helping his brother. Steve, on the other hand, had made peace with his fate. He was tired of the wasted years on the road and wanted to make the most out of whatever time he had left – he just didn't have the heart to tell his brother. Or me.

Maya continued. "Now that he has returned and captured both of your brothers, Corabas intends to reclaim Chris as his vessel."

"And what about Steve?"

"It was Steve's sacrifice that saved Chris. He is also the one that banished Corabas back to Hell using an incantation from my family's spell book. The demon is sure to exact his revenge on your brother in brutal fashion."

"Okay, so how do we stop the creep?"

"I believe the key to our success lies in you, literally. Raga is bound to Corabas and is therefore attuned to his power. We can use the demon to locate the remaining anchors and sever Corabas's connection to this world."

Not going to happen.

"That sounds great," I said. "But how am I going to force Raga to help? She isn't going to do anything that might piss off her master, and she's damn close to taking over my body."

So close.

"I have given some thought to this and have a plan that I think will work, but first I need to know how far the demon's possession has progressed." Maya held me in her stare. "Tell me, are you still in control of your actions?"

I couldn't handle her unblinking gaze. My eyes fell to the kitchen table. "Mostly, I guess."

Maya reached across the table and grabbed my hand. She squeezed gently. "It's all right, child. Tell me what's going on."

"I thought I was in control until this morning. That's when Raga decided to hijack my mouth and start talking to me."

"I see. I suppose that was to be expected. It may end up working to our advantage in the long run. The stronger the connection between demon and vessel, the more potent the magic. As long as we can keep Raga in check, we should be able to use the demon's energy to pinpoint the location of the anchors."

"Okay, but what's to stop me from going all Linda Blair on you in the middle of Glenn Dale?"

Maya released my hand and reached into her pocket. "I have something for you that may help us." Pulling a green beaded necklace out, she said, "This is a family relic worn by my mother and my mother's mother before her. The wearer is given great power over dark spirits. It will tame the beast raging inside you and let you channel its energy."

"So...why am I just now hearing you have a magical necklace that could have helped me control Raga all along?"

"At the time I believed the charm I gave you would be sufficient to subdue the demon until I could exorcise it, but given the current state of things, it is clear such hopes were dangerously naïve. You have my apologies for that. Consider the necklace a tool of last resort. It is quite powerful and should be used with the greatest of caution. It is also a family heirloom and precious beyond measure."

The yaya looped the necklace a couple of times to shorten it before standing in front of me and saying, "Take this with my blessing, and use it to command Raga."

My hand shot up and grabbed her arm. I looked at her as Raga spoke. "Get that piece of trash away from me, or I'll snap your wrist in half!"

Maya's fierce eyes stared through me at Raga. "You will *not* take this girl today. Summon your courage, Kate. Push the beast back into its cage if only for a few seconds. You can do it."

It was the strangest thing, staring at my hand but not being able to control it. I focused on my index finger first, willing it to loosen ever so slightly. Next, I moved onto my middle finger and then so on. One of the few things I still had control over in my life was my body, and I wasn't about to give it up to some psychopathic, Twinkie-eating demon without a fight.

After a few seconds, Maya was able to wrestle free and drop the enchanted jewelry around my neck. As the beads touched my skin, a tingling sensation cascaded down my body. It was as if a switch had been flipped, and suddenly I was back in control.

"Are you okay?" Maya asked. "Is the demon subdued?"

You bitch.

After a heavy sigh, I said, "That's affirmative. Locked up and pretty pissed off about it."

"Excellent."

The necklace was warm to the touch and prickled my fingertips. "Wow. This thing has some serious mojo."

"Not mojo, child, Palo."

Take it off.

"Raga says she doesn't like your gift."

Maya smiled. "That is not a surprise. You now have the power to control Raga."

I bet you look ridiculous wearing it. Like some cheap hooker that –

"Quiet," I commanded.

Raga fell silent.

"Wow, this thing works."

"Of course it does," Maya said. "We can now use Raga to locate the remaining anchors and alert us when Corabas is near. If the need arises, you can even summon the demon's other abilities such as preternatural perception, strength, and agility."

I thought back to popping the lock on Jake's patio door like it was made from aluminum foil. "Really? So I can lift cars over my head and leap tall buildings and junk like that?"

"This is not like the comics, Kate. How strong you are and how high you can jump depends on Raga's raw power and the degree to which you are connected to the demon. But I must warn you, the more you rely on Raga's abilities, the closer your bond with the beast becomes. In the event you lose the necklace, the risk of being overtaken by the demon is enormous."

"Okay, so don't lose the necklace. Check."

"There is one more thing we need to consider. With your brothers' help, I found and removed the first anchor, but soon after that, Corabas descended upon us. It was as if he knew we were coming."

I thought about Jake's apartment and the map. "Could Corabas have an accomplice? Would a demon ever employ a human as a spy?"

Maya scratched her chin. "Perhaps. Why do you ask?"

"There is this guy I'm dating – *was* dating. His name is Jake and he had some strange things in his apartment."

"What kind of strange things?"

"He had some old newspaper clippings of murders in Bowie and also a map of the town pinned to a wall. There were circles on it with dates, dates people were murdered in Bowie."

"He showed this to you?"

"Not exactly. I sort of broke into his apartment and snooped around."

"What kind of girlfriend breaks into her boyfriend's place?"

Even though I had ordered Raga to be silent, I could sense she was amused by Maya's comments. "It's not like that. He lied to me about taking care of his sick mom. When I went over to visit him, he wasn't home."

"I see." Maya didn't sound convinced.

"Plus, there was no mom. Can you believe that?"

The witch smirked. "Uh-huh."

"So that's when I broke in. Heck, I didn't even really break in. His patio door wasn't locked." I had no idea why I lied to Maya about the door. "Anyway, that's when I saw the map. Also, there was this weird charm. It looked like a chicken foot with a bunch of beads wrapped around it."

Maya's eyes turned into slits. "A chicken foot you say? Was it painted black?"

It seemed a weird question, but we left Kansas a long time back, so I rolled with it. "Um, I'm really not sure. There was a lot going on at the time. Why? Is that important?"

"In Palo Mayombe, chicken's feet are often used as charms or to curse someone. The foot could be a mere protective token, but if colored black it would be used to hex one's enemies."

I closed my eyes and tried to visualize it. "I'm pretty sure it wasn't black, but it's hard to tell for sure. It was all dried up and old. I suppose it *could* have been black..."

When I opened my eyes, Maya was staring at me. "Very enlightening," she said.

"Look, I'm sorry." Pointing to my head, I said, "There's a lot going on up here, not to mention the fact that I'm sharing the space with a demon, so sue me if I can't recall if the damn thing was black. It's a strange thing to have to remember anyway."

Maya laughed softly. "I suppose you're right, but these are strange times. Your friend clearly knows something about the dark arts. Whether he is using this knowledge for protection or to cause harm is uncertain. Tell me, did he know your brothers and I would be at Glenn Dale last night?"

"He did, and when I mentioned it he started acting weird. He got real distracted and said he had to go take care of his mom."

"And after that you went to his house to find that he was not there and there was no mother?"

"Bingo."

Maya sighed. "You would be wise to be wary of your friend. He may be in league with Corabas."

"That's what I'm afraid of."

"Now let us prepare. It's time we go to the hospital, find your brothers, and rid the world of this demon forever."

CHAPTER 27

By the time we got to Glenn Dale, the sun sat low on the horizon. Shadows stretched out from the abandoned hospital's buildings, and a bitter cold settled on us. On the drive over Maya explained that Corabas was using Palo Mayombe to mask his activities at the hospital and that she had managed to alter his spell in the hope that we too wouldn't be caught by security or law enforcement.

After pulling into the parking lot in front of the Children's Hospital, Maya shut the engine off and turned to me. "Two anchors remain. We'll have to destroy them both before confronting Corabas and rescuing your brothers; otherwise, he will be impossible to stop. The anchors are located underneath the Adult Hospital and Finucane Hall."

With Raga now caged, I was feeling better than I had in a long time. I was also very much looking forward to seeing the expression on Chris's face when he discovered he was being rescued by his kid sister. "So let's get to it then," I said grabbing the door handle.

"Not so fast," Maya chided. "Corabas has them protected by kilombos."

"Kill what o's?"

"Kilombos are powerful spirits. These ones are particularly nasty as they have been forced into servitude by Corabas. The demon must have learned from his first encounter with your brothers to protect his anchors. I have the power to free the spirits from bondage and destroy the anchors, but I must be afforded the time needed to perform the rituals. You, Kate, must keep the spirits at bay until my work is done."

"How exactly am I supposed to do that?"

"Using Raga's eyes, you will be able to see the spirits' true forms, and with the demon's strength you can restrain them."

"So I'm going to fight ghosts. That's what you're telling me?"

"Your supernatural muscle should prove equal to the task," Maya responded.

"*Awesome*. What about the Goatman? Am I going to have to fight him too?"

Maya laughed. "You wouldn't last ten seconds against Corabas. He is ancient and formidable and cannot be destroyed by anything on Earth."

The wave of adrenaline I was riding suddenly crashed. "Then what the heck are we doing here if we can't hurt him?"

"Calm yourself. You will need a clear head for the challenges to come. I said we cannot destroy Corabas. We can harm him though. More to the point, we can send him back to Hell permanently."

As the encroaching wave of panic subsided, I said, "You probably should have opened with that. So how are we going to send the bastard off? You have some special spell you're going to zap him with?"

"Not exactly," Maya said reaching into the leather satchel slung over her shoulder and pulling out a monster revolver that looked like it came straight out of *Dirty Harry.*

"Oh snap! Do you have one of those for me?"

"I only have the one. Each bullet is marked with the sign of Watariamba to guide it to its target and the sign of Centilla N'Doki for potency."

"And that will take care of Corabas? What about the person he's possessing?"

"The only way to defeat the demon is to deprive him of a vessel. Now come, child. We must go."

The coldness of Maya's response surprised me. "We have to kill the person he's possessing?"

"Corabas cannot be exorcised as easily as Raga can. Unlike your dilemma, the demon's host had to let him in. That's why the bond is so strong and the creature so dangerous."

Remembering how Chris had almost become Corabas's vessel, I asked, "So that's it? A bullet is the only way?"

"The host, whomever it is, has not just accepted the demon willingly but has engaged in the slaughter of countless people. He or she has tasted human flesh and is beyond saving. Do you understand?"

"I suppose." Meeting Maya's gaze, I said, "But you didn't answer my question."

"There are always other ways, but this is the most assured means of defeating Corabas. Now, command Raga to give you her eyes. We must move before Corabas is alerted to our presence."

I did as I was told and watched in amazement as a silvery blue aura surrounded Maya. "Whoa. Did you know that you're glowing?"

Maya smiled. "I carry a protective charm. You can see its power now."

"You didn't happen to bring an extra one, did you?"

Her smile faded. "In your current state, I'm afraid the charm would do more harm than good. It would be in direct conflict with Raga, and you would be most uncomfortable. Remember the stone I gave you?"

The prickly heat the red rock caused came to mind. "Ugh, never mind. Don't want to go through that again."

After we exited the car, I remembered that I had silenced the demon. "You can talk now, Raga. Tell me, are we headed in the right direction?"

If you wish to die, then absolutely.

My groan got Maya's attention. "You need to be specific in your questions if you want to get anywhere with the demon. Although Raga must obey your commands, she still serves another master. She will mislead you if she can."

"Okay, Raga, one more time. Is one of the remaining anchors in this direction?"

Yes.

"Can it be reached by the tunnels?"

Yes.

For the last several days, I hadn't been able to get Raga to shut up. Now the demon seemed incapable of providing more than one-word responses. "You can speak freely, Raga. Just don't get on my nerves, or I'll order you to zip it again."

Soon Corabas will capture you, and you will be mine as he promised.

"You think so, huh?"

Of course.

"I wouldn't be too sure of that. From what I've learned of Corabas, he doesn't seem like much of a team player. Once he has Chris back, he won't have much use for a demon sidekick, will he? The way I understand it, your job was to keep an eye on Chris until Corabas could possess him. After he has what he wants, what does he need you for?"

To do his bidding, of course.

"Which is what?"

It's…well…it's none of your business. That's what it is!

I had struck a nerve with my line of questioning. The demon was unsure of herself. I felt her doubt as if it was my own. "Whatever you say, but maybe you shouldn't be so eager for us to meet Corabas, since it's pretty clear he doesn't need you anymore."

That's not true! We'll see who needs who soon enough!

"Fine, fine. Whatever you say."

Bitch.

Raga fell silent.

"It may not be wise to antagonize the demon trying to possess you, Kate," Maya warned.

There was a method to my madness that Maya failed to pick up on. In teasing Raga, I found the demon was as confused as I was about what was going on. Apparently, there had been no communication between Corabas and Raga, and I got the feeling that her return wasn't so much intended as it was an accident. When Corabas came back into power, perhaps the evil he'd conjured up ten years ago had simply returned with him. If that was the case, then maybe it was true that Corabas had no need for his lackey.

An image of Chris nearly decapitating the Bunnyman flashed into my brain as we entered the tunnel system from the basement of the nurses' dormitory. I followed Maya in silence until we came to the intersection where I had stumbled upon the first anchor. The mark of the horned god had been wiped off the brick wall.

"The stain of Corabas proved hard to remove," she said patting, the canvas bag looped over her shoulder. "But the next one will be no match for what I have prepared."

"What are you packing? Some Mr. Clean?"

Maya scowled. "That would do nothing to remove the anchor. Cascarilla mixed with fresh ground bat skull. *That* is the way to strip evil from just about anything."

"Of course. Bat skulls. Why didn't I think of that?"

The wooden sign affixed to the wall said Finucane Hall. Below it an arrow pointed into a pitch black corridor. Maya nodded toward the darkness. "The next anchor is down there, and it is sure to be protected. Stay close and be on guard."

Aiming her flashlight down the long, narrow tunnel, Maya led the way. Though I needed no light to see, the yaya did. A subtle funk gradually permeated the air the farther we went, and claustrophobia ensued, which was bizarre because I had never before experienced a fear of closed-in spaces, including on my prior trip into the tunnels. The smell became almost unbearable after a dozen more yards. "What the hell is that stink? It's like someone had a lunch of rotten eggs and then pooped it out."

"I smell nothing," Maya responded.

"You're kidding, right? It's like a loaded diaper filled by a baby that was force-fed Indian food. I can barely breathe. And what's with this tunnel? Is it narrowing, or is it just me?"

Maya stopped and turned to me. "The tunnel has not changed in size." Gazing into my eyes, she asked, "The smell, would you say it could be sulfur?"

"Does sulfur smell like used diapers?"

The witch grinned. "It does. We are on the right trail. This place must be warded against trespassers. The charm I carry protects me from its effects."

"That's great for you, but I'm about five seconds away from hurling."

"You have Raga's eyes; now command the demon to give you her strength. That should be sufficient to neutralize the spell's effects."

"You heard the lady," I wheezed to my demonic roommate. "Give me your strength, Raga."

A spike of adrenaline rushed through my body, killing all claustrophobic feelings and clearing the stench from my nose. I said the only thing that came to mind. "Jesus."

Maya's grin grew. "Not quite. I take it that worked?"

"Heck yeah it did."

"Good. Let us continue."

A couple of minutes later, we emerged into a basement that had to have been at least a thousand feet long and wide. The paint had not yet started to peel on its mildew-stained walls, and no traces of graffiti were visible.

"This is Finucane Hall. It served as a dormitory for hospital staff," Maya said, shining her flashlight around the room until its beam froze on a bunch of sagging ceiling tiles. "Stay clear of that," she warned.

"What is it? Another magical booby trap?"

"No, it's asbestos. This place is full of it."

Holding our breath, we tiptoed around the cancerous material and between a hodgepodge of rusting cots and rotting furniture before coming to an open area. Maya knelt and drew a series of arrows and squiggly signs on the ground that bore a striking resemblance to the symbols I saw her scribbling on her dining room floor not so long ago. I watched as she pulled a small stick from her satchel and placed it in the middle of her artwork.

"That looks familiar," I said.

"It should. It is the same spell I used the night you were spying on me."

"Won't the stick just point to me again since there's evil in me?"

"No," she said as she continued drawing. "The necklace you wear not only gives you control over Raga. It also masks the demon's aura." Maya whispered a few words as she flicked the stick clockwise.

As if balanced on a tack, the tiny piece of wood spun for several seconds before the sharp end came to an abrupt stop, settling on a series of tall metal filing cabinets abutting a wall to our left.

"You think Corabas might have actually filed the anchor?" I asked as we moved to the cabinets.

"Unlikely," Maya answered while trying to open several drawers.

After having no success, she peered around the side of the column of drawers to her right and shined her light. "It looks like the cabinets are mounted to the wall at the top. I can see what looks like runners."

"And then there's this," I said, pointing to a numbered keypad mounted on the wall adjacent to the cabinets.

Maya's eyes met mine as we both said, "Secret room."

The witch pointed to a small section of floor to the left of the cabinets that was clear of debris and grime. "See the clean area? These cabinets must slide in that direction. I bet that keypad was used to open them."

"Maybe six or seven years ago it was," I said, pushing different combinations on the lifeless keypad. "But this thing hasn't been used in a looong time."

Maya sighed. "Someone has moved these cabinets recently. The tracks in the dirt look fresh." She grabbed a handle of one of the drawers and tugged. The cabinets moaned in protest but failed to budge.

After once more commanding Raga to lend me her strength, I tapped Maya on the shoulder and said, "Step aside, little lady." A tingling sensation shot down my arms and into my fingertips as I placed my hands on the right side of the cabinets. Leaning my shoulder in, I pushed. A cacophony of clanks and pings followed as hidden gears slowly turned. The metal monstrosity yielded an inch or two at first but surrendered completely when I dug deep and put my legs into it. With a hollow whine the block of cabinets slid to reveal a nondescript steel door that had been forced open.

"That was awesome!" I shouted like the spaz that I was.

The tone of Raga's voice was one of smug satisfaction. *You're welcome.*

From the way the metal frame bent inwards, I knew that something powerful had pushed the door open. One word slipped from my mouth. "Corabas."

CHAPTER 28

Rows of beds lined both sides of the room before us. Four to each wall, they were supported by an array of gizmos. Some of the stuff looked like medical equipment I'd seen on television, including IVs and blood pressure monitors, but most of it was foreign to me.

"Why would they have patient beds in a hidden room within the staff dormitory?" I asked.

Maya scanned the room with her flashlight. "That is a good question."

Opposite us was another metal door. I slowly made my way between the rows of empty beds. "This medical equipment has got to be worth some serious cash, but no one has looted the place."

"The beds, they're all made," Maya whispered.

A large oak desk occupied the far right corner of the room. On it was an old calendar, an inbox stacked with yellowed paper, and a keyboard and monitor. I ran my fingertips over the Apple II logo emblazoned on the decade-old machine. "I think my dad had one of these."

"What *is* this place?" Maya asked.

I grabbed the papers sitting in the tray and blew the dust off the top one. "This looks like a patient record. It has their age, sex, and blood type along with some lab work. At the bottom it says they're prepped for phase 2 testing, whatever that is."

"Project Bellerophon," Maya said.

I glanced up and saw her paging through files from one of the cabinets lining the wall. "According to these records, it looks like terminal patients were eligible for phase 2 of the project," she said.

"So what do you think that's about? Some radical new therapy or drug meant to help people who are near death?"

Maya looked back at the rows of patient beds and the hidden door we had entered through. "I do not. I think it was intended for something terrible."

"I kind of got that vibe too."

"We can't afford to get sidetracked. Where is the anchor? We need to destroy it and leave this place as soon as possible."

A placard was posted on the far wall next to the second door. *Genesis Chambers* was engraved on it. The anchor was close now – the bees buzzing in my head told me so. Pushing the unlocked door open, I said, "The anchor is somewhere in here."

A dark corridor loomed before us. Maya unholstered her gun with her right hand and rested it on her left, which gripped the flashlight. With both pointed forward, she swept the hall while we crept along. Seconds later a steel-framed door appeared on our left.

"Chimera Twelve," Maya whispered while reading the sign affixed to the door.

"What does that mean?" I asked.

Ignoring the question, Maya raised her flashlight to a window in the door and looked through. I snuck up behind and peered over her shoulder. In the center of the room, a pile of bones sat in a pool of black goo. Based on the extent of decomposition and the way the bones were splayed out, it was hard to tell whether the remains were of a person or animal. A thick chain lay in the middle of the mess and extended out a few feet where it was bolted to the floor.

"What is that?" I asked.

Maya stared at the long-dead thing for a few seconds before losing interest. "Come," she said turning her attention back down the corridor. Whatever was running through her mind would be kept private for the moment.

Soon enough we came to another door labeled *Chimera Six*, and once more we peeked inside. A similar mound of nastiness in the corner of the room had one notable difference. In the middle of the muck, a wolfish skull grinned at us with two rows of jagged teeth.

"That was definitely not human," I whispered.

"No, that *was* chimera number six."

"What the heck is a chimera?"

Maya looked at me. "In mythology and the occult it is a monstrous creature made up of different animals. To the Greeks the chimera was part lion, part goat, and part snake, and it breathed fire."

"Wonderful."

"It was killed by the hero Bellerophon, while he was riding Pegasus."

"Wait. I thought Perseus flew Pegasus. You know, like in *Clash of the Titans*."

Maya frowned. "It was Bellerophon."

"Okay, but in the movie—"

"Focus, Kate. We have work to do. Follow me." Maya moved on.

Not wanting to be left alone in a secret lab buried beneath the remains of a haunted sanitarium, I naturally followed. The buzzing sound intensified as we passed the rooms for Chimeras Seven and Ten and reached hive-level activity when we approached the last remaining cell. The sign on the door read *Chimera Two*.

"It's in there," I whispered. "The anchor is somewhere in that room."

Maya opened her satchel and retrieved a jar of red liquid and a handful of iron nails. "The kilombos will attack anyone who attempts to reach the anchor or to free it from servitude. The second part may sound contrary to the spirit's desires, but remember it is under Corabas's control."

"Why don't you just shoot it?" I asked.

"The bullets have been fashioned with a singular

purpose, to destroy Corabas's mortal shell and send him back to Hell. They will do little good against an enraged spirit forced to do the demon's bidding."

"So what do you need me to do?"

"I will need time – not long – to complete the incantation that releases the spirit. Once my work begins the kilombo will become…agitated."

"Okay," I said pointing through the tiny window in the door, "but as long as it's in there and we're out here, what's the problem? If we just keep this door shut, you should be able to hocus pocus the spirit out of here no problemo, right?"

Maya dipped an index finger in the jar and painted a large circle on the floor in front of the cell door. "In order for the spell to work, the spirit must enter the ring. When this is done, I will speak the words and free it from its bonds."

"Is that blood you're using?"

"Yes."

"Human blood?"

Dipping her finger back in the bottle, Maya spoke. "Of course. Human blood is the most potent."

Even though Maya had saved my life and helped me control the demon trying to possess me, she still scared the crap out of me sometimes. When frightened my go-to coping mechanism was humor. "Is it from anyone I know?"

She smirked as she continued drawing. "Do you know that annoying little fat boy that lives in the house on the corner of Spindle and Belair?"

"Cody Johnson? Are you telling me that blood is his?"

Maya stopped drawing and looked at me, grinning devilishly. "No, but I did tell him if he let his dog poop in my yard one more time, I would gut him like a pig and serve him up at the next neighborhood barbeque."

She's spooky.

It was the first comment Raga had made in some time, and I had to agree with her.

"It's my blood," Maya said as she went back to work. "I always keep some for such occasions."

I made a mental note never to cross Maya and watched in respectful silence as she finished her gruesome finger painting.

She produced a towel from her satchel and wiped her scarlet finger clean. "Now comes the tricky part. The kilombos must be physically surrounded by the spell, by the symbols I have drawn on the ground."

"How are we going to do that?"

Wearing a blank expression, Maya waited patiently for it to dawn on me.

The terrible truth slapped me in the face like a wet fish, and a cold sweat washed over my body. Maya wasn't just asking me to protect her. She needed someone to lure or wrestle the kilombo into the middle of the magical trap she had laid for it. "Oh…well, shit."

Putting a hand on my shoulder, Maya said, "It will take just a few seconds for a few words to be uttered. I have no doubt you can do this; otherwise, I would not ask."

Feeling the weight of her gaze, I stammered, "I—I guess I could try."

She pointed to the necklace around my neck. "Trust in my handiwork and in Raga's power. Do you understand?"

The metal door holding Chimera Two rattled. Maya and I looked at each other before glimpsing in its window. A whirlwind of dust, bones, and what looked like fur had whipped up. The faster it spun, the more it coalesced until eventually gaining the shape of a humanoid figure roughly seven feet tall. Furry arms stretched out from a decaying torso, which ended in a long serpentine tale. The kilombo's skull appeared human save for a pair of fierce-looking fangs jutting out from its mouth. Glowing amber eyes zeroed in on me.

I could barely breathe. "I am so screwed."

"That thing is nothing more than a construct assembled by the kilombo to guard the anchor," Maya said. "It is not truly alive, so do not worry about hurting it."

"Don't worry about hurting *it*? Are you frigging kidding me? It has fangs, Maya. Fangs. I don't have fangs. Maybe you should be asking that freak show not to hurt me."

Ignoring my comments, Maya nodded toward the door. "It is time."

"You hear that, Raga? It's go time. So unless you want to lose your vessel and never taste a Twinkie or slice of pizza again, I suggest you lend me some muscle."

Seconds passed and I was getting a little nervous when *bam!* The jolt of energy almost knocked me clear out of my Vans. "Awwwesome!"

With a mere gentle tug, I popped the lock on the metal door and pushed it open, but even in my jacked up state, I hesitated when I stared into the kilombo's terrible eyes.

Apparently, a sixteen-year-old girl decked out in denim and sporting a bitchin' necklace was not as imposing a sight as I had hoped because the kilombo did not hesitate. Using its coiled tail like a spring, the creature launched itself at me.

Claws and fangs were seconds away from tearing me to shreds when I raised my arms and started spastically flailing. "Ahhhhh!"

Bones, scales, and fur flew in every direction, and an unexpected silence descended on the room.

"You were supposed to bring the kilombo into the circle, Kate, not annihilate it."

I took a knee and a couple of deep breaths before answering. "In my defense, I have never been in a fight in my entire life. Considering the fact that my first one was against a reanimated chimera, I think I did just fine."

You did not. That sucked.

"Fine will do us no good unless we can remove the anchors and send Corabas back to Hell," Maya said.

I raised an arm and pointed to the anchor painted on the back wall of the cell. "So there it is. Why don't you go ahead and scrub away? One down, one to go, right?"

Maya rolled her big brown eyes and motioned to the ground in front of me. "That's why."

Swirling up into the air, the shredded remains of the chimera combined once more, this time into a slightly larger version of the creature.

"Well, that sucks."

"Grab the kilombo!" Maya shouted. "Bring it into the circle!"

Do what I tell you to.

"Come again?"

"I said, bring the creature—"

I put a hand up to silence Maya. "Not you. Raga is talking to me."

You don't know what you're doing, so just do what I tell you to. That way you won't get killed, and I won't have to watch you act like a complete spaz.

Spaz wasn't a word I had heard Raga use before. For a moment I wondered if our time together had not just changed me but the demon as well. "Okay, Raga. What do you think I should do?"

Follow my lead. You will feel a compulsion to move in your arms and legs. Just clear your head and go with the flow.

Go with the flow was also a new one for Raga, but I got what she was saying. Grinning, I said, "I think I can do that."

As the chimera sprang at me, I felt a jolt in my legs, pushing me to the right. Surrendering to the demon, I moved as directed, letting the kilombo pass. Another jolt shot through my right arm, sending it up and then looping it under the same arm on the beast. An instant later I had the chimera in a full nelson.

"Good!" Maya shouted. "Quick, drag it into the circle!"

Keeping a chimera in a wrestling hold was the strangest experience of my relatively short life. First of all, the stench of moldy fur had me gagging. Second, the creature's bizarre amalgam of decayed flesh, bone, and scales was slippery and gross, so gross. As the chimera nipped at my arms in vain while squirming to get free, Raga and I slowly hauled it into the center of Maya's trap.

She threw a handful of dirt on both of us and started shouting in Spanish.

Unfortunately, my mouth was open at the time. Spitting out, I yelled, "Hey, c'mon!"

Maya ignored me and continued throwing more fistfuls of dirt as she circled us and chanted. The chimera lashed out furiously with its tail, striking my back repeatedly but causing no real damage, thanks to Raga. Seconds seemed to stretch into hours, and just when my burning arms were ready to quit, the chimera convulsed and crumbled through my fingers into a pile of dust.

Leaning over, I coughed up a mouthful of earth.

"Here, child," Maya said, handing me an open flask.

I took a swig and felt liquid fire rolling down my throat. After a fit of wheezing, I shouted, "Jesus, Maya! What the heck is that?"

"A potion. It's intended to provide strength and protection."

"By potion do you mean moonshine?"

Maya smiled. "For full potency, the ingredients needed to be purified with powerful spirits."

Putting a hand to my mouth, I mumbled, "My lips feel numb. So does my tongue."

"A common side effect. You will regain sensation in a minute or two."

I want some more.

"Raga likes it," I said.

Fumbling through her satchel, Maya said, "That's hardly surprising."

She produced a small jar and approached the anchor. "Now it is time to cleanse this place." Maya smeared a paste of bat skull and cascarilla over the anchor and began chanting once more.

That is a bad idea.

"Why?"

Once she removes the anchor, Corabas will know we are here. He will hunt us down.

"So why are you telling me this? Don't you want your master to find us?"

Not like this. If he finds us and I am not in control of you, he may decide to kill you. If that happens, I go back to Hell. I don't want to go back to Hell. It sucks there.

"I see. So are you going to help us? If you do, maybe when this is all over I'll treat you to an all-you-can-eat buffet."

All-you-can-eat? That sounds amazing! But…to challenge Corabas is madness. Perhaps if you remove that horrible necklace, I could be of more assistance.

"Nice try, but the necklace stays."

Suit yourself. I imagine your death will be quite painful. It is an ugly necklace by the way.

"You really do suck, Raga."

I looked at Maya and smiled. "Raga says that Corabas will know we are here the instant the anchor is removed."

Wiping her fingers, Maya stepped back from her work. "Of course he will. But, if we are swift, we should be able to destroy the remaining anchor before he can stop us. Once the final one is gone, I will send Corabas back to the abyss, this time for good. It was my bloodline that brought this plague upon the world, and it is my responsibility to rid it of the demon. Look now." She pointed at the anchor. "The anchor is severed and we are closer to ridding the world of Corabas."

I watched as the gunk Maya had spread over the anchor changed from yellow to an oily black. When she cleaned the mess from the wall, the symbol was gone. Before either of us could get a word out, a terrible rumble shook the room, knocking us to our knees.

He knows.

CHAPTER 29

Goosebumps rose on my arms. Shivering, I slowly stood and turned to see a shadowy figure in the doorway.

"I feel it too," Maya said. "We are not alone, are we?"

I looked to where a face should be, but all I saw were swirling colors, mostly gray, indigo, and black. "Nope."

She is free.

The words were not spoken, but I could hear them in my head all the same. I knew immediately the ghost was referring to the kilombo Maya had liberated. "Yes, she is," I answered.

You are like the one who keeps us here.

The ghost sensed Raga. It must have thought I was like Corabas. "No. I'm here to help you." Waving a hand toward Maya, I said, "We're here to help."

"What is the spirit saying?" Maya asked.

"It thinks I'm evil because of Raga's presence, but I'm telling it we're the good guys."

"Ask the spirit where the last anchor is. With its help,

we can find it quicker, and time is of the essence."

Dropping back down to my knees, I drew the sign of the horned god in the dust. "Can you tell us where to find the remaining anchor?"

The ghost backed up, clearly disturbed by my drawing.

"Wait!" I said, wiping the symbol away. "Please, we need your help. We are here to send the other one back to where he came from."

The shadow stood silent as if contemplating my words. Finally, it spoke. *It is close. You must free us. All of us.*

"How many are trapped?" I asked.

Not just trapped. Used. Used like oil or fire wood...until we are no more.

"What did the spirit say?" Maya asked.

"The anchor is close by. It's asking us for help. It says they are trapped here and being used like some kind of fuel."

Maya muttered something in Spanish and looked to me with widening eyes. "It's worse than I feared."

"What does it mean?"

"That vile creature, Corabas, has not just imprisoned these poor souls and enslaved them as he did with the kilombos. He has done a far more terrible thing."

It was hard for me to fathom a crueler fate than being stuck in Glenn Dale for all of eternity. "What could possibly be worse than being trapped here?"

"He is also draining their life force for his own

twisted designs."

"So it's almost like he's like killing them all over again?"

"That is a wickedly apt description."

Being held captive in such a sad and lonely place was bad enough, but the thought of having your spirit slowly sucked from you in the process was almost too much to bear. "That's messed up. I mean, *really* messed up."

"Indeed."

Turning back to the ghost, I said, "We'll help you. By the way, what's your name?"

In the years I've been here, I have forgotten much, including my name. Call me what you will.

"Okay then. Let's go for something simple. How about...Casper?"

Very well.

"So, Casper, what can you tell us about the one that keeps you here? Has he been at Glenn Dale for a long time? Is he close by now?" I asked.

The evil one arrived many years ago, but time blurs when you are no longer among the living. His power has infested every brick, mound of dirt, and blade of grass in this place, so it is difficult to feel his presence until he is upon you. Now, come with me.

We followed Casper out of the secret lab and up a flight of rusty stairs, exiting Finucane Hall at ground level. Once outside, I noticed we had guests, lots of them. Tall, short, thin, and fat, swirling shadows loomed across the moonlit nightscape for as far as the eye could see.

"Wow," I whispered.

"There are many?" Maya said.

"Hundreds," I mumbled in awe. The sight of so many victims of Corabas's wickedness stirred something savage and vengeful inside of me. I was no longer here just to save my brothers and myself. I was here to save Glenn Dale from the demonic disease that tormented both the living and the dead.

Casper spoke. *The destruction of the anchor brought them here. They are anxious to be free of the demon's yoke. Follow me. The final anchor is not far.*

As we reached a side entrance to the Adult Hospital, Maya said, "Corabas must be purged from this place. When we destroy the remaining anchor, he will be vulnerable. Now," she motioned to the thick wooden door before us, "if you would be so kind."

"Okay, I've seen this done on television," I said raising my right leg. "Just gotta plant the foot next to the door handle."

Summoning Raga's strength, I swung my foot up. Instead of popping open like the doors in *Miami Vice* always did, the darn thing splintered into a thousand pieces.

Maya was silent as she picked pieces of wood out of her thick black hair.

I chose to focus on the result rather than the execution. "Door's open."

"Please be a little more careful when we meet the next kilombo. I would prefer not to be washing bits of it out of my hair later."

"Oops. I'm still getting the hang of this. I'll try to do better from here on out." Putting a hand over my heart, I said, "Promise."

A long corridor extended before us with multiple patient rooms on each side. The doors were all open, revealing broken windows, rusted cabinets, and crumbling plaster walls. As we walked past them, I reflected on the poor souls trapped in this decaying world and an immense sadness came over me.

"Did you know about this, Raga? Did you know what Corabas was doing here?"

I sensed hesitancy on Raga's part.

"Answer me."

No.

"You don't sound very convincing. Are you telling me you had *no* clue what was going on here?"

I didn't say that. I did not know what my master was doing with the souls trapped here, but it does not surprise me. He is merciless and consumes what he desires, be it living or dead.

If I didn't know better, I'd say Raga's words were laced not with awe or respect but with dread. Before I could delve more into that puzzle, the buzzing in my head returned. "We're getting close."

The hall opened up to a foyer with a pair of stairways, one going up and one down. I didn't have to wait for Casper to offer directions. The buzzing was coming from below.

"Look," Maya said, pointing to the floor.

Tiny black circles speckled the cracked terrazzo tiles, leaving a trail of mysterious dried droplets that continued down the steps.

Leaning over, Maya spit on one of the beads and swirled her finger in the mix until it turned scarlet.

"Blood?" I asked.

"Yes. Spilled within the last couple of days, if I were to guess. Come."

We descended into another large room filled with dusty bedframes, rotted mattresses, and rusted chairs and tables that had been stored and forgotten. The layout reminded me of the basement in the Children's Hospital all the way down to the series of three by three metal doors along the wall.

"Super, another morgue," I said flatly.

Casper's words were ominous. *There is an evil in the air that I cannot abide. Good luck to both of you. The fate of many rests in your hands.*

The ghost retreated into the shadows.

Maya shined her flashlight on the trail of dried blood, following the tiny drops to the mortuary cabinets. A bloody handprint was visible on the middle door.

I started toward it, but Maya grabbed my shoulder.

"Don't you feel it?" she asked. "The last anchor is behind that door. This is a trap."

"So where's the kilombo then?"

Maya opened her mouth but paused as the earth

began to shake.

The floor in front of the mortuary shelves burst wide as dirt spewed forth. Whirling about, the hellish cyclone gobbled up debris from all corners of the room. Wood, glass, metal, and wire, such things coalesced within the furiously churning mass of dirt, forming a humanoid figure that brushed up against the ten-foot-high ceiling. From beneath the golem's earthen flesh, shards of glass, wooden stakes, and twisted spirals of metal jutted outward and formed a type of spiked armor. Blue flames burst to life in a pair of plum-sized eye sockets.

Maya's eyes grew wide. "This kilombo is bigger than the last one."

Pointier too.

Addressing both Maya and Raga's comments, I said, "Thanks, guys. Real encouraging."

Shall I take the lead?

As much as I needed all the help I could get, I was getting used to my newfound strength and agility. Now knowing what I could actually do gave me a confidence I didn't have when we first stepped foot in Glenn Dale. "Thanks, but I think I'll start this dance myself."

"Stick to our plan!" Maya shouted as she dropped to her knees and began drawing. "Buy me time to complete the trap and then bring the creature to me!"

The golem made a move for Maya, but I darted between them. "How the heck am I supposed to get that thing into your circle? I'll get cut to shreds!"

Maya paused from chanting long enough to shout,

"Improvise!"

Grabbing the end of a nearby cot, I swung the hunk of tetanus between myself and the mud monster and lunged forward, driving it back against the wall. The golem gripped the other end of the cot and pushed hard. Metal groaned as we twisted and pulled its frame in a crazy-ass game of tug-of-war until it finally snapped in two with a high-pitched *twang*.

This wasn't working. I needed to find a way protect myself and get the golem into Maya's trap. After chucking my half of the cot at the creature, I surveyed the room for anything to help me. More cots, chairs, broken glass, old desks, and a butt-load of rotting mattresses. *Mattresses*. Ducking as the golem's section of cot flew over my head, I snatched up a nearby mattress. With my shoulder leading the way behind the mattress, I charged the monster, driving it back into the wall with the force of a charging bull. Dirt, splinters, and tiny slivers of glass soared through the air.

"That's good!" Maya shouted. "Now bring it over here!"

"You gotta be kidding me," I muttered under my breath.

Getting the kilombo to Maya's circle was going to be ugly any way I sliced it. The true question was how much damage would I have to take in the precious seconds the witch would need to free the spirit.

You can do this.

It was the strangest thing, words of encouragement

from the demon trying to possess me. Stranger still was their invigorating effect. Kicking it into fifth gear, I squeezed the golem like a hungry python and pivoted. I headed to Maya's trap, holding the golem like it was a giant burrito of squirming evil.

When the monster's fist smacked down on my back, it felt like someone had slammed a brick into me. Glass and wood pierced my skin as the creature grabbed my shoulder in a vain attempt to free itself.

Screaming in pain, I doubled down, tightening my grip and pulling harder until we made it into Maya's circle. While I struggled to keep the golem within the confines of the ring, a wicked grin grew on its face, spreading until it cut halfway through the creature's head. As if loaded on springs, the golem's mouth popped open, revealing row after row of gleaming glass shards.

Oh crap.

With a *chomp*, it snapped down within inches of my face and continued biting at the chilly air as it slowly drew closer. Dirt was flying from Maya's hands again, and she was shouting in Spanish. Why the heck was her spell so damn long? Why couldn't she just say abracadabra or hocus pocus and be done with it?

With the golem's glass teeth millimeters away from my cute little button nose, I lost my footing. Dropping to one knee, my grip loosened and the world around me turned gray.

You got this. Just a few seconds longer.

Closing my eyes, I summoned what remaining

strength I had and made it back onto two feet.

The golem wailed and began trembling. As it's terrible groans increased in volume, its convulsing became nearly undearable.

I think it's gonna blow.

I released the kilombo and grabbed the fallen mattress with my right hand. With my left I snatched Maya's wrist and shouted, "Get down!" She understood and fell to the floor as I dropped beside her and heaved the grimy cushion over our heads. Moments later came a thunderous *boom* followed by a shower of glass, earth, and wood.

Pushing the shredded mattress off us, I stood and waved the dusty air away from my face. "Wow, that was…awesome!"

Maya rose and pointed to the bloody cabinet. Coughing to clear her throat, she said, "We must act swiftly. Corabas will be upon us soon."

As Maya reached to open the cabinet, something thumped on the door from the inside. Hand outstretched, Maya looked to me.

Thump!

I assumed a fighting stance. "Who's there?"

A muffled voice answered. "Kate?"

My friend's trembling voice was unmistakable. "Jackie?"

"Wait a minute," Maya cautioned.

It was too late. I was already pulling the door open.

A welt the size of a jawbreaker swelled on her left

cheek, and a trickle of blood had dried just below her split lip, but it was definitely Jackie. Helping her out of the mortuary cabinet and onto shaky feet, I asked, "How the hell did you get here?"

Ignoring my question, Jackie looked at Maya with wide eyes before turning her gaze to me. "I saw his face," she said.

"You saw whose face?" I asked.

"It was terrible! His eyes, Kate. They're blood red! And those horns! They coiled out of his head like snakes. But the worst were his teeth. They were black, Kate, *black*." Jackie started shaking uncontrollably.

I pulled her in close and hugged my friend.

"I thought I was dead," she said. "I was sure I was dead. Am I dead?"

"No, beautiful," I answered. "You're not dead. You're safe now."

Jackie pushed back. "No, I'm not! And neither are you...or her." She pointed at Maya.

Grabbing Jackie's hands, I tried to calm her. "It's okay. We're here to send him back to where he came from so he can't hurt anyone again. Soon this will all be over and you'll be—"

Jackie yanked her hands away from me and shook her head. "You don't understand. We were so freaking stupid, so naïve."

"What are you trying to say, child?" Maya asked.

Jackie's blue eyes were on fire. "It's Jake, Kate. Jake is the Goatman."

CHAPTER 30

Even though I had a creeping suspicion Jake had been up to no good, the words still hit me like a sucker punch to the gut. "Come again?"

"I knew something wasn't right about him when we first came here and he up and vanished. Who does that?" Jackie asked.

"That's not enough to go on by itself," I said.

"You're right. Which is why I followed him last night after we spoke on the phone."

"Are you crazy?"

Jackie nodded. "Maybe a little bit. Anyway, he came here. I thought I was being cool and following at a safe distance. I didn't think he was on to me, but I was wrong. Looking back, I'm pretty sure he knew I was following him from the very beginning."

"Then what happened?" Maya asked.

"I tried to stick behind him in the tunnels, but it was so dark, and all I had was a lighter. I remember there was a sign with the words 'power plant' on it. That's when I turned to leave, but a hand grabbed me from behind. The last thing I saw was his face – its terrifying face – before everything went black." Jackie shuddered. "When I woke up I was in the cabinet. I shouted and banged on the door for a while, but it was no use. Eventually, I faded back off to sleep, and that's when I heard the two of you raising holy hell out here." Tears formed at the corners of Jackie's eyes. "At first I thought it was *him* coming back for me. Thank God it was you two!"

Jake. The Goatman. It was all real, all true.

A deep breath later I regained my composure and confidence and hugged her again. "You're safe now. Why don't you head back to Maya's car and chill?"

Jackie was shaking her head before I finished my sentence. "As if! You aren't leaving me alone in this place. Not by a long shot." Her face scrunched. "What's *she* doing?"

I turned to see Maya applying her bat skull goop to the last remaining anchor. "That? It's kind of like magical Mr. Clean. It can get rid of dirt, blood, cursed symbols, etcetera."

The frown stayed on Jackie's face. "Really?"

"Observe," Maya said, stepping back from her handiwork.

Just as before, the symbol faded and then disappeared as the magical concoction absorbed it. A rumble shook the whole building, causing a torrent of dust and plaster to fall.

Jackie jerked upright like she'd been zapped by lightning. "Gah!"

Grabbing her shoulders, I smirked. "You get used to it."

"That was the final anchor. The trapped spirits are now free of Corabas's power. He is vulnerable," Maya said.

"And pissed," I added. "Very pissed."

"Vulnerable?" Jackie said gaping. "How can something ten feet tall with razor-sharp claws and horns be vulnerable?"

I sighed. "I guess it's time you knew. I have super strength from a demon that's sort of possessing me, and Maya has a magic gun."

Jackie snapped her fingers in front of my face and then pointed to her own. "Look into my eyes, Kate. Did the Voodoo Queen maybe give you something to smoke?"

"Nope. But she does have a magic potion that has some kick to it."

Jackie cast suspicious eyes on Maya. "I bet she does."

"It's not like that," I said, grabbing one of the morgue's cabinet doors. "Check it out." With a metallic squeal, the door came off in my hand.

Jackie smiled. "Wicked!"

"Right? And that's not all. I can see and talk to ghosts."

"Ghosts? Actual ghosts?"

"Yep, and they're all around us."

Jackie's head swiveled left then right as she scanned the room. "Seriously?"

"Uh-huh. Maya can even cast spells to get rid of them if they're causing us any trouble. Those types are called kilombos."

Facing Maya, Jackie said, "That is so cool. It sounds like you guys might actually be able to pull this off. Got anything for me, like an Uzi or lightsaber or something?"

"I don't know. Do we, Maya?"

Casting a cool look at Jackie, Maya said, "No. We have no Uzis or other weapons for your friend."

"Bummer. Sorry, Jackie. We didn't really plan for anyone else to be joining us. Stick close to us and you should be fine, okay?"

"Yeah," Jackie said dejectedly. "I guess so. Just don't wander off without me."

"No way, homegirl."

After letting out a long sigh, Maya spoke. "Time is now against us. Corabas is no doubt aware of our presence and waiting for us. I have a feeling we should go to the power plant. My intuition tells me that's where we will find him and your brothers."

CHAPTER 31

After entering the underground tunnels through the Adult Hospital entrance, we headed east back in the direction of the Children's Hospital. Being the only one with supernatural vision, I led the way, followed by Maya and then Jackie. After ten uneventful minutes of slogging through pools of muddy water, we were back at the intersection where we first encountered the Bunnyman. To our right were two tunnels with signs reading *Finucane* and *Children's Hospital*. To our left was one labeled *Power Plant*.

As we started off toward the power plant, I heard a shout from Maya followed by a large splash. Turning, I saw Jackie and Maya both sprawled out on the muddy ground. Maya was ranting in Spanish and cradling her right leg.

Scrambling to her feet, Jackie blurted, "I'm sorry! I couldn't see in the dark."

I knelt down next to Maya. "Are you okay? How bad

is it?"

Tears welled in the witch's eyes as she shined her flashlight in Jackie's face. "I told you to be careful and watch the ground! You were supposed to step where I stepped!"

"I know. I'm sorry. I must have stepped too soon. I didn't mean to."

"Can you stand?" I asked.

Maya shook her head. After another round of cursing, she shouted, "Christ, child! How much do you weigh?"

Putting my hands up to silence the two of them, I said, "Okay, everyone just chill for a sec. Maya, any chance we could splint it and you could lean on me?"

Maya stared at me like I had a third eyeball growing out of my forehead. "Do you *see* any sticks around here, Kate? Even if there were, by the time you had me bandaged, standing up, and hobbling, it would be too late. Time is critical, and I am no longer of any use thanks to your friend. Here," Maya shoved the gun in my hands. "Take this and shoot the demon. Do not let him speak to you. Just aim at his chest and pull the damn trigger."

The weight of the gun in my hands surprised me. "So, just point and shoot? What about a safety?"

"It's a revolver, so it doesn't have a safety. Just point the barrel of the gun at the demon and squeeze the trigger like you'd squeeze an orange to get the juice out of it."

"What if I miss?"

Maya shut her eyes and spoke through clenched teeth. "The gun is loaded with six bullets. If you miss all six times, you can kiss your ass goodbye."

Jackie sidled up next to me and held a hand out. "This is all my fault. Please, let me help. My father taught me how to shoot years ago."

"No!" Maya shouted. "This is Kate's responsibility. It has to be her." Her eyes popped open and turned a blistering gaze on me. "This burden cannot be passed along so recklessly. It was *ours* to see through to the end. Now it is *yours*. Do you understand?"

"I guess so. The help would be nice, but if you're saying—"

Maya reached up and grabbed my hand. She flinched as she spoke. "Your fate is up to you and not to another. Keep your wits, and do not be tricked or threatened by the beast. I am sorry I cannot go with you, but I have faith that you are up to the task, that you will do the right thing when the time comes."

"But what about you?" I asked. "You're defenseless here."

Despite her pain, a tiny smirk cracked on her face. "A yaya is never defenseless. If any shadow, spook, or ghoul is foolish enough to cross me, they will regret it. I promise you that." She waved me off. "Now go. Hurry. Send Corabas back to Hell."

We left Maya at the underground nexus and proceeded down the tunnel toward the power plant. Though the witch had given Jackie an extra flashlight from her satchel, I still led because I could see better without the light.

We were well into the tunnel and out of Maya's earshot when Jackie tugged my arm. "Hey, Kate."

"What?"

"I get what Maya was saying about you needing to be responsible for your own fate and all, but…"

"But?"

"But she's not here anymore, and I feel totally worthless. Why don't you let me help you? A few minutes ago the witch was planning to shoot Corabas. Why can't one of your best friends do it instead? You know, like one who actually knows how to shoot."

Now would normally be when Raga interjected with some wisecrack, but the demon had fallen strangely silent. If I had to guess, I'd say it was because she dreaded meeting Corabas in her current subdued state. But this wasn't exactly the best time to psychoanalyze Raga, so I pushed it from my mind. Having never shot a gun before, I wasn't pumped with the idea of my first target practice being against a murderous ten-foot-tall demon that harbored a mega grudge against most of my family. Maybe Jackie was the right choice for the job after all. I gripped the pistol and was pulling it out if my waistband when a *thump* echoed down the corridor from in front of us.

Instinctively, I yanked the gun out and pointed it into the darkness. "Who's there?"

The sound of sloshing footsteps answered. They

grew steadily louder as something approached.

"I said, who's there?"

"Kate? Is that you?"

Jake's voice was unmistakable.

"Don't move," I ordered as Jackie shined her flashlight on him. He was filthy but otherwise appeared normal.

"Oh God! It's him!" Jackie screamed. "It's the Goatman! Shoot!"

Jake's eyes flared as he whirled around to stare into the blackness behind him. "Where? I—I don't see him!" he shouted, backpedaling closer to us.

I trusted Jackie, but she was known to panic from time to time, and I had to be sure before I pulled the trigger. Cocking the hammer back like I'd seen it done on *T.J. Hooker,* I shouted, "Put your hands in the air, and turn around, Jake!"

Hesitant to turn his back on the dark corridor, Jake was slow to follow my orders. When he did a scowl formed on his face. "What are you doing?"

"Shoot him, Kate! Quick, before he changes!" Jackie pleaded.

Jake waved his hands. "Whoa, say what? Why the heck would you do that? What's wrong with you two?"

Something didn't feel right. If Jake was the Goatman, why bother playing innocent? He would know that Jackie would call him out as soon as she laid eyes on him.

"If you can't do it, give the gun to me, and I'll take

care of things," Jackie said. "Hurry though. A few more steps, and the gun won't even matter. Corabas will snap our necks before you can pull the trigger!"

Jake stopped moving. "What the heck is a Corabas? Look, I've been hiding out in these tunnels for the past couple of days trying to figure out a way to rescue your brothers."

Something had been gnawing at me since Maya and I first found Jackie, but it took Jake's words to jog my memory. In all our conversations regarding Corabas, Jackie had never asked who Maya and I were referring to. So how could Jackie know—

"Shoot him!" Jackie screamed.

I spun and pointed the muzzle at Jackie. "How did you know the Goatman's true name?"

"What the heck are you doing? Aim that thing back at Jake or we're dead."

"Answer the question. How did you know the Goatman's name was Corabas?"

"I don't know. I guess you or Maya must have told me. What difference does it make?"

Shaking my head, I said, "Nope. Uh-uh. Neither of us said anything to you before you started referring to the Goatman as Corabas."

"Well, it must have been Theresa or Mike that told me."

"Bzzt! Wrong answer! They don't know who Corabas is. You're lying, Jackie."

Her hand was lighting fast, striking the side of my

face like a sledgehammer and sending me crashing to the floor. The world went gray as sparkling stars danced in my peripheral vision. She was saying something, but the words came out warbled as I fought to remain conscious.

"You weak-willed child! How could you ever consider yourself capable of stopping me, even with the help of that mongrel witch?"

"Jackie?"

"Not quite. Right under your nose these many months, and you didn't have a clue." Corabas looked down at his open hands. "I have to admit, possessing a girl has been a unique experience. Enduring the lunacy of high school, the puerile chattering of teenage girls, and the pathetic courting attempts from hormone-crazed boys has been maddening. However, one of the benefits of wearing such an innocent shell is the freedom of movement and utter lack of suspicion. The last three people I dined upon didn't see it coming until I had already ripped out their throats. Simply amazing! It really was an exponential improvement over Jackie's grandfather. But he served his purpose. How does the saying go? Any port in a storm?"

I watched Corabas pick up Maya's gun from where I had dropped it. Gripping the barrel, he squeezed until it flattened like a pancake. "You really shouldn't play with such dangerous toys."

From the corner of my eye, I saw Jake pull a knife from his jacket. Was he actually thinking about stabbing

Jackie? Was that the only way to free her from Corabas? My vision started to clear, but my mouth was still playing catchup. "H—How? Why?"

"Tsk, tsk, tsk. You still don't understand, do you? I suspect Chris would have fared better in uncovering my ruse. To answer your succinct questions, before you knew Jackie, she was far from the picture of health you now see. Childhood leukemia had ravaged the unfortunate child, leaving her in a constant state of pain and misery and silently longing for death. When her beloved pop-pop came for a visit and made her an offer of perfect health, it was simply too good to pass up."

"You tricked a dying girl into letting you possess her?" Jake said, grimacing. "You really are despicable."

"Tricked is such a distasteful word. I simply explained that she would never get sick again and would live a long healthy life. Unlike you, I never lied to get my way."

"What's Corabas talking about, Jake?"

"Yes, Jake, what am I talking about?"

Jake's icy blue eyes locked onto me. "So here's the deal. My real name is Jake Sullivan, and I grew up here – in Bowie. I lived over on Buckingham Drive. Anyway, back in summer of seventy-seven my mom went missing. A year later, after the police raided the house owned by the Butcher of Bowie, they found some of her bones in the basement. Dad and I moved away soon after that. There were just too many memories here. Anyway, after I got out of high school, I started investigating stories about witchcraft and the supernatural. That's when I met up with your brothers. It was about a year ago, I guess. They bailed me out of a sticky situation in Poughkeepsie and taught me a few things."

"Wait. After you *got out of* high school? Exactly how old are you?"

"Eighteen."

I breathed a sigh of relief. For a minute I thought I might have been dating a guy as old as my brothers. Eighteen wasn't so bad.

Corabas sneered, clearly enjoying the exchange between Jake and I.

"I came back to Bowie when I heard the news reports of the decapitated bodies. It seemed familiar to me, just like ten years ago right before the police raid on Edward Hutchinson's house. I enrolled at Bowie High figuring it would be a good way to get the latest info on what was going on around town. You'd be surprised how easy that was to pull off."

"And when you found out I lived on the same street as the Butcher of Bowie you figured what? That you'd cozy up and find out if I had anything of value to share? Is that all I am to you? A source of information?"

It's not too late for us to kill him.

Jake shrugged. "No, not really."

"Not *really*?"

"You didn't let me finish," Jake said. "When we first met, yes, I wanted to find out what you could tell me about the Butcher of Bowie. I figured there was either a copycat out there or somehow the Goatman had reemerged. But it didn't take long for me to fall for you. You have great taste in movies, a wicked sense of humor, and your smile can light up a room. Kate, you're actually kind of awesome."

Maybe we don't have to kill him after all.

"Enough," Corabas interrupted. "Now that we are all reacquainted, I believe it's time to slip into something more comfortable." Blood doused blond hair as the demon's horns burst through bone and flesh, coiling round and round in wicked spirals. With an unearthly shriek Corabas dropped to all fours and commenced to convulse and groan as if spellbound in a bizarre fit of agony and ecstasy. Shiny black claws split fingertips and bulges of muscle and fur tore through clothing as Corabas stretched into ten feet of literal hell on earth. The stench of brimstone permeated the air. Smoke poured from the demon's mouth as it spoke. "I remember your mother, Jake," Corabas teased. "A plump little thing, correct? She really was a tasty little hen, that one."

"You piece of shit!" Jake shouted.

Jake moved in before I could tell him to stop, not that it would have done any good. I watched Corabas effortlessly backhand him, sending him flying into the tunnel's brick wall where he fell unconscious to the floor like a sack of rocks.

The demon's searing red eyes shifted to me. In the dark they looked like burning coals. "Fortunately for you, I need you alive – at least for the time being."

Corabas grabbed Jake by an arm and heaved his

limp body over his shoulder. "If you want to see your boyfriend or brothers again, I suggest you meet me in the power plant within the hour. Otherwise, well, all of this exertion has left me a bit peckish, and I may have to snack on one of my guests. Oh, and Raga, you will have some explaining to do when next we meet."

Oh crap.

CHAPTER 32

By the time I backtracked to Maya's location, she was applying some type of poultice to her ankle. With the gun gone and Jake captured, I was freaking out.

"What happened to your face?" Maya asked.

I touched the side of my head and flinched as a current of pain shot to my brain. "Funny story. Turns out Jackie is possessed by Corabas. All this time and the Goatman was right in front of our faces."

Maya spat on the ground and cursed in Spanish. "I should have known. Corabas has been playing us for fools, and we've fallen straight into his trap."

"Speaking of, why didn't we know who he was? I can see ghosts thanks to Raga and you have your witchy gifts."

"Corabas is too smart for that. He must be using a glamor spell to mask his demonic aura. Where's the gun?"

"Trashed," I said. "Corabas squished it."

Maya huffed and muttered, "I practically handed him the only weapon we had."

"He kidnapped Jake and said to meet him in the power plant within the hour. What I don't get is why he didn't just try and kill me then and there."

Bitter laughter slipped from her lips. "How could I have been so blind?"

"What's going on, Maya? What were you blind to?"

"This has been his plan all along. I was too obsessed with finding the spell book to see it."

Maya's cryptic comments were starting to rattle me. "To see what? You're freaking me out a little."

The witch's fierce gaze grabbed hold of me. "Think about it, Kate. Once Corabas possessed Jackie, he could have gone anywhere. It would make sense to move to a place distant from Bowie and start again, but Corabas chose to stay and begin killing again. Why?"

"Old habits maybe?"

"Nothing Corabas does is without careful thought and meticulous planning. That is how he has remained on the Earth for so long. It is also how he managed to escape Hell's clutches when your brothers tried to send him back ten years ago. Kate, don't you understand? We are caught up in the web Corabas has spun. There is only one thing the demon has thought of in the past ten years, only one thing he has wanted."

"So what is it? Revenge?" I asked.

"Yes, but that is not his primary objective. He seeks to finish what he started."

The light bulb finally went off. "It's Chris, isn't it?"

Bingo.

Maya nodded.

"But why? Corabas has another vessel now. A younger one."

"The demon spent a great deal of time selecting and then grooming your brother. He was the prize, the prize that was stolen from him. Now he wants it back, and he wants to punish those responsible for depriving him of it."

"That would be Steve."

"To begin with, yes, but I imagine his killing spree won't stop there if he gains possession of Chris. All of those who helped your brothers will be targets."

The witch is correct.

I shook my head to try and clear it. Something wasn't adding up. "That plan won't work. There is no way in hell Chris will allow Corabas to possess him. Didn't you say the vessel has to be willing?"

Maya's response was a whisper. "Yes."

"So his plan is destined to fail. Now all we have to do is figure out a way to save my brothers and Jake. Maybe we can whip up some type of distraction, you know, draw Corabas away from his lair. Then I'll swoop in and free everyone with a little help from Raga. Once we're hell and gone from this place, you can get another gun and mojo up some more magic bullets. We'll come back and—"

"Kate."

"Don't interrupt. I'm on a roll here. If we could just—"

Maya put a hand on my knee. "Kate, you should go."

"Go get him? Sure, but we need a plan first."

"No, you should leave this place. Fly as far away as you can."

Slamming the brakes on my train of thought, I looked at Maya to see if maybe she was in worse shape than I initially believed. Though she no longer appeared to be in excruciating pain, she wore a sad, almost defeated expression. "Come again? I think your busted ankle might be clouding your judgment. How would me bailing help the situation? I'm not abandoning my friends or family. You said it yourself, this is my responsibility."

Maya's smile was wistful. "I did say that, didn't I? But you misunderstand me. You are the key, Kate. You always have been. It's because of you that your brothers returned. It's because of you they are now Corabas's prisoners."

"You're going to lay a guilt trip on me now? Can't this wait?"

"It cannot. Don't you see? *You* are all Corabas needs to get what he desires. You are correct in assuming Chris would rather die than let Corabas possess him. But if your brother felt he could save a life – your life – in exchange for giving the demon what he wants, Chris would not hesitate."

And just like that my world came tumbling down. I was the final piece of the puzzle. I was all that was needed for Corabas to succeed. And if I left now, Chris would refuse Corabas and everyone would be killed… but at least Corabus wouldn't have my brother.

"Now you see why you must go. Deny Corabas his prize. Your brothers would want you to."

I opened my mouth to speak, but lacking anything to say, I shut it. We had come all this way. We had fought kilombos and destroyed the Goatman's last remaining anchors and for what? The best-case scenario was that my friends and family would die. Here I was thinking I was making a difference, thinking I was the hero about to save the day, and it turns out I was nothing more than a pawn being used by the demon to get what he wanted. It was all so heinous. "This is bullshit," I muttered.

Grabbing Maya's hand, I looked her in the eyes. "What's the backup plan?"

"This is the backup plan. The smartest thing for you to do would be to leave this place. Take yourself out of the equation."

"I didn't ask what the smartest thing was. I know you, Maya, and I know you don't go anywhere without being prepared. I don't believe for a second that you would come this far without a plan B. So out with it. What's our plan B?"

An awkward silence descended as the strangest staring contest ensued. Peering deep into the witch's dark brown eyes, I searched for a glimmer of hope, some twitch of the lid or shift in her gaze to indicate she was holding out on me. But Maya refused to yield. Her unblinking eyes revealed nothing, no clues or hints as to a backup plan. Just when I figured it was a lost cause, she finally relented. "With the anchors now removed, we may have another option on the table, but it is a long shot."

"I knew it! So what is it? What's the plan?"

"With nothing tying Corabas to this world aside from his current vessel, there may be a way to send him back."

"I don't think Corabas is going to wait around while you draw circles on the ground and then promenade with me into one of them."

Maya shook her head. "No circles." Pulling her hand out of mine, she pointed to my chest and said, "The key is in you. Literally."

"Raga?"

I don't like the sound of this.

Maya continued. "Having summoned Raga to the mortal world, Corabas is connected to her. That is why Raga manifested in you as Corabas's strength returned. That is also why we couldn't exorcise Raga from you. With the anchors now removed, if one demon is sent back to Hell, theoretically the other one can be as well."

I definitely don't like the sound of this.

"But there's a catch, isn't there?" I asked. "There's a reason you chose the gun over this plan."

"In order for this to work, the demons must be connected. Physical contact between the vessels is required."

"For how long?"

Maya's eyes smoldered with hidden power. "Long enough for you to command Raga to leave your body and return to Hell. With Raga still bound by the necklace, she will have no choice but to do as you say. When she leaves, Corabas should be pulled into the abyss with her."

Let's go with the smart choice and just leave here.

"So I need to get close enough to grab Corabas and then order Raga back to Hell."

"Yes."

"And that will be that?" I asked.

"I...believe so."

I wished she sounded more certain. "What happens to Jackie?"

"She should be fine, at least physically. What she will remember of her possession is another matter. She might lose all memory from the time she was first possessed, or she may remember fragments."

"Still, that's a lot better than how she would have ended up under plan A," I said.

"Perhaps. I suppose that depends on how much she recalls."

Slowly standing, I said, "It's settled then. Plan B it is."

"There's more. There is much to lose if you fail."

"No kidding? You mean like my life, my brothers' lives, the life of my boyfriend, and, let's not forget, yours."

"That is only the beginning," Maya said. "To take

something innocent, something pure, and to corrupt it is a terrible thing."

"Sure," I said, nodding. "But Corabas is an evil douche, and that's what evil douches do."

"Listen to me carefully, Kate. The greater his vessel's fall, the more powerful Corabas becomes. One of the main reasons he chose your brother was his innocence, his kind soul. If he could take such a pure thing and corrupt it, he would be…unstoppable."

I thought about Steve telling me how Chris used to be. That he was a caring, compassionate brother. "Those bullets. They weren't just for Corabas, were they?"

She stared into my eyes. "Only if there was absolutely no other choice."

"You're a cold woman, Maya. And if you think I'd ever kill my brother, you're out of your frigging mind. Now if you'll excuse me, I'm going to go send Corabas back to Hell."

As I walked away, Maya's words echoed down the corridor. "You must not let Corabas join with Chris."

CHAPTER 33

The walk to the power plant was a lonely one. For the first time since the craziness began, I was on my own – except for Raga.

I still think this is a mistake.

"Sorry, Raga. It's nothing personal at this point. To be honest, in a weird kind of way it's been fun. Thanks to you, I've been suspended from school, serenaded Jake with a little Def Leppard, kicked some kilombo butt, and eaten my body weight in pickles and Twinkies without gaining an ounce."

We walked in silence for another minute.

I had fun too. The food was good, Jake was hot, and smashing things is one of my favorites.

"We made a pretty good team, you and I."

Seconds passed before Raga spoke again. Are you scared?

"Absolutely."

Me too.

Raga's words surprised me. "What are *you* afraid of?"

What you said before is true. Corabas is displeased with me. Even among our kind, he is feared for his cruelty and vindictiveness. He has always been heavy-handed, but this time I fear his punishment will be…severe. The same malice that drives him to seek vengeance on your brothers will be directed against me.

"I guess I get that. Even for a demon he's an asshole, huh?"

Exactly.

"Raga?"

Yes.

"Thanks for lending me a hand in those fights…and for the advice. I couldn't have done it without you."

Agreed.

"Guess we have one more coming."

Guess so. Can I ask you a question?

"I think we're beyond the point of you asking permission. What's up?"

You were mad at Chris. You called him a dickhead the last time you spoke to him.

"Thanks for reminding me. So what's the question?"

Why are you risking your life for him now? It doesn't make sense.

Sometimes I forgot I was actually talking to a demon. Human emotions and relationships were probably as foreign to Raga as her behavior was to me. "Just because I was mad at him doesn't mean I want to see him hurt.

Sure he can be a pompous ass sometimes, and he's definitely bordering on psychotic, but deep down I know he loves me. That's the reason he's been acting the way he has. He's trying to push me away so he can protect me."

Then why not do as he would wish, and leave like the witch said?

"Because as much as he cares and worries about me, he doesn't truly know me. If he did, he would understand that I'd never abandon family. Also, I'm a little sick and tired of everyone thinking they know what's best for me, as if my brothers are some shining example to emulate."

Humans are confusing.

"I suppose we are."

The more I talked to Raga, the more she surprised me. Despite her murderous tendencies, she possessed an almost childlike innocence. "Raga, were you always a demon?"

Why do you ask?

"Just curious. You seem very different than Corabas."

In Hell Corabas is a lord. His power is great, and he holds much authority. I am a mere thrall. And yes, I was always a demon, spawned to serve those such as Corabas millennia ago.

"So you've been working for buttheads like that since the day you were born?"

Spawned.

"And you have never left Hell except for when you possessed me?"

Correct – except for a brief trip to Tibet about five hundred years ago. It didn't go well.

As I chipped away at the enigma that was Raga, the less she seemed like a terrible monster hell bent on serving her bloodthirsty master and the more she resembled an abused child, born in subjugation and knowing nothing but misery. No wonder she was so desperate to stay topside.

"Raga, I hope you know if there was some other way to—"

It's not your fault.

A hush followed as I sloshed down the dank corridor. As nuts as it sounded, a part of me was actually going to miss Raga, and not just because I could eat whatever I wanted without turning into a lardass. There was an absurd blend of craziness and sincerity about her. True, she was a demon, but she was my kind of demon.

Raga was the one to break the silence. *I think you and Jake make a good couple. He's cute, and you are pretty.*

The unexpected compliment made me chuckle. "Thanks, but I'm not so sure of that. He did lie to me, after all, and I'm pretty sure you were ready to kill him for it."

That's when I thought he was cheating on us – I mean, you. That's when I thought he was cheating on you.

"I don't know. Even if he is a little older, he is cute and sweet. Maybe in a couple of years, if we somehow survive this nightmare, we can give it another shot. But now's not the time to think about it."

Why not?

The smell of burning wood drifted down the tunnel. Corabas was close.

"Because now's the time for us to kick some ass. Can I count on you?"

My question was answered with silence. It was understandable given our situation, but the feeling of aloneness that pervaded me earlier returned tenfold.

Up ahead firelight flickered along the walls of the corridor. I closed my eyes and focused on breathing to ready myself for what was to come.

Trust isn't necessary. You have the necklace.

It was better than nothing.

CHAPTER 34

Rusted pipes, broken gauges, and split holding tanks danced in the light cast from an immense bonfire burning in the middle of the power plant basement. Corabas stood behind the inferno, his spiraling horns nearly scraping against the vaulted ceiling. He turned and cast a hideous smile, revealing rows of ebony fangs that gleamed in the firelight. He was terrifying to behold.

Corabas beckoned me to enter with a clawed finger. "Please, make yourself at home."

Stepping through the entrance on rubbery legs, I caught sight of Steve, Chris, and Jake shackled by their arms to the aging machinery. I prayed they were just unconscious and not dead. A symbol of the horned god had been drawn on Chris's forehead, and on the floor next to the fire, a cluster of crimson arrows and circles were scrawled in dizzying patterns. Corabas had been busy.

The demon slowly circled the fire. "Ten years ago I

was cheated out of my vessel and had to make sacrifices to avoid perdition. My power was greatly diminished, and I returned to the one location where I was still bound to the mortal world, this hospital. Since then I have bided my time, growing stronger and laying the foundation for my return. I would be lying if I denied having dreamt of this moment countless times."

"That must suck considering how badly this is going to turn out for you." The strength of my voice surprised me.

"*This* will be splendid for me," Corabas replied. "The question is how will it turn out for you? If you are a good little girl and do as you're told, you may just walk out of here in one piece. Unfortunately, the same cannot be said for others present. I know you're there, Raga. I can smell the stench of your failure from where I stand. Raga, the demon who couldn't control one teenage girl any better than she could keep an eye on a fifteen-year-old boy ten years ago. It was clearly a mistake to summon such a wretch to assist me. After things are set straight, your punishment will be meted out."

Oh crap.

"Raga can't come to the phone right now. But on her behalf, I'd like to say you can kiss both of our asses."

Why did you say that?!

Laughter oozed from Corabas. "I must congratulate you, Kate. Time and again you've proven yourself more resilient than I could have imagined. By now my gluttonous servant should have assumed control, but I can see you've got the better of her. It must have something to do with that abominable necklace you're wearing. It has a most repugnant aura about it."

I had to distract him, play for time while working my way to within arm's reach. "So why my brother? What's so special about him?"

"The pact we made in the summer of 1978 was a potent one, intended to be executed on All Hallows' Eve, the night of the black moon. The falling of this astronomical alignment on such a sacred date is exceptionally rare and would have ensured a singularly powerful merging of demon and vessel. Although the possession spell was undone, your brothers failed to send me back to Hell. As such, the potency of the initial bargain still lingers, waiting to be rekindled tonight when I possess Chris as I was destined to."

Corabas did a sudden about face and stepped in front of Chris. He brushed the side of my brother's cheek with his gnarly clawed fingers. "I must admit, I am quite impressed with Chris's progression. Even without my presence, the darkness within his soul continues to spread and fester. I feel it calling to me even now. You must have noticed it. The quick temper. The bloodlust. I sowed such seeds of iniquity him years ago. I'm almost tempted to set him free just to see what kind of monster he turns into."

"How about you quit talking about my brother as if he's anything like you? It's creepy, and it's bullshit."

More laughter bubbled up from the demon as he

touched an ugly wound below his left eye. "Chris's skill with a knife is extraordinary, matched only by his anger. Even with my carefully laid trap, your brothers were within a hair's breadth of subduing me. They make quite the team. Chris with his fury and Steve his wit. It's a shame to break them up, but as much as I have enjoyed my current host," Corabas pointed to Chris, "he is the real prize. I thought I had lost him forever." An unnerving sneer grew on the demon's face. "Kate, you have no idea how thrilled I was when you told me they were coming back home. And to see what kind of killer Chris had become! Oh, what a treat! As absurd as it is, I feel the strangest pride in him…almost as a father would for a son."

I had to give credit where credit was due. Corabas had played us for suckers, lining us up like dominoes just so he could tip one over and watch the rest fall. But this wasn't going to end up like he wanted it to. Rolling up my sleeves, I took a step toward Corabas and shouted, "Chris is nothing like you, you buttface!"

What are you doing?

Corabas sighed. "Come now, Kate. Don't pretend like you haven't seen the changes in him. Steve knows what his brother has become. Why do you find it so hard to accept? Do you actually hold out some hope that Chris isn't damned already? How sad."

"I'm tired of your blathering. I think it's time I whooped some Goatman butt. What do you say to that?"

What are you doing?

"The game is over, child. I have won. There is no need for you to be injured."

"Not afraid of a little girl, are you?"

"Your generation thinks they're invincible, don't they? That is until you end up splattered across the hood of a car or die from an overdose. I suppose it's a sign of the times." Corabas stretched out a clawed hand. "Perhaps I'll just snap an arm, give you a nice clean break so you don't end up crippled. As long as you are alive, I can use you to bargain with Chris."

I needed to get close, but in order to grab Corabas, I would have to work him over a bit and hopefully catch him off guard. Muttering under my breath, I ordered Raga to lend me her strength.

This is a bad idea.

The demon's power surged through me like a lightning bolt. I watched the smile drop from Corabas's face as he recognized my determination.

"You're as big a fool as your brothers," he said.

I hurled one of the bullets from Maya's gun at the demon's face.

Corabas caught it without batting an eye. "Throwing rocks? Perhaps I overestimated your intelligence. What's this?"

Smoke slipped between the demon's fingers as the enchanted bullet seared his flesh like a hot coal. Opening his hand to drop it, Corabas roared.

Using the distraction, I dashed forward with supernatural speed and landed a solid uppercut, sending

Corabas stumbling backward. Before he could regain his balance, I moved in and swept his leg Cobra Kai style. The demon fell hard.

It appeared Raga's strength was sufficient enough to stun Corabas if not outright defeat him. Psyched by my immediate success, I decided to go for it, leaping onto the demon's prone body in the hopes of putting a quick end to the fight. As I soared through the air, a hand the size of a watermelon swatted me like I was a fly.

"How dare you!" Corabas thundered.

I shot across the room, careening into a row of pipes and slumping to the ground. Fortunately, Raga's durability saved me from broken bones or severed limbs. Wheezing, I got to my feet.

Corabas was already standing again. "So you can summon Raga's strength and speed. I presume the trinket around your neck is responsible. The witch really is talented. Still in the tunnels, is she? After I am done here, I will retrieve the spell book and rip her limb from limb. No one steals from me and lives."

"Technically you stole the book from one of her ancestors, so that makes *you* the thief," I countered between gasps for air.

Corabas's eyes blazed like tiny suns. "Enough of your idiocy!" His mouth stretched wide as he heaved forward and launched a blast of hellfire from his mouth.

I juked to my left in time to avoid the attack, but the smell of singed hair caused me to momentarily panic. Patting a hand on my head to verify there were no flames, I shouted, "You can breathe fire? What the hell! Raga, did you know Corabas could breathe fire?"

Sorry. Forgot.

"Can *we* breathe fire?" I asked.

Don't be ridiculous. Of course we can't.

The ground shook as Corabas lunged toward me.

I stayed low and opened up into what I guessed was a tackling stance. Now was my chance. If I could take the hit, latch onto Corabas monkey-style, and say the words, it just might work.

He plowed me straight to the ground with the strength of a bulldozer, but I managed to grab a tuft of fur and hold on. Shutting my eyes, I said, "Raga, I command you to—"

The words died in my mouth.

I was falling into darkness. Looking up, I could see light. Corabas was there, and he was holding my necklace in his hands. He spoke. "Get up, wretch."

I obeyed.

"Really, Raga, to be outwitted by a mere child. You stand on a razor's edge, fiend. Do as I say, and perhaps I will let you serve me as a slave. Fail me and it's back to the pit. You remember the pit, don't you?"

"Please, no."

It was my voice, but they were Raga's words. I was no longer in control of my body.

"Fetch me the tome from the witch," Corabas commanded. "It is valuable and will be of great use for my future plans. By the time you have returned, I will have roused Master Dwyer."

Without another word, Raga turned and entered the tunnel.

Raga, you don't have to do this. You don't have to do what he says.

"If I don't, he will send me back to Hell. It's terrible in Hell. Weren't you going to send me there a minute ago? I think it's best if you don't pretend to be my friend. All you want is to send both of us back."

That's not true.

"Really?"

Well, that's not entirely true. I definitely want Corabas in Hell, and I want my own body back, but I have no beef with you.

"I would like to have beef with or without you. It's delicious."

Think, Raga. If you bend to Corabas, he will abuse you for the short time he allows you to stay on Earth, and then he will kill me and send you back anyway.

"Maybe, but at least it won't be today or tomorrow. At least I will have some time."

I tried to think of something to say that would dissuade Raga, but she was just as much a prisoner as I was. I felt the fear Corabas instilled in her; it was absolute. We continued in silence for the next several minutes until...

"Kate, is that you?"

The voice was Maya's.

Raga said nothing, trudging along in silence until she stood in front of the witch.

Maya frowned. "It's no longer Kate, is it? That's most unfortunate. So what do you intend to do, Raga?"

The demon reached into Maya's satchel and pulled out her family's spell book. "My master wants this."

"Is that all he wants?" Maya asked in a mocking tone.

Raga's hand shot to the witch's throat. "No."

What the hell are you doing? Maya isn't your enemy. She hasn't done anything to you. Why are you trying to kill her? Corabas never said to.

Raga began squeezing. "It was implied."

Do you think this will make things better between you and him? Maya has never hurt a soul. She is a friend.

"She tried to exorcise me, and then she made me your slave." Raga's fingers closed tight.

Maya tried in vain to pry herself free as the life was being choked out of her.

True, but she was also ready to kill Corabas. She was trying to save me and my family too. Please, don't do this. Just bring the book back, and tell Corabas that she was gone when you got here.

"He will know I am lying. He always knows."

Do it as a favor for me, as a parting gift for someone whose body you have taken possession of. Raga, I'm begging you.

Raga's grip loosened the slightest bit. "A favor?"

It's what friends do for one another.

Raga's hand popped open, and Maya slumped to the ground.

Is she okay?

"She is unconscious, but she will be fine."

Thank you, Raga.

With the book in hand, we turned around and headed back to the power plant. It was bizarre being the one in the cage. I could still see, hear, and feel things, but I wasn't the one in control. Even stranger, I sensed Raga's emotions. She was both anxious and conflicted, but above all she was terrified. It was strange; I found myself wanting to comfort the demon that was possessing me.

Raga.

Crickets.

Raga, I know you can hear me…it's okay to be scared.

"I'm not scared. I'm a demon, born of Hell and feared by millions."

Millions?

"Perhaps not millions but thousands."

Thousands?

"Yes, thousands…a lot. A lot of people fear me."

The demon was utterly petrified. *If you say so. But it's okay.*

"What is okay?"

It's okay to be scared. People are scared all the time.

"I know. I felt it at Glenn Dale when the Bunnyman was after us. I also felt it when we fought the foul spirits protecting master's anchors."

Just don't let it control you. Don't let other people use it to manipulate you, like Corabas.

"I have no choice but to serve Corabas. It was he who pulled me up from the abyss and gave me purpose."

He did that for himself, not for you. You owe him nothing, Raga.

"You're just saying these things because you're scared."

I am – and so are you.

CHAPTER 35

By the time Raga and I made it back, Chris was waking up. Steve and Jake remained immobile, and I was optimistic that they were simply unconscious. My guess was Corabas wanted bargaining chips and dead brothers and boyfriends made for poor ones.

"The witch is no more?" Corabas asked.

"Escaped. But I have the book."

Corabas snatched Maya's spell book from Raga's hand. "It's of little consequence. She will meet her end soon enough.

"Kate, is that you?" Chris asked in a slurred voice.

"Not exactly," Corabas said mockingly. "No, your sweet little sister is currently under my control."

"Raga," Chris mumbled.

"Precisely. The real question is how much is your sister's life worth to you?"

Chris stared at Corabas through half-open eyes. "Have you gained weight? You look like a pile of crap."

Corabas's hand flew, striking Chris across the face. "You should be more respectful to the one who holds the lives of your brother and sister in the palm of his hand."

Chuckling, Chris spat out blood. "So it's that old game, huh? Kill everybody if I don't offer up my body? I figured in the past ten years you would have moved on. Maybe found yourself a nice Mrs. Goatman to settle down with. Really, what makes me so special?"

"You know the answer to that. I will make this a simple choice for you. Your sister's life for yours. If you surrender to my power, I will let her go free."

Chris snorted. "As in free but possessed by a demon? No thanks."

"I offer you Kate's life and her freedom in exchange for yours. I believe it's an immensely fair trade considering I could kill the lot of you right here and now. So what do you say? Your sister leaves this very night if you acquiesce."

The blood began boiling in my veins. "But, master, you promised me Kate. You said she was mine."

Corabas turned his hellish gaze on Raga. "Shut up, you fool! By the end of this, you will be lucky if I let you remain in a dog's body! Honestly, Raga, how did a little girl get the best of you for so long? Yours was a simple task. Terrorize the child until her strength wavered and then take possession of her. An imp could have done it, not that you're a far cry from one."

A terrible rage welled within Raga. "Kate is strong, master."

"Is it Kate now? Are you two chums all of a sudden?" Corabas chortled. "Enough with the excuses. I don't know why I thought this time would be any different. Ten years ago you let a little boy trick you and ruin what should have been my greatest victory. This time you almost allowed a similar disaster to happen. I don't know why I put up with such incompetence."

Chris cleared his throat to get Corabas's attention. "Sorry to break up the reunion, but Kate and Steve have to go free; otherwise, there's no deal."

"You expect me to release the one that thwarted my plans, the one who robbed me of my prize and nearly sent me back to Hell? This I cannot do."

"It's okay, Chris," Steve muttered as he too roused. "This has gone on long enough. Fifteen years of my life sacrificed, and we're still no better off for it. If we can protect Kate, keep her safe from the demon's wrath, then at least we would have accomplished something."

I sensed the confusion pouring into Raga and mixing with her anger. Despite her time on Earth, humanity was still an alien concept to her.

Stumbling to his feet, Chris said, "Listen up, Corabas. For the last ten years, I've felt nothing but regret, and I'll be damned if I'm gonna let you take ownership of this body without knowing my sister and brother are safe. Given the amount of time and energy you've spent trying to possess me, I would say sparing their lives is a small price to pay. Wouldn't you agree?"

The demon's burning eyes turned to Steve. "You and

your sister will leave this place. You will travel far away and never return, elsewise face my fury. My patience grows thin. This is my final offer."

"What about him?" Steve asked, nodding to Jake's motionless body.

"He and the witch are mine. They pose a threat as long as they live, and I am hungry."

Shaking his head, Steve said, "I'm not leaving—"

"It's a deal," Chris blurted.

"A wise choice," Corabas said.

Another wave of anger inundated Raga. Apparently, she did feel something for Jake. *You okay?*

"I'm fine," Raga whispered.

We watched Corabas grab one of Chris's hands and turn it palm up. With the care and precision of a surgeon, he sliced my brother's flesh with a razor-sharp claw. A ghoulish grin crept across Corabas's face as he studied the blood on his talon. "The final ingredient."

He knelt by the fire and scrawled a series of symbols on the floor. "Ten years of meticulous planning finally bear fruit. Tonight I am born again, stronger than ever before." Corabas closed his eyes. "Perhaps I will travel. See the world and enjoy its many delights." A noticeable chill slithered into the room as he began chanting.

From the corner of my eye, I detected movement. Jake was awake and had somehow managed to free himself of his chains. From his waistband he unsheathed a wicked-looking knife and snuck up on Corabas who was occupied with his incantations. Jake pounced on the back of the demon, driving the twelve-inch blade deep between Corabas's shoulders.

With a bloodcurdling howl Corabas jumped to his feet and flung Jake into a large boiler tank like a rag doll. He reached over his shoulder and yanked out the blade. "Miserable insect! You will die now!"

Raga tensed.

Corabas is going to kill him if we don't do something.

Corabas bounded to where Jake was slumped on the floor and grabbed him by the neck. Raising Jake off his feet, the demon said with a smile, "I suppose a little snack before finishing the possession will do no harm." Drool dripped from his wolfish mouth as it gaped opened.

A blue ball burst in Corabas's jaws. He dropped Jake and fell to his knees, retching up water as wisps of steam curled up out of his mouth. He gagged and sputtered.

"Hey, asshole!" Mike shouted raising another water balloon. "Get your hands off my boy unless you want another face full of holy water!"

Theresa slipped out from behind Mike. She had a baseball bat cocked back over her shoulder like Wade Boggs. "Hurry, Kate! Help your brothers while we distract him!"

"What are your friends doing?" Raga asked me.

They're trying to rescue us.

"But they're going to die. Why would they do something so foolish?"

Because that's what friends do. It's just like what family does for each other.

"But there is nothing to gain and everything to lose."

"You insolent little shits!" Corabas bellowed as he rose. "How dare you! You will beg for death before I am through with you!"

That's not the point. What matters is making the effort. Didn't you feel it a few seconds ago when Corabas was about to kill Jake? You wanted to help him.

"That's different," Raga mumbled.

"Kate, why are you just standing there?" Mike blared.

Corabas moved with lightning speed, darting across the room and knocking Mike to the ground with a vicious blow to the chest.

"Mike!" Theresa screamed as she swung. With a *thud* the bat landed square on Corabas's ribs.

The demon smiled as he tore it from Theresa's grasp and backhanded her, driving her down beside her stunned boyfriend. Splinters flew as Corabas snapped the bat in two like it was a twig. "I must thank all of you!" he shouted. "You have saved me the effort of hunting you down and killing you individually. How thoughtful!"

Placing a foot on Mike's shin, Corabas snarled and pushed down. The sickening *snap* of fractured bone was followed by Mike's high-pitched scream.

"Raga," Corabas said pointing back to Jake, "make yourself useful for once and dispose of that one."

Though he swayed on rubbery legs, Jake was back on his feet. "Run," he whispered to Raga, thinking he was speaking to me.

Reaching down, Corabas grabbed Theresa by the leg and raised her into the air until her face was inches from his own. "I think I'll slit your throat and let you bleed out. That way your friends can watch you die, not that they'll have long to mourn for you."

"Stop."

Corabas turned to Raga. "What was that?"

"You should stop. Leave my friends alone."

Theresa dropped to the floor next to her wailing boyfriend. Laughter rose from Corabas's belly, growing in volume as it bubbled from his grinning mouth. "Friends? *You* think you have friends? Raga, you are the most pathetic creature I have ever known, both on Earth and in Hell. And that's saying a lot."

Don't listen to that creep. You are not pathetic.

"I'm not pathetic," Raga answered.

Corabas opened his mouth to speak, but hesitated. Smiling, he said, "Now is not the time for you to grow a spine, demon." Waving a dismissive hand, he continued. "Do as you're told, and help me clean up this mess. We can have a nice long chat about exactly how pathetic you are later."

"Corabas, you're a creep."

Way to go, Raga!

Smoke curled out of Corabas's flaring nostrils. "So who is it I'm talking to now, Raga or Kate? Because it sounds like that little girl has managed to trick you into thinking these people actually care about you. In case you have forgotten, Raga, you're a demon. All of the people in this room fear you and hate you as they do me, or do you think otherwise?"

The cruel smile on Corabas's face widened as he approached Raga. "Do you actually believe that Kate or any of these humans feel something for you? Do you think they would hesitate to kill you if they could? The idea is beyond absurd."

That's not true, Raga. Not anymore. I'm your friend no matter how this turns out.

"Corabas, you're a bad master. You never had a kind word for me, and I don't think I want to help you anymore."

I trembled as a warm sensation spread from head to toe. Raising both hands of my own volition, I wiggled my fingers. Raga had relinquished control of my body back to me. I felt her slipping to the recesses of my mind.

"I'll miss you," I whispered.

You too.

It was go time.

I scooped up Maya's necklace from where Corabas had dropped it. Taking a deep breath, I stretched my arms out. "You know what your problem is, Corabas? I bet you were never loved as a baby demon. I think all you need is a big hug!"

Using Raga's supernatural speed, I sprang forward and latched onto Corabas like a spider monkey. Before he knew what was happening, I was commanding Raga to return to Hell.

Surprised by my boldness, Corabas tried in vain to

pull me off. "Raga, you fool! What have you been duped into doing?"

I'm positive I heard Raga giggling. The strength ebbed out of me as she slipped away. "Raga wasn't tricked," I said. "She just decided that she likes us more than she fears you."

With the deed done, I released Corabas and backed away.

Tall and black like sparkling obsidian, Raga's true form remained to wrestle with Corabas. She was nothing like I envisioned. Her lithe form wrapped around him and wrenched his wicked essence from Jackie's tiny body.

My friend fell to the floor unconscious.

"This is not possible!" Corabas shrieked. "If it takes a thousand years, I will return! Raga, you will pay dearly for this betrayal!"

With powerful arms Raga kept hold of Corabas as a stygian rift broke through the room's cement floor. Slithering up, a sinister black fluid enveloped them, pulling them into eternal darkness.

Raga was strong and formidable, but above everything, she was frigging beautiful. Her triumphant laughter drowned out Corabas as the two departed this mortal world. I felt her presence within me dwindle to that of a candle's flame. Before it flickered out, I heard one last word. *Goodbye.*

CHAPTER 36

"This is the second day this week they've served pizza for lunch," Theresa said, looking at her tray in disgust.

"No complaints here," Jackie said before taking a bite of cheese-covered dough that had been dabbed with the slightest amount of tomato sauce.

"Here either," I added, downing the last bite of my slice.

It had been weeks since the showdown at Glenn Dale, as it was referred to by all of us save for Jackie. Since that time she had seen a variety of specialists to help with her memory loss. The story Theresa and I concocted was that Jackie slipped and hit her head when practicing a backflip for one of her cheerleader routines. The lump she took after being freed of Corabas and falling unconscious added authenticity to our lie and convinced her parents and doctors alike. It even accounted for her partial amnesia. Fortunately, in all the tests, scans, and lab work performed, no trace was found of the childhood leukemia that had plagued Jackie before her possession.

From my brothers to Maya and my friends, we had all sworn an oath not to let Jackie discover what had happened to her. Perhaps it might sound cruel to those who can't fully grasp what she went through, but knowing what we did, we were unanimous in feeling she would be better off unaware of the evil that once lurked within her. It was actually kind of fun getting to know the real Jackie and become friends with her all over again. She was a pretty awesome chick.

Already reaching for the peanut butter brownie on Theresa's tray, I asked, "You're not gonna eat that, are you?"

Scrunching her nose at the tan blob, Theresa shook her head.

"Have any of you ever heard of the Jericho Covered Bridge?" Mike asked while snacking on his girlfriend's fries.

"Oh my God," Theresa said, grabbing one of Mike's crutches. "I swear I will beat you to death with this if you start in on another one of your crazy-ass adventures."

Jake had taken Mike to the hospital after Corabas trashed his leg. Figuring the less complicated he made the lie, the easier it would be to convince hospital staff of its truth, Jake explained that the break happened when they were exploring Glenn Dale, and Mike took a bad fall down a stairwell. That story worked too.

"Shh," Jackie said, raising her hand. "I want to hear about it."

Mike leaned in close to Jackie and lowered his voice. "So the story goes, you drive onto the bridge and stop. Then you put some baby powder on the trunk of your car. You get back in the car and put it in neutral. Now, the car shouldn't move at all because the bridge is perfectly flat, but if you give it a few seconds, it will start moving forward on its own."

Jackie's eyes grew wide. "That is so creepy."

I cast a knowing glance at Theresa.

She caught it and winked back.

"And that's not the freakiest part," Mike continued. "Once you get off the bridge and look on the trunk, you'll see little kids' handprints all over it."

"Oh, man!" Jackie squealed. Grabbing Theresa and me by our arms, she said, "Guys, we have to try that. It would be so wicked."

Despite having the use of just one leg, Mike clearly couldn't help himself. If there was something dumb and reckless to do, he would always be first in line. Glaring at him, I asked, "So who's gonna drive us there, genius?"

"We'll get Ja…" Mike's voice trailed off as he realized his blunder. "Oh yeah, never mind," he said sheepishly.

After the showdown at Glenn Dale, Jake hadn't been back to school – which kind of made sense considering he wasn't a high school student in the first place. It was still weird not seeing him around though.

"Have you talked to him recently?" Theresa asked.

"Just a couple of incredibly uncomfortable phone calls. He told me that he'll be moving back home in a few days. He asked if we could meet up before he leaves."

"And?" Theresa persisted.

"And...I said yes."

"It's bogus that his family has to move during his senior year," Jackie blurted. "His dad must work for a bunch of dicks."

With Corabas back in Hell and Jake's mother avenged, there was no real reason for him to stay in Bowie. We talked a few times since everything went down, but the conversations were mainly about how Jackie was holding up, when were my brothers leaving, etcetera. True, I was still a little steamed at him for lying to me, but in all honesty I kind of missed him.

"Don't worry about it, Kate," Theresa said. "You still have plenty of school year left to find a date for prom. I wasn't going to bring it up, but Tim Shuster has been asking about you."

"Tim Shuster? Why?"

Theresa frowned. "Because he needs a study buddy for chemistry. Why do you think, doofus? It's common knowledge that you're back on the market, and rumor has it he's liked you since the ninth grade."

With Jake leaving, Jackie's amnesia, and my brothers continuing their quest to reclaim fifteen years of Steve's life, the senior prom was the last thing on my mind. "Theresa, I just can't deal with that shit right now."

"Come on, Kate," Jackie blurted. "You only have one senior prom, and Tim is super cute. Chad is renting a limo for us, so if you go with Tim, we can all share the limo together. It will be awesome."

Life is funny. Just three weeks ago Jackie was about to kill us all and take possession of Chris, and now she was talking about her date for the prom. In her defense, she was possessed at the time, but it was still weird as hell.

"I don't know. I guess I'll think about it," I said.

After choking down a mouthful of pizza, Theresa asked, "Will Chris and Steve be hitting the road soon?"

Most times when I was questioned about my brothers it would grate on my nerves, but ever since Glenn Dale things had been better between us, and the subject wasn't quite so irritating. "Yeah, they decided to stay through Thanksgiving before heading out. I have to admit, it's actually been nice having them around. They had some funny stories to share from when they were kids, and I've even gotten Chris to lighten up a little on the whole big brother act. Now if I could just get him to lose the damn mullet."

"What's wrong with mullets?" Mike asked with a bewildered expression.

Patting her boyfriend on his arm, Theresa said, "I'll tell you when you're all grown up."

CHAPTER 37

My brothers and Maya had made several trips back to the abandoned hospital since the showdown to ensure the area was clear of all remnants of the Goatman. Except for a traumatized pooka roaming the grounds, all was more or less quiet. Maya claimed that without Corabas around to warp the fairy's mind, the pooka possessed more bark than bite and would satisfy itself by simply scaring the crap out of people. At least that's what she told me, and I knew better than to second-guess a yaya.

As it turned out, Maya had known my brothers for many years and even worked with them on occasion. That revelation explained some of the more cryptic comments she had made about them in the past. It also kind of ticked me off that none of them thought it was worth mentioning earlier.

With her family's spell book back in her possession, Maya worked tirelessly to find a way to help Steve reclaim the years he had sacrificed to save Chris, and after much research she came upon a spell that she believed would work – with one small catch. The nganga used for the incantation would need to harness a significant amount of spiritual energy. This would require special bones, specifically those of a powerful witch or sorcerer. Not wanting to give up any of her own, despite her affection for my brothers, Maya came upon a story of a fearsome witch that went by the name of Moll Dyer who lived in southern Maryland in the late 1600s. After delving a little into the darker side of Maryland's history, Maya discovered where the witch was allegedly buried. Preparations for a road trip were underway.

Since Corabas's defeat and learning of a way to reclaim his brother's lost years, Chris had changed dramatically. The bright smile I remembered from my childhood returned to his face, replacing the cynical smirk he wore for so many years, and the snide comments and orders he used to bark at me had also ceased. Yes, he was still a smartass from time to time, but I'm pretty sure some of that was mandatory under the big brother code.

"Everything loaded up?" I asked Steve as he tossed a duffel bag in the trunk of the Monte Carlo.

Nodding, he said, "Think so. The hollow point silver bullets came in yesterday, and thanks to our fairy godwitch, we have enough wormwood, yarrow, and devil's claw to choke a horse. Also, I picked up some iron arrowheads for the crossbow bolts."

"What about Maya's charms?" I asked.

Chris and Steve stuck out their arms, exposing the

leather-bound red stones strapped around their wrists.

After a sip of coffee, Chris asked, "What about the duck tape and stun gun?"

Frowning, I turned to him. "What do you need that stuff for?"

Before Chris could answer, Steve said, "Check. And by the way, it's duct tape not duck tape. It's not made from duck."

"Really?" Chris said, rummaging through the car to produce a roll of the silver tape. "Then how do you explain this?" he asked, holding up a roll labeled *Duck Tape* to Steve's face.

After a heavy sigh, Steve countered, "That's just the brand name of the tape. It's the Duck Tape brand of duct tape. Get it?"

Shaking his head, Chris said, "That doesn't change the point that it's Duck Tape. If you want some Jell-O, you don't say please give me some gelatin, do you?"

Steve grinned. "There's no point arguing with you, is there?"

"Absolutely pointless," Chris answered.

I took the cup of coffee from Chris's hand and sniffed it. "Just coffee?"

Taking it back, he smiled. "Damn skippy. Got to be clearheaded if we're gonna steal old Moll Dyer's bones and put an end to this mess once and for all."

Standing on the curb as my brothers packed their car with guns, knives, potions, and a couple of small explosive devices, I couldn't help but smile. Yes, they were going on a literal witch hunt, and true, they could get hurt or even worse, but the last couple of weeks with them had been some of the best we've ever had together, and it just made me happy.

"Hey, Dwyers!" Maya shouted, coming up the street from her house. "All set to kick some undead witch butt on your little adventure?"

"As ready as we'll ever be, babe," Chris said.

"Babe?" I said, scowling at him.

"Chris!" Maya bleated with a mischievous smile.

"Sorry," he replied, slipping his hand around her waist and kissing her cheek. "Couldn't help myself."

As the world around me fell into chaos, I said the only thing that sprang to mind. "What?"

After playfully smacking Chris on the chest, Maya turned to me. "We weren't planning on letting you know about us until your brothers returned. Chris and I have a…complicated relationship."

"Uh-huh. And how long has this," I waved a hand in front of them, "been going on?"

"What would you say?" Chris asked Maya. "We met taking down that pack of werewolves outside of Scranton, right?"

"No, guapo. That's when we were first together. We met destroying the vampire nest in Lansing."

Holding up my hands, I shouted, "Okay! Got it! I don't need to hear any more about the first time you two did it."

Chris closed his eyes. "Oh what a night."

I should have been pissed about them holding out on me, but for some reason I wasn't. I now considered Maya a friend, and if being with my lunkhead brother made her happy, then oh well.

Pointing to my neck, Maya said, "I never pictured you for the sentimental type. You know the charm is no longer necessary."

I touched the polished green beads and smiled. "Guess it's kind of grown on me."

"I'm glad you like my handiwork, but be warned, sometimes such tokens can hold residual energy from the powers they were intended to contain. Let me know if you experience anything strange."

"Kate *is* nothing but strange," Chris said with a wink. "It's one of the things we like about her. Normal is boring and lame."

Chuckling, Steve said, "In that case we must be the most interesting people ever." He nodded in approval at his packing job. "I think that's it. Between the firepower and bag of tricks Maya provided, we shouldn't have any trouble with a four-hundred-year old witch."

Chris slammed the trunk closed. "Let's get this show on the road. We're burning up daylight amigos."

After hugs all around, Steve and Chris got in their car. Before heading off to God knew what kind of mayhem, Steve shouted from the driver's seat, "We'll call after we get settled!" Looking at me he continued. "If we need the big guns, we know who to call!"

CHAPTER 38

Jake and I decided to meet up at Allen's Pond before he left town. I thought I was prepared to say goodbye, but seeing him crouched near the edge of the pond, skipping stones along its surface as he stared off to the horizon, brought a flood of emotions back. "Hey."

He jumped at the sound of my voice, speckling the water with pebbles from the shore. Standing, he smiled and said, "Didn't hear you come up."

"I can see that. Looked like you were deep in thought."

"Guess so. It's been a crazy few weeks. I'm still trying to process it all, figure out my next moves, y'know?"

"I get that," I said with a smirk. "It's not every day one defeats the legendary Goatman of Bowie."

Jake scratched the back of his neck. "Still can't figure how we came out of it alive. Last thing I remember was stabbing that son of a bitch and them whammo, everything went black. When I came to, Mike's got a broken leg, Jackie and Theresa are passed out on the floor, and the Goatman's gone. From what everyone said, you were the one to save the day."

Hunching my shoulders, I said, "Had a little help." I wanted to say more, but now wasn't the time. Jake had some explaining to do, and I was going to make damn sure he did it – with some arm twisting if needed.

"Well, I don't know how you pulled it off, but I'm damn glad you did."

An uncomfortable silence followed as a group of ducks casually floated by.

Grimacing as if recalling something painful, Jake continued. "So, I know we haven't talked about it since Glenn Dale, but I really am sorry for not telling you the truth about me sooner. It's just, when I came back to Bowie, my plan was to find the Goatman and take him out. I wasn't lying when I said I met your brothers on a monster hunt before – they actually saved my life. Afterwards we got to talking, and that's when I found out they had a run-in with the Goatman back when they were kids. Chris was sure they had gotten rid of him, but Steve didn't seem convinced. Anyway, I kept tabs on Bowie happenings, and when news reports of missing persons surfaced, I decided it was time to pay a visit to my hometown."

"Yeah, Steve and Chris told me about helping you out in Poughkeepsie. But why infiltrate the high school, and why take an interest in me?"

"I figured Bowie High was the quickest way to get

the lowdown on the bodies that were turning up. I was looking for any patterns or similarities to the Goatman's victims from a decade ago. That's when I first bumped into Theresa and she let slip that one of her friends lived on the same street as the Butcher of Bowie. You see, I knew from Chris that was an alias for the Goatman. Anyway, that's when I met you."

"And that's when you figured you'd cozy up?"

Jake's eyes dropped to his feet. "It's not like that. Sure, I thought I'd hang out with you and your friends and get some intel that way, plus Mike's obsession with all things spooky seemed a good fit. But..."

"But?"

He looked back up and smiled. "But I never planned to fall for you."

My heart made a concerted effort to jump clear out of my throat.

Grabbing my hands, Jake said, "Since we met, I thought you were the funniest, cutest, and strangest girl I'd ever met. What happened with us wasn't planned. It just...happened. And I'm not sorry for it."

Had to hand it to him. Jake sure knew what this girl wanted to hear. "Neither am I." Chuckling at the memory of our first date, I said, "You decided to ask me out even after having met my brothers? I have to say, that's pretty ballsy."

Jake snickered. "I thought Chris was going to kill me that night when we were parked in front of your house."

"Knowing my brother, I'm a little surprised he didn't.

So what now?"

"Think I'm going to head back home and hang out with the old man while I figure out what's next. After Mom passed it was rocky between us. I'd like to see if we can patch things up."

"Mmm. That's a good plan."

"Thanks. I see you found your good luck charm. I'm glad. It looks nice on you, very…natural."

Touching my necklace, I said, "It's kind of grown on me."

Jake leaned in and hugged me. "I suppose I should be going. Maybe I could pay you a visit sometime down the road."

Closing my eyes in the hopes of holding back the building tears, I returned his embrace. "That would be nice." As he pulled away, I kissed his cheek and whispered, "Be safe."

Jake winked and turned away without another word.

A familiar voice echoed in my head as I watched him leave.

I'll miss Jake. He's got a butt I could really sink my teeth into.

"Shh, Raga, you're ruining the moment."

EPILOGUE

Funny thing about anchors, they don't have to be magical symbols carved into trees or painted on tunnel walls. As long as there is a strong magical link between the object and the entity, an anchor can be just about anything: a rock, a favorite book…even a necklace.

A week after the showdown at Glenn Dale, I actually found myself missing Raga's unique take on life, boys, and prudent dietary choices, and in this nostalgic state of mind, I put the necklace Maya had given me around my neck. That's where I discovered my old friend, patiently waiting for me.

According to Raga, after she dragged Corabas back to Hell, she was considered a bit of a hero. See, Corabas had been topside so long that the infernal powers were mega pissed at him. Apparently, even Hell has its rules regarding possessions, and Corabas had broken oodles of them. With her former master now in the hot seat, Raga was left to roam free, but the poor girl had no clue what to do with herself. That's when she felt the call of the anchor.

She described it as if it had been a dream, flooding her mind with a mix of sights, sounds, smells, and tastes from her time in my body. Through the shadows of Hell, Raga followed the call of the necklace until it reached its loudest volume. Closing her eyes, she willed herself upward toward the source. Then *plop*, she found herself back in the necklace watching me from where it sat on my dresser. After a few days she got bored and tried calling to me through the anchor, and that was when I put it on.

I've considered telling Maya and even my brothers about Raga's return time and time again, but for now it's our secret. Maya would no doubt warn me of entering into a friendship with a demonic being, and Lord knows I'd get an earful from my brothers. The understanding I've reached with Raga is pretty simple, but it works. I promise to wear the necklace a few times a week so she can experience things through me much as she did before. In return she promises to behave – not that she has a whole lot of choice considering she's still compelled to obey my commands. But I don't like to order her to do anything – somehow it just feels wrong.

She enjoys pizza nights and anytime mint chocolate chip ice cream is on the menu. I tend to leave her at home on dates, lest she become a little too feisty. We've reached a kind of comfort zone over the last few weeks, but who knows what the future holds? I'd like to think that things happen for a reason and that just maybe there's a purpose for her return to me other than to let me pig out without gaining a pound – even though that's frigging *awesome*. But sometimes in the back of my mind, I wonder if a day will come when I need Raga's strength once more…

About the Author

Raised in Bowie, Maryland, Mark Reefe moved his homestead to the beautiful Shenandoah Valley some years back, where he lives with his lovely wife, two boys, one dog, and the sweetest mother-in-law. After many years in federal law enforcement catching drug smugglers, money launderers, and fugitives, he decided to scratch the itch tickling him and start writing. Mark's earlier published works blended his experiences along the southern border with supernatural elements in haunting tales that have received numerous accolades.

Most recently, his fondness for the urban legends of his old stomping grounds spurred him to write *Spindle Lane* and *The Ghosts of Glenn Dale*. These darkly nostalgic stories feature teenage friends exploring many of Bowie's spookiest places and encountering some of their more infamous residents.

Writing credits: *The Ghosts of Glenn Dale* (Apprentice House Press, Loyola University Maryland, October 2023), *Spindle Lane* (Apprentice House Press, Loyola University Maryland, October 2020), *The Road to Jericho* (Burning Willow Press, November 2015 and The Three Furies Press August 2020), *The Valley of Hinnom* (Burning

Willow Press, January 2018), and *El Sendero* (Burning Willow Press, November 2017).

When Mark's not writing, he enjoys woodworking, camping, breaking small appliances when they don't appear to work, apologizing to his wife for breaking the previously mentioned appliances, and bourbon (not necessarily in that order).

Apprentice
House Press
Loyola University Maryland

Apprentice House is the country's only campus-based, student-staffed book publishing company. Directed by professors and industry professionals, it is a nonprofit activity of the Communication Department at Loyola University Maryland.

Using state-of-the-art technology and an experiential learning model of education, Apprentice House publishes books in untraditional ways. This dual responsibility as publishers and educators creates an unprecedented collaborative environment among faculty and students, while teaching tomorrow's editors, designers, and marketers.

Eclectic and provocative, Apprentice House titles intend to entertain as well as spark dialogue on a variety of topics. Financial contributions to sustain the press's work are welcomed. Contributions are tax deductible to the fullest extent allowed by the IRS.

To learn more about Apprentice House books or to obtain submission guidelines, please visit www.apprenticehouse.com.

Apprentice House Press
Communication Department
Loyola University Maryland
4501 N. Charles Street
Baltimore, MD 21210
Ph: 410-617-5265
info@apprenticehouse.com • www.apprenticehouse.com